BIG H(

SHÓⁿGE TOⁿGA WA'U

BIG HORSE WOMAN

SHÓⁿGE TOⁿGÀ WA'U

BARBARA SALVATORE

BIG HORSE
BOOKS
VERDIGRE NEBRASKA

STORY, ART © 2022 BARBARA SALVATORE
ALL RIGHTS RESERVED

The within material is copyrighted work. This First Edition is circulated for comment and review, with the understanding that it is available for critique, correction, update, and edits, particularly in relation to the Ponca Language, which should be communicated directly to the Author.

It may not be reproduced, in whole or in part, without permission from the author and artist, who is the sole owner of copyright, trademark and all other intellectual and property rights therein.

BIG HORSE WOMAN is a work of fiction. Though historical context and extensive research inform the story- most names, characters, places and incidents are products of the author's imagination and dreams.

Barbara Salvatore

www.bighorsewoman.com
bighorsewomanbooks@gmail.com

Paperback: 978-1-957861-04-3
Hardcover: 978-1-957861-05-0
Kindle: 978-1-957861-06-7

[**Historical images**: credits noted in Illustration Index – page 334]

*To the Ponca
and the Niobrara*

*To the
Heart of Everything that Is*

*To the dreams we follow
that change us forever*

"everything on the earth has a purpose,
every disease an herb to cure it,
and every person a mission.
This is the Indian theory of existence."

—*Mourning Dove (1888-1936) Salish*

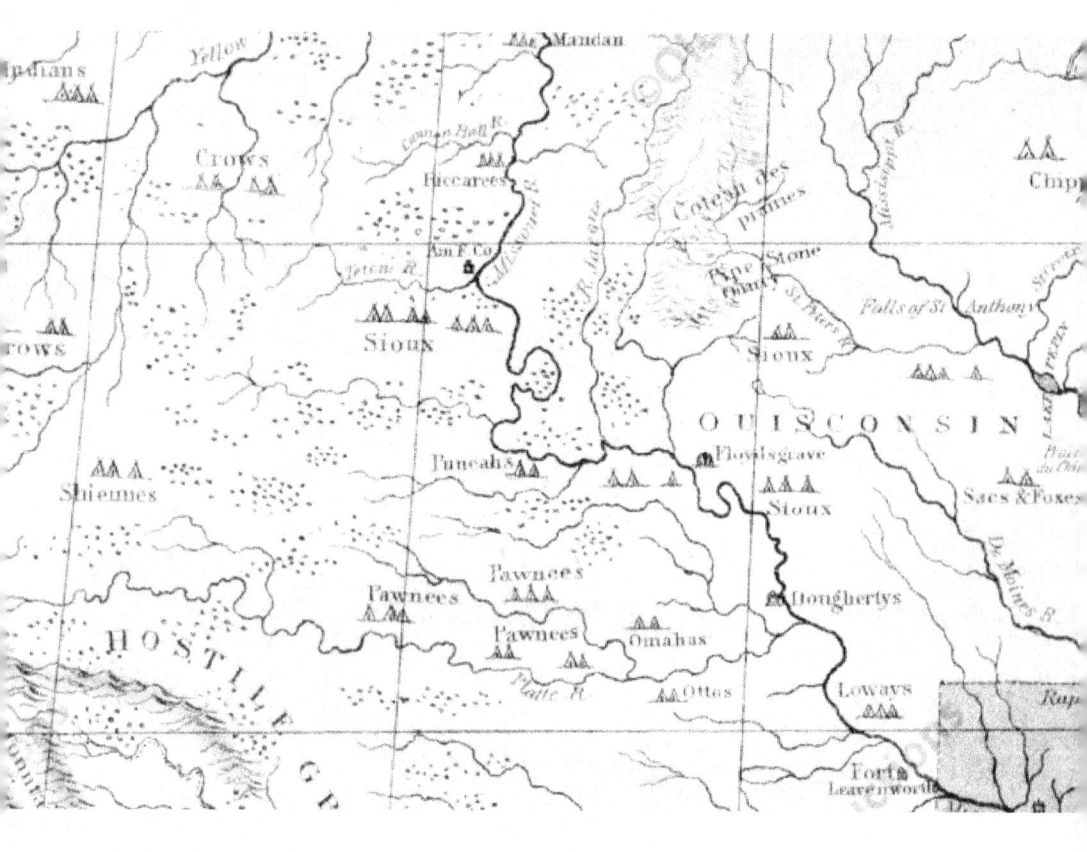

Outline Map of Indian Localities in 1833, George Catlin.(detail)

CONTENTS

BIG HORSE WOMAN 1
BIRTH PLACE 4
GREEN CORN 6
SHOOTING STARS 10
SEED CARRIER 14
NIGHT FALL 17
SIOUX 19
PIPE 24
PLANTING CREEK 28
PLUM TREE WOMAN 30
RAIN WALKING 31
BEAR MEDICINE 32
FACING THE WIND 33
THEIR HORSES 34
MOONS 35
PLANTING 36
BEAR MEDICINE 40
FIRST HUNTER 47
THE PROMISE 50
FIRST DOE 54
CORN FIELDS 56
BUFFALO RING 58
CALICO RAG 64
NETTLES 71
LODGE 77
FUNERAL PYRE 84
RAIN WALKING 88
SHE HAS CHANGED 91
MORE MEN 92

SACRED	97
BLOOD	99
PREPARATIONS	101
BLOOD ROBE	108
MOON LODGE	112
SORE EYES SUN RIVER	114
JOURNEY	127
DROWNING COLT	131
SUNFLOWER SEED AND BEAR GREASE	137
BIG HORSE WOMAN	144
LONER	146
CURLEW	148
PULLING UP THE BLANKET	153
VENGEANCE	156
KILLING	157
PAINT	161
STIRRING	165
A WOMAN!	168
PLENTY OF PEOPLE	173
SEEING	174
BLACK BEAR	175
VISION	178
PACKING	183
STORM CLOUDS	186
COUP	192
MOURNING SONG	197
SCAFFOLD	200
MOURNING VISION	204
HIDDEN MEDICINE	209
RUBY DAWN	212
MULLEIN	214

VOICES	217
DEER	218
WATER	220
RABBIT	221
MORNING FORAGE	224
DOCK ROOT	227
DREAM	229
WOOD WALKING	230
MOON STREAM	231
POULTICE	235
THE ROOT OF IT ALL	239
SUMAC AND CEDAR	242
BLACK EYES WOMAN	245
TRAIL OF MEMORIES	248
CORN SEED AND TEETH	252
GHOSTS	256
PINE GROVES	258
NETTLES	265
SQUEEZE	267
BLUE DAWN	272
BLUE SKIRT	276
ROSE	280
GONE	281
FOUND	283
SUN DOWN	285
SMOKE	287
CAMPFIRE IN THE VALLEY	290
FISH CATCHING	294
SKY FAWN	296

ADDENDUM

The Ponca Language 300
Pronunciation Guide 302
The Names 303
The Five Ðhégiha Tribes 306
Timeline of Recorded Visitors – Niobrara and Missouri Rivers 308
Mormon Timeline 326
Footnotes 328
Moons 331
Historical Images 334
Bibliography 335
Illustrations 340
Four Book Series 341
MAGGHIE 342
Acknowledgments 347
Testimonials 352
About the Author 361

FOREWORD
Clifford Taylor III

It seems like Barbara Salvatore's life and mine were braiding together long before we first met at that fated open mic, in Lincoln, NE almost a decade ago.

We were both artists from an early age, writers and poets, had had our lives profoundly changed by ceremony and the old culture, and more specifically, almost so specifically that there might be no more of our ilk currently than can be counted on one hand. We were both combining all of our skills and inspirations to write something large and dream-given for my tribe, The Ponca Tribe of Nebraska, and all the concentric rings of others composing the rest of our audience connected to that heart-carried core. When we started talking and she told me that her contacts with the Ponca Tribe were the folks who just happened to be my great Aunt and my great Uncle, we both just got wide-eyed and happy and started laughing; the synchronicities were almost too much; O the joy of meeting another soul on your same frequency; O the joy of meeting another writer who wanted us Poncas to have some beautiful books, representation, and all the good medicine that comes with that too.

Not too long after that night I learned the full story of the quadrilogy that has been so much of her life's work over the past 20 years, the first volume of which, *Big Horse Woman*, you are now holding in your hands. Even the first book carries the weeping, grand energy behind all of these precious, poetic books, of the heroines and times that inhabit them: one night Barbara had a vivid dream of an Indian woman on a big horse satchelled with seed-bags and a dog right down beside her, photographically detailed bluffs and river behind them. This woman was an ancestor, a woman who once really lived on this earth.

The dream instantly began to flower within Barbara and her life as a story, as the life-story of this woman from the old days. More dreams came, sketching out and delivering the story as Barbara began to write it, flooding her with more from that Other World as soon as she was ready in this world, and some-times before. Barbara wrote, painted, drew, researched, recalibrated so much of her life towards the work and its quality and authenticity, eventually moving from New York to Nebraska to take a two year Omaha language (our close relatives with a huge overlap linguistically) course at UNL in Lincoln, which is where we met. When you talk to the woman or hear her read from this tremendous work you feel the journey that she's been put on by the ancestors to imbue Big Horse Woman's story with as much ancestor-endorsed soul and cultural authenticity as possible; *it is always moving and amazing to see the ways our relatives in the Other World are ingeniously communicating their help and influences into our lives, giving us a bridge back, a pathway to the indigenous consciousness that unites us and that'll ultimately heal us, which I believe this book so magically and beautifully is.*

So many times, while reading Big Horse Woman I would have to set it down in my lap and let myself travel away into all of those character-defining feelings and memories that the book returned me to. All those places in Niobrara- the homelands of our Ponca people- I would hear my dad talk about spending his boyhood in, and then that I got to know as I got older and went up there for powwow, funerals, Sundance, to camp and fish, or just to visit; they were all there, rendered in poetry and clean prose, embellished and embedded with our language, home to a story that felt like such a gift to be experiencing. Our Ponca people before the event of Contact, making their lives with all of the material and spiritual culture the world around and beyond gave them along the Niobrara, flourishing, hardy, rich, sophisticated and wise, and then some of what happened once a different sort of civilization did come into our midst.

What a special book Barbara has crafted into being for all those who wish to visit the priceless depth and magnificence of those under-remembered and under-told stories and times. *We Indians know of the healing that comes from hearing the stories of our ancestors. Here is a book that beautifully holds that healing in its pages for all sorts of readers that only time knows the full scope and number of.* I imagine that old triangulated Ponca ancestor looking down at Barbara's finished telling of her story and proudly saying, Mission accomplished.

Barbara and I have talked many times about that Ponca book shelf that needs growing, so that the young people and others who're drawn to it have some substance and variety to choose from, so that they can feel good and know the good they're capable of when they read of their own people pulling off awesome, sublime, heroic things. I myself am hard at work on a couple of books that I hope to do my part in helping to grow this book shelf with someday. I would like to thank Barbara for her contribution to the people's bookshelf with *Big Horse Woman*. Thank you for receiving these seeds from the dream world and handing them out to us and all of our sons and daughters with this dream of a book.

And thank you Big Horse Woman.
Thank you for the dream and thank you for this book, too.

Clifford Taylor III
Ponca Poet, Writer, Storyteller
Ponca Tribe of Nebraska

PREFACE - NOTE TO READER:

PLEASE REFER TO THE **PONCA LANGUAGE, PRONUNCIATION GUIDE** and **NAMES GUIDE** at the back (pages 300-305) as needed, while reading the story.

I am in no way a spokesperson or representative of the Ponca Tribe of Nebraska, or the Ponca Tribe of Oklahoma.

This book and these stories are my own, as any mistakes are my own.

BIG HORSE WOMAN has been reviewed by Ponca Tribe of Nebraska Tribal Historians, Cultural Directors, and Cultural Committee, many Ponca Tribe of Nebraska and Ponca Tribe of Oklahoma tribal members, and numerous Ponca and Omaha Language and cultural consultants, in Nebraska, Oklahoma and Kansas.

With linguistic and tribal assistance, I have aimed for correct and appropriate portrayals, correct use of the embedded language, tradition, culture, clan and gender etiquette, of the Ponca (Pónka), Omaha (Umónhon), Sioux (Sicangu, Lakota, Santee, Dakota) and Crow (Apsáalooke).

References, extensive Footnotes, and further Resources are available upon request.

This is a First Edition. *Corrections are welcomed.*
Any assistance with accurate and proper usage of the Ponca language, will allow me to make corrections in future printings. My hope is that this book can be used as a learning tool
for Ponca Language learners.

Sharing and passing this story on to relatives is encouraged!

Wíbthahon

Barbara Salvatore
Verdigre, Nebraska

www.bighorsewoman.com
bighorsewomanbooks@gmail.com

BIG HORSE WOMAN
SHÓᴺGE TOᴺGÀ WA'U

>"Certain trees, certain animals, certain birds,
>certain clouds, are yours to keep-
>those you are born by.
>The Willow, the horse, the ears up dog,
>are my kind.
>I keep the ermine at my waist,
>morning rain at my fingertips.

Willow talks to me soothing.
There is no sadder tree, no better trunk, to cry on.
Her roots, deep in sandy water, she drinks up tears,
and they flow through her.
So it always was with me,
Thíxu wíⁿ.
Water Willow.

I thought myself one of them,
being so named Willow from birth.
And I *was* the Willow for my people.
If I had not been born there, *then*,
under that tree, those stars –
only spirit knows –

I would never have been able to bend to the times
that were coming....

So I was - born under a twin black willow tree
on the west bank of the Nínshude.
The sky was full of shooting stars,
showering in every direction, so they say.

Yes, I saw them-
the changing stars that saw my way to earth.
I would say that birth is very much like seeing stars...
It was for me.

I landed among the people
at the Beginning of Cold Weather,
on a cold, snow covered night.

Thíxu wiⁿ.
They named me.
Water Willow
I was called.

You would have thought they'd name me for the stars...
But the stars are magic. Sacred.
Xúbe.

They...the stars ... our ancestors, our babies, our unborn.

No. Grandmother gave me the name of the Tree.

The Tree, gave me its ears and voice."

Shóⁿge Tongà Wa'u
Big Horse Woman, 1852
(Thíxu wíⁿ
Water Willow,
being her child name)

BIRTH PLACE
MOᴺZHÓᴺ THÒᴺ ÍDATHAI

November 13, 1833

Kímoⁿhoⁿ stood far from the twisting black willow tree, where
KóⁿdehiWiⁿ chose to give birth. Her body and Grandmother's
were obstructed from view by the tightly woven willow
birth hut, nestled under the twin black willow tree. The birth
lodge was covered with buffalo robes. Sweetgrass smoke
rose steadily from the smoke hole. The cold earth floor,
lined with dry reeds and grass, buffalo robes and blankets,
sage carefully placed. Mist floated down river, melting and
carving the closest snowy banks.

Kímonhon did not remember ever seeing a hut so skillfully
constructed, with such speed. But then, he'd never been
so near a birth, never watched the women work. He was
noticing what he'd never noticed before. It was all new.
Nothing he was seeing, was anything he knew.

He thought to this day many times; imagined his own ideas
of what would be. He had not pictured himself in such
proximity.

But the voices ...
His ears followed the sounds of the women inside,
and the voice he loved most, singing to the stars.

> 'Mikà'e wíbthahon.
> Wíbthahon mikà'e.'
> Thank you, stars.
> Stars, thank you.

He listened, mesmerized – by her song,
still the same curious fellow he was taunted as
when they first met, remembering ...

GREEN CORN   Summer 1832
WÁHABA

Kímonhon crept along the field's edge, towards the green corn. He and friends were out stealing green ears; something they weren't supposed to do, but always did. There were always boys out stealing corn this time of year. And girls were watching on the stands, protecting their fields from predators and birds, and boys. The songs they sang from the field-stands were mostly the same.

> "Oh you silly niashinga,
> too young to go out hunting,
> your arrows are good for nothing
> but shooting up into the sky!"

This tormented him. What did they mean?
Why did they always turn their backs and giggle?
Girls were so strange.
That was, until the day he heard *her* singing.
Then, he stopped creeping for the green ears and stood stalk still. Her voice mingled with the rustling corn leaves. He closed his eyes to determine that the song came from near the river, east.

The song fell in and out of the summer river rushing by.
He listened for a long time to the corn leaves, and the river,
and her voice. Her song was new and these words were
meant for *his* ears,
> "love boy, don't steal my mother's corn,
> Don't be a coward in my field.
> Don't run and hide like a Crow hopping,
> in my field, stand tall!"

She dared him. He stepped out from the shadows and he
stood tall, and then he saw her on her scaffold, grinding the
sweet, milky kernels. She was not supposed to look at him.
She should have turned her back. But she did not.

Her friend on the platform was é'kithe related, Wihéto"ga,
to his mother's clan. So, when invited to refresh himself
with sweet corn drink, he could politely accept this offer,
along with the opportunity to gaze at his sister's
new friend.

It was only then, that he noticed the girl's
Mother standing in the nearby cornfield.
Her mother, who had noticed him long
before, and was watching him closely.
She rested, leaning on her antler rake
as he approached.

The field felt big that day. He thought he'd never reach the platform. When he finally did, he climbed the three short steps up the log ladder, to her.

His cousin passed the gourd ladle to him, from which he gratefully drank. He had nothing to say. Except that he wished her friend would go on singing. They answered his request with another river of giggles.
He shyly stepped away, attempting to overcome his unfamiliar blushing.

When he looked back over his shoulder, he saw the girl's Mother- her mouth covered with one hand and holding her rake from jiggling off her laughing shoulder, with the other. He saw his cousin and her friend, still giggling.
All the laughing was too much,
but her face was just enough.

Kímonhon knew he would see her again.
He was so overcome that he felt himself growing merely at her thought. He had not expected this and did not know what to do. But he easily discovered that shooting towards the sky was an answer.

~

He would listen to her singing, whenever he was nearby, throughout summer. Otherwise, he was out hunting, gathering gifts that would bring her closer to him.
The sooner he could ask, the sooner he could have her. Right now, there seemed nothing he wanted or needed more. He was brave all right. She brought it out of him.

~

When the young hunters went out for birds, Kímoⁿhoⁿ returned with a young eagle. He gave KóⁿdehiWiⁿ's father a wing, and many eagle feathers to adorn his pipe and shield. He gave away his own fine hunting horse and three of his best buffalo ponies.

The next day, KóⁿdehiWiⁿ was in his arms. After all the dancing and much feasting, they were given their own lodge. They were joined.

At the Beginning of cold weather, Kímoⁿhoⁿ and KóⁿdehiWiⁿ packed their horses and moved ahead of winter to her mother's home.

Kímoⁿhoⁿ was well received by her family and clan.
He took his place among them.

SHOOTING STARS
MIKÀ'E ÚXPÁTHE

November 13, 1833

Now, here, at the Beginning of next winter, Kímonhon watched the last light fade behind the birth hut and realized the song had stopped. The sky grew black with no moon, and time stood still.

Kímonhon paced and waited for what seemed far too long, in silence. Then the first stars caught his eye and his attention drifted to the sky. He saw a shooting star, and another...
and *another!*

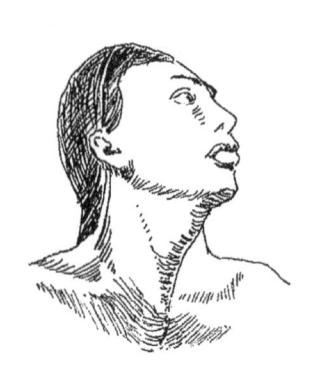

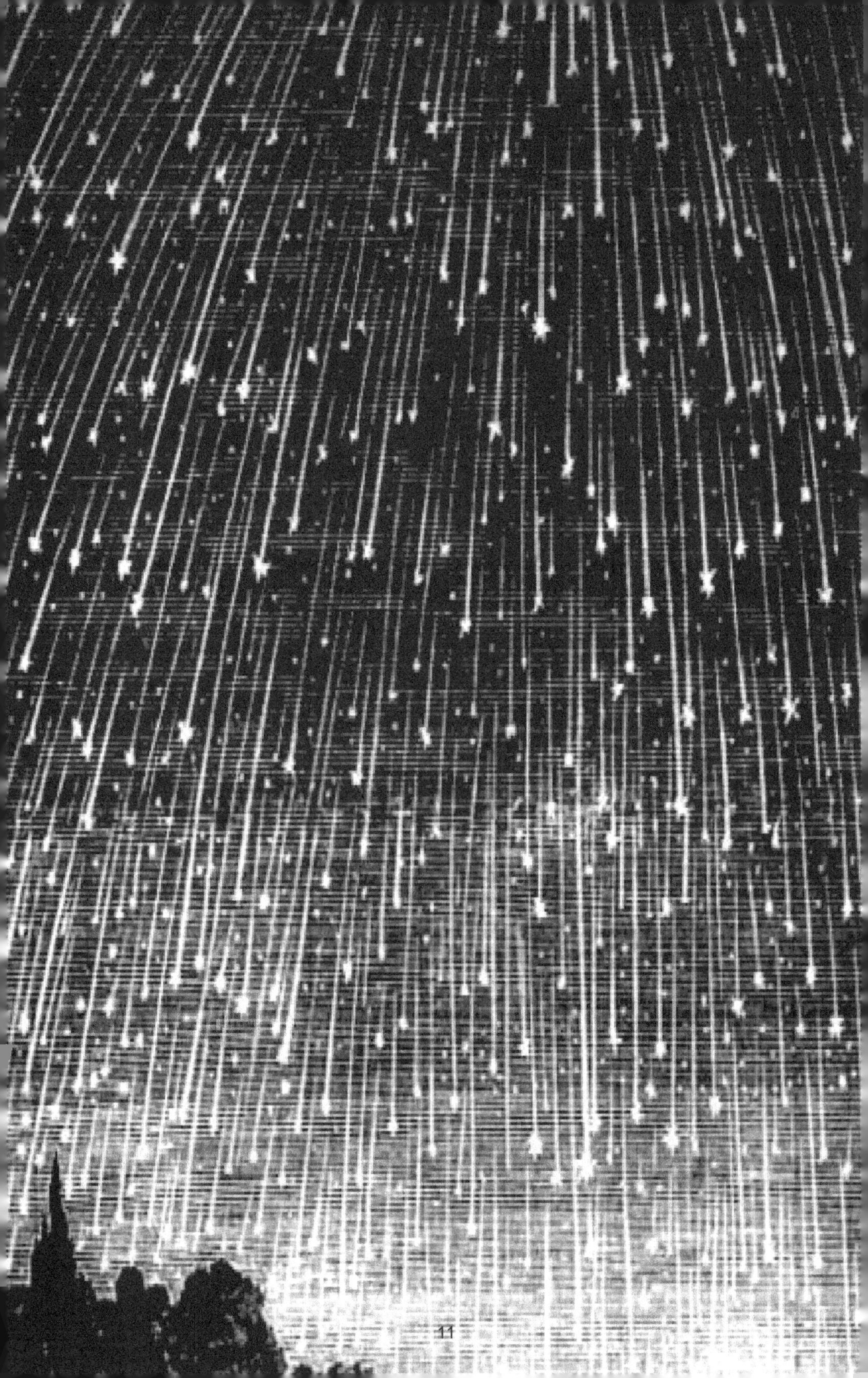

The sky above him danced with stars.
He stood and watched them fall in disbelief.
Time leapt forward in full motion.
The stars streaked by, crowding the sky.

He heard the distant wailing of women in the village,
followed by muffled screams from within the snow-covered
earth lodges. He watched the sky and heard the brisk steps
of his new father rushing towards him.

Máⁿchu Máⁿkaⁿ came up the well-paced path towards the
river, his eyes never leaving the sky. Wrapped in thick
buffalo robes and high boots, he stood beside his son,
face turned up.

> "Kímoⁿhoⁿ you are a fortunate man
> to be given a child tonight.
> The skies shower us.
> Shooting stars fall to earth.
> I have heard the words they sing
> and know it will mean
> this child of yours will know
> a different world
> than the one she is born to.
> The eastern skies sweep down on us
> like prairie fire across the plains.

A great wave is coming
with many deaths,
and many births.
This child comes through the tunnel tonight
with the stars and their sight."

They stood, craning necks to the sky.
Watched in wonder at the rare magic they witnessed.

Kímonhon sank from standing, his knees melting into the
snow. Head back, he watched the stars shower above.
Thought of the love that brought this birth.

Noise from the hut made him tremble, as the silence broke
with deep moaning, short breaths, steady song, all as he
moved dizzy towards the willow.
The willow shook, with the force of KóndehiWin as she pushed
the baby out. He heard Grandmother, Nónzhin Mónthin,
her song now rising above the labored breathing of his wife.

When he heard the baby, he was just paces from the door.
When the baby wailed, he froze in place.

He was a father!

SEED CARRIER
WAMÍDE-Íⁿ

Her mother held her, touched her lips with sacred water,
nursed her, welcomed her. Her grandmother named her.

In the early days, every woman carried seed
for their families, for their village, for the tribe.
But not every woman knew the seeds to carry
of medicine.
Those that did, carried these seeds wherever they went.

Rain Walking was such a seed carrier.
Nóⁿzhiⁿ Móⁿthiⁿ carried the seed of every medicine that crossed
their path. When her daughter, KóⁿdehiWiⁿ, gave birth-
there and then Nóⁿzhiⁿ Móⁿthiⁿ recognized Water Willow as one.

Rain Walking had the seeds of knowing to pass on,
and she saw that Water Willow would be fertile ground.
She saw in this new child, the heart and hands to carry seeds.
She whispered to her new granddaughter,
> "Witúshpa...
> For every medicine, there is a plant.
> For every plant, there is a seed.
> For every people, a Seed Carrier."

And thus, she blessed her.

Rain Walking was close to the seeds, knew when they were thirsty, and could call on winds when they grew desperate to drink. When Rain Walking beseeched, these winds would gather up clouds and press rain from them.

And that is how she got *her* name.

Rain Walking would keep the rain making in her fingertips, until Water Willow was old and strong enough to move winds and water. But first, she would speak with trees.

And so her name was - the tree she was born under.

Thíxu wiⁿ, *Water Willow,* she was called.

~

When they opened the door to Kímoⁿhoⁿ, he saw his child glowing red, thick vermilion grease coating her skin. They wrapped her in an ermine trimmed blanket and placed her in his arms. The wind was a spiraling zephyr, blowing circles around them.

Stars were yet falling from the sky.

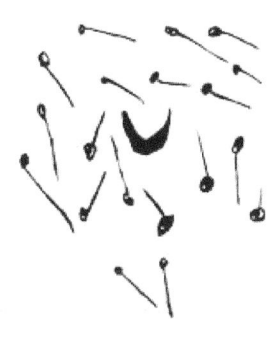

*

*

*

Ho! Sun, moon and stars,
All that move in the heavens,
Listen to me!
Into your midst
New life has come.
Make its path smooth.
Ho! Winds, clouds and rain,
You that move in the air
Into your midst
new life has come
Make its path smooth!

Omaha Prayer * Birth of a Child [1]

NIGHTFALL
HÓᴺDOᴺ AHÍTEDI

Water Willow was born into a many horse clan. The ponies, her first playmates. Red Pony, a lead mare, adopted Water Willow as her own, often sheltering her between front legs, under shield of her chest.

One time, KóⁿdehiWiⁿ found Red Pony's neck curled around Water Willow, fast asleep in the sweet grass, her head pillowed on a mossy rock.

KóⁿdehiWiⁿ scooped her up and carried her, still sleeping, back to their lodge. But Water Willow dreamed she was still curled up, her ear still pressed against the mossy stone, the sound muffled...

but she heard it...

the hooves of many horses running,
drumming up warnings...

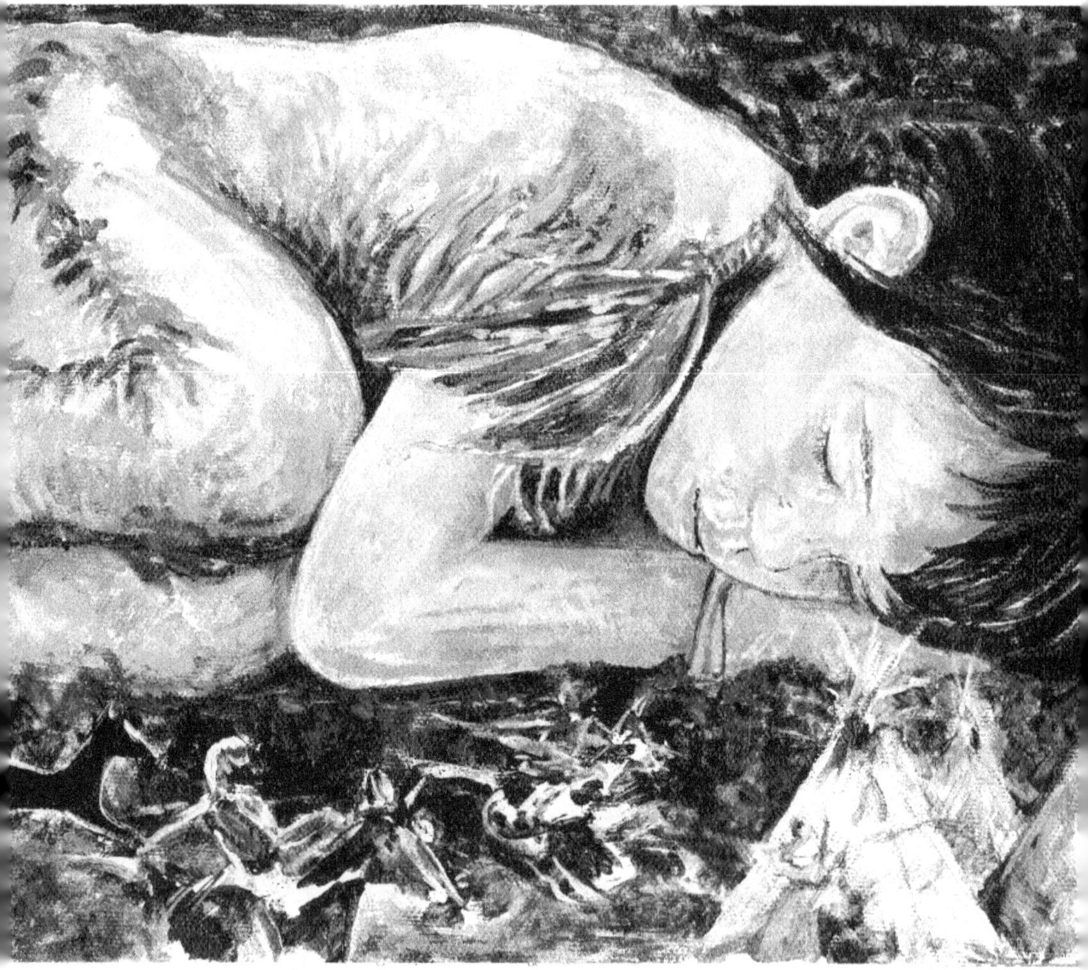

SIOUX   1838
SHÁᴺXTI
The Real Sioux

Water Willow dreamed Sháⁿxti would soon invade their camp and woke to the sound of many horses, drumming in her ears. She told Grandmother they should run away.
> "Many horses are coming!
> The black-faced warriors are coming!
> We do not want to die!"

Grandmother woke slow and half-asleep, spoke,
> "My pony is so old...I have no bow strung...
> Go back to sleep.... The warriors will go away..."

Water Willow cried, *"No Grandmother!*
> *We have to go!*
> *They will capture us!"*

Grandmother, squinting in the dark, saw Water Willow's fear. It struck her as very real.

Grandmother poked a stick across the tepee into her
daughter's back. Water Willow's mother and father woke
to her crying. They thought it no more than a child's night-
mare, and tried to quiet her. Grandmother knew better.
    "Water Willow has had a dream."
She told KóⁿdehiWiⁿ to send Kímoⁿhoⁿ to bring word to
their Chief.

Grandmother moved about in the dark, as she packed.
She made a generous bundle of t'agát'ubè [2], corn powder,
pumpkin seeds, dry squash, and bear grease for Granddaughter.
Then she and KóⁿdehiWiⁿ packed everything else.

Water Willow took her bundles, blanket, and beaded hide-
scrap pony out under the stars. She looked back at people
waking, moving sluggishly about, ignoring the alarm she
clearly felt. She looked up the wide river, waiting.
How could they not feel it? The threat rang through her.
Water Willow wrapped her blanket tight around her
shoulders, and whispered to her hide-scrap pony,

    "Grandmother will tell them, you'll see,
    and we'll be gone...
    Don't worry...
    There is a big white tree...
    big and wide...
    waiting...
    to hide us..."

As neighbors woke, Grandmother spread word. As word
spread, the people packed, while awaiting the call to unlash
tepees. Scouts were sent over the hills north, west, and east.
Kímonhon scooped up his daughter by the river and brought
her to the council fire, where she curled up on her mother's
lap. KóndehiWin stroked Water Willow's winged eyebrows,
until she drifted back to sleep.

Grandmother offered willow tea, and willow bark for
their pipes, as the council debated late into the night.
All were told of the Dream.

Water Willow had seen only four winters. Many people did
not know her, but they *all* knew Grandmother, Nónzhin
Mónthin

The council measured and considered all that they could
move, all that would be lost, and, *if* they did move,
where to go for winter camp.
It was the Beginning of Cold weather.
The Ponca had just returned from a grueling hunt.
Fresh buffalo hides and robes lay washing, pegged down
in the river. The Great Muddy River scraped sand and silt
across the robes, carrying loosened flesh and bloated scraps
down river. The soaking wet robes were too heavy to carry.
The butchered meat was not yet dried, not yet smoked,
would turn bad if put early in packs.

This would bring predators. Camp dogs would fight
amongst themselves...driven wild.
Sháⁿxti would easily follow such a trail,
and then all could be lost.
But leaving behind the robes and meat, meant another good
hunt or rounding-up would be necessary before snow fell.
Warriors were mixed as to what to do.
They might not find buffalo again before snow,
or the yearly migration, that would separate them...

They were considering all of this for the dream of a child,
when Water Willow woke from her mother's lap
to the sound of hoof beats...

A scout came whooping into camp, with reports that a
Sháⁿxti war party *would* be there by daybreak.
The call was given and tepee poles came down in swift
rhythm. Hides flapped loose along the river, in the dark
wind. Babies were lifted in their cradleboards, tied to
strong backs, hung from saddles and travois.
Some never woke to the rhythmic motion.

Lodge covers were un-pegged, rolled and folded, poles
lashed to the horses, piled well with baskets, parflêches,
food, blankets. Cooking hearths and praying altars became
invisible. Fires were buried. Food stores well covered or dug up.
Saddle bags, feed and seed sacks, filled to capacity.

They assembled on the hill that sloped silently away
from the Muddy River.
Dogs nipped at the heels of horses that strayed.
A group of mares and foals trotted in a tight pack,
to join their leaders on the trail.
Ants filed out, carrying cornmeal prayers away,
grain by grain.

The People followed the road of the buffalo, heading west.
They traveled over the packed earth in the dark of night,
many miles, before they stopped.

Scouts sent messages forward. Sháⁿxti were following still.

PIPE
NINÍBA

It was then that Chief Shúde Gáxe went alone from his people, to an eastern slope. There he sat beside his horse and prepared the sacred pipe.

His back was to his people,
but they read his every move
and joined him in his long and silent prayer.

He unfolded the long pipe bundle.
Lifted its long ash stem from its bed of dry sage.
Held the smooth bowl in the palm of his left hand, filled it with nínígahi - his own smoke mix of sunflower, sumac, mullein, willow.

Scraping his flint until a stroke set bright sparks, he then puffed gently until the bowl was burning orange. He exhaled and raised his pipe to the east. He raised the pipe and blew smoke to the south, west, north, to the sky and to the earth.

He held the pipe bowl close to his heart, and again offered it up.

Chief Shúde Gáxe touched the earth with strong weathered
hands, palms flat against her, withering grasses tickling
every finger. He closed his eyes, smelled this new earth,
and asked
> *Where will we be safe?*

He felt the tickle quicken now, and wind come up behind.
He stood and smelled the cold breeze as it passed.
Heard it whisper...
> *To the north...*

So he returned to them with direction that shifted their
path. They moved straight north as the sun rose and warmed
their backs. They walked on, to hilltops and narrow valleys
where they had never been.

When they finally stopped, it was by a wide bright stream,
with an ancient white sycamore beside it.
Water Willow recognized it.

The tree opened her arms to them, its limbs pushing out
over the water, branching wide over the ground.
Some of them had never seen a tree so distinctly beautiful.
Every white finger of it beckoned them.
Water Willow went to the white tree
and wrapped her arms around it.

They did not camp directly under it. They camped away
on a southern flat, facing the tree, and the rising sun.
From there, they could revere it.

Well protected on four sides, there were cliffs. The scouts
came back with reports of clay in hidden gulches, gathering
in pits, of branching streams, and buffalo tracks.
They rested, waited, made certain they remained far from
the Sháⁿxti. Next morning a scout returned with news
that the Sháⁿxti had finally turned back.

The Council was resumed. They invited Water Willow.
The Chiefs and Headsmen spoke, and finally Smoke Maker
addressed the people, saying all that mattered.

> "Our robes lay in the Muddy Waters still,
> and it is all that we have lost.
> We have this dreaming child to thank for
> our lives. We will honor her family in our
> new home. We will pray for the buffalo to
> replenish our stores. We will provide
> Water Willow's family with meat for our
> coming winter. We will live safely in these
> hidden hills, on these abundant creeks,
> hidden among cottonwood, pine and
> sycamore.

>We will work together, in gratitude for our
>new home. We will build a round corral
>for the buffalo, shadowed by these cliffs,
>and run them into it.
>Later it will be a safe haven for our horses,
>when winter winds bring snow."

And he presented his son, to offer a gift, saying,

>"Water Willow, here is your first bow.
>You will learn to use it.
>My own son, Kíka Toⁿgà, will hunt with you.
>It will do us honor."

When he finished speaking, all remained silent,
allowing his words to sink in.
When it was a picture in everyone's mind,
that they all shared a piece in,
they responded with heads nodding
and a warm welcoming of Thíxu wiⁿ,
Water Willow, their dreamer child.

PLANTING CREEK
WACHÍSKA ÚZHI ZHI WA-A I TE

So it was that they moved from the Muddy Yellow River, on the warning of Water Willow's dream.

They named this Planting Creek, because the corn grew well and tall and loved it there.

For three winters following, Water Willow was welcomed and listened to stories told at the fires of both women and men. She was made welcome at the fires of everyone. She had become a real person to her clan and was closely watched.

Each of her family shared their own best gifts with her...

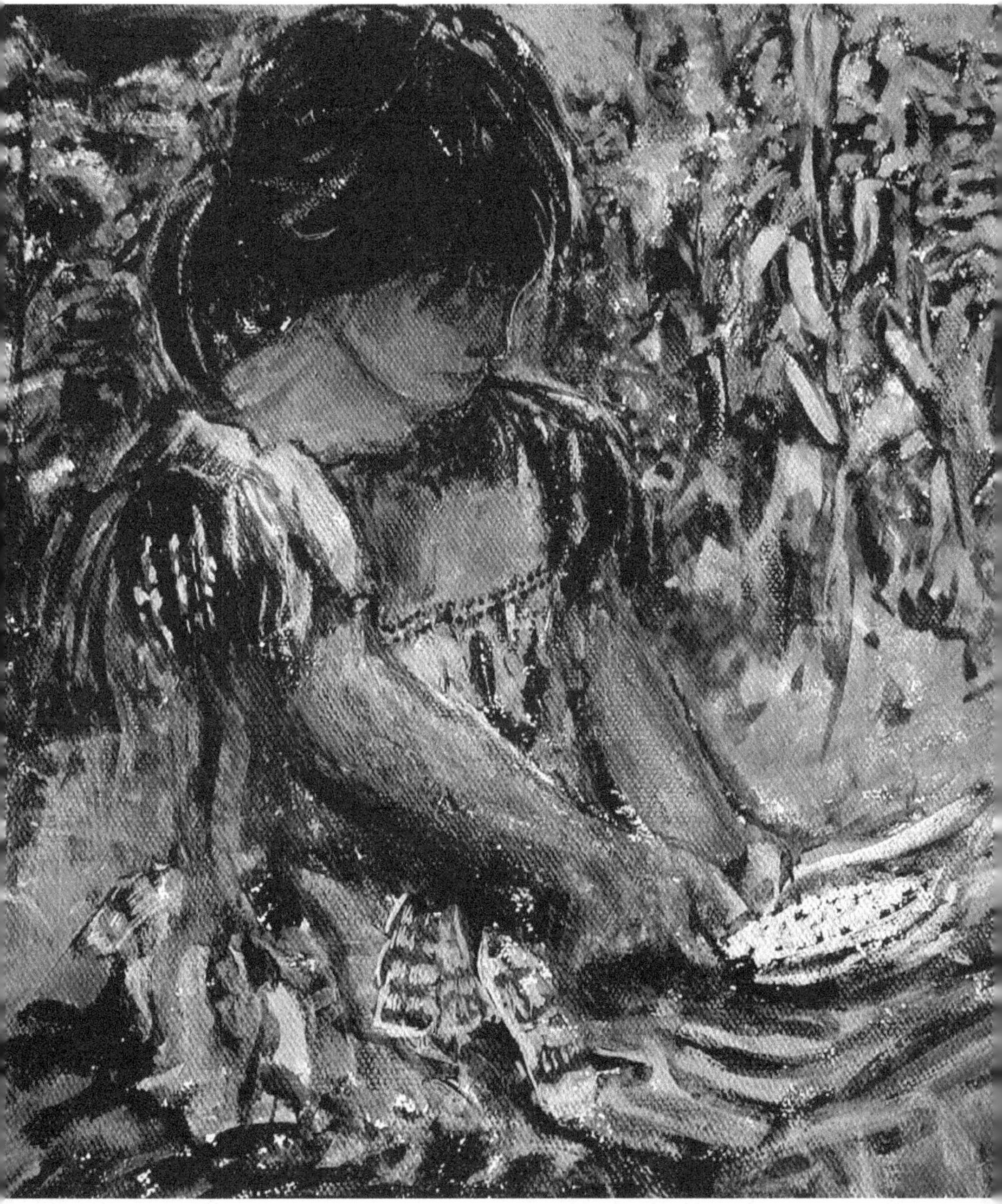

PLUM TREE WOMAN
KÓᴺDEHIWIᴺ

Her Mother was a strong skinner, her doe and buckskins fine and supple. Her arms were woven of sinewy muscle, strengthened by scraping buffalo robes. She never rushed her work or her rhythm. Water Willow watched her mother's forearms and hands, glossy with grease and fat, stained from years of tanning.

Scraping was usually accompanied by songs or stories, daily lessons. KóᴺdehiWiᴺ reminisced to Water Willow, how it was her singing that had snared Kímoᴺhoᴺ. It was hard to resist KóᴺdehiWiᴺ's voice. She made beautiful clothing and moccasins, parflêches and flat bags, deer, rabbit and mole skin pouches. In trading, her work brought seeds, beads, rare shells, quills and teeth, weapons, tools, and even horses.

She passed on common knowledge, practical advice to her daughter...

"If you are willing to remain ignorant and not learn how to do things a woman should know, you will ask other women to cut your moccasins and fit them for you. You will go from bad to worse: You will leave your people, go into a strange tribe, fall into trouble, and die there- friendless."[3]

RAIN WALKING
NÓNZHIN MÓNTHIN

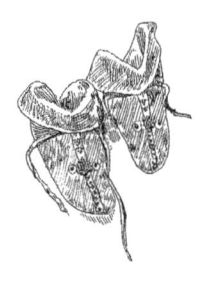

Grandmother showed Water Willow that with quills and beads she could express the beauty of symbols, pattern and color. She showed her the talking spirit of pictures- what meant earth, sky, thunder, sun, water, footstep, cloud, fruit, star- all sewn in shining, talking beads. Animals, birds, and flowers were all beaded in pictures.

She learned to make bone needles and pull long sinews through them. Grandmother's squinting eyes could no longer see to string the needle, but she certainly could see to sew. Her beadwork was still most beautiful.

Water Willow learned too, about living things, from Grandmother, Nónzhin Mónthin, who mostly talked about plants and barks, or how to make paint, boil buffalo marrow, collect fish oil, how to make a meal-powder from grain or seed.

By the fires with Grandmother, she saw and learned how to cook corn, beans, meat and squash. She learned how and when to harvest, prepare and use certain plants, how to make medicine.

BEAR MEDICINE
MÁⁿCHU-MÁⁿKAⁿ

The dreams she had that mattered, Water Willow spoke of, to Grandmother, or to Grandfather, Máⁿchu Máⁿkaⁿ. They were good listeners.

Máⁿchu Máⁿkaⁿ was named for his strong Bear Medicine.
He knew the root medicines that healed broken bones
and arrow wounds and helped in child-birth. Bear Medicine
took her into the deep woods, rambled with her over
high ridges, uncovered secrets the bears revealed to him.

Of plant powers such as these, small amounts were carefully
dried and powdered, very sparingly and cautiously used.

Jack-in the pulpit, Míkasi-máⁿkaⁿ [4], was one of them.
They followed the trail of recently dug corms, and even
Water Willow noticed how the bear tracks eventually wove
and staggered. Máⁿchu Máⁿkaⁿ explained - that the animals
knew many strong poisons that were also strong medicines.
That they could get drunk on berries,
but stand up to poisons.
But what a bear could bear,
was often much more than any person.

FACING THE WIND
KÍMO^NHO^N

Her father, Kímoⁿhoⁿ, was the one who showed her the hunt, and basic weapon making skills.

He was not a talker. Talk was wasted, in his eyes, and long speech was saved for matters he shared with his wife.

He did not show emotions unless they ran up his spine and forced their way through his throat. And then his voice had the guttural power of a snarling wolf.

When honored with the role of wáthoⁿ, he directed and led the buffalo hunt, managed the approach and chase, straight nosed and forward, as a good leader would. He protected his family and clan, with fierce tenacity and loyalty.

Water Willow learned from him how to sharpen her own claws, keep her ears up, snarl at threats and nip any hand that threatened her.

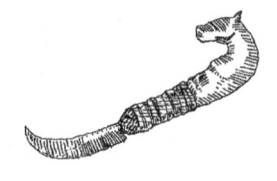

THEIR HORSES
OᴺSHÓᴺGE-MA

Early on they were taught how to ride their horse backwards,
for many reasons, it could save them, to know this trick.
A herd of children riding their ponies backwards
made you think you were seeing things.

You could fool someone distant, long enough to gain
sufficient ground for escape, them expecting you to get
closer, but instead see you moving smaller, away.
Or when having to aim at the predator coming from behind,
the shot to bring him down.
Every child that could ride, forward or backwards,
was a trick of the eye, horse magic.

They were taught to disappear *beside* the horse, to flatten
against his ribs, one leg hooked over his hip or shoulder,
disappear into a herd, hide when passing enemy camp.

And then, to ride the neck, to swing freely up and down off
the ground, the horse's head lifting you up onto his back.
This skill and speed was not acquired by all.
But Water Willow was one, with her horse.

MOONS
NÍO^NBA AMA

People knew the earth's smells and tastes on which their lives
depended. Knew when something was ready to be planted,
plucked, dug, tracked or hunted.
The naming of their days, of their moons, reflected this.
Each moon was named for food, or lack of it.
She was born at The Beginning of cold weather.
The next full moon brought Snow, and frozen water.
Deer pawed the snow, in search of food, under a hungry
hardship moon.
When Geese came back, trees snapped free of ice.
The Sore-eyes moon signaled the end of glaring snow.
With Rains came tender grass.
They planted under the moon Spring begins,
when leaves held potent medicine.
Hot weather, and they dug Núgtha.
As the Green Corn grew, so the Buffalo fattened.
Prairie roses bloomed in the middle of summer and they
picked Chokecherry. Corn in silk, with the Moon of ripening.
When all leaves had color, Elk bellowed at the moon.
Then they Stored food in caches, to prepare again,
for the Beginning of cold weather.

PLANTING
ÚZHI ZHI

After the full Sore Eyes Moon, glaring snow melted and the earth softened. They all began the daily treks to their fields and clearings outside camp. They assembled willow branches and old lodge poles to repair the family borders that wove around the edges.

They raked fallen branches, brushed dead grasses into piles. They were careful to leave cold, wet earth, banked around the edges, so the fires they set over the garden fields could not travel past to surrounding trees and grass.

Very early next morning, while winds still slept and moisture hung cool and heavy in the air, they set flame to the dead wood and brush, and smoke hung low, until the garden fields were all burned in, the ash stirred up.

They raked black ashes into earth with antler rakes. Worked together to turn the dirt. Stirred the earth with buffalo and elk-shoulder hoes. When plum trees blossomed, the seeds went in.

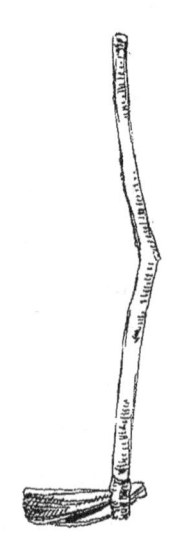

The women went out, planting poles in hand, seed bags at their hips, poking holes and planting corn, beans, squash and pumpkins.

As the seeds thrived, they hoed and pulled wild greens that grew naturally in profusion between the rows and beds. They ate these fresh and dried, in soups, teas and medicine.

Water Willow's Grandmother always let the wild plants grow in around the edges, because she knew their many uses. Every harvest, they saved some of the wild plant seeds, as well as the best ears of corn, for next year.

Summer brought melons, beans, sunflowers and corn. They'd harvest, dry, and Store Food in Caches, as yellow cottonwood leaves shook, then fell.

Sometimes, these stores of squash, beans, and corn lasted all winter. Sometimes they fell short.

Water Willow felt a hunger to know what everything was, how it grew, how it lived, what it became, how it was used, how it died. She collected seeds of every kind, wrapped in little scraps and bags. As a child, she had her own part of the garden, planted with some of everything. From her seed and nut collection, came her own circle of discovering. She discovered things that everyone knew and discovered things no one else noticed.

She could not sit still long. She rode fast, always looking out ahead and moving on. It was not long before Water Willow saw that the...

> *River ran through the sky.*
> *Sky was in the river.*
> *Earth was in the plants.*
> *Plants were in the earth.*
> *Sun was in the stars.*
> *Stars were in the sun.*
> *Animals were part of each other.*
> *Animals were part of her.*
> *Bees and flowers made honey.*
> *Butterflies were the flowers they drank from.*
> *Buffalo were the grasses they grazed on.*

She spent most of her summer days in the creek.
She loved water. Or foraging on the sandy shores.
Her mother, KóⁿdehiWin, told her it was because
she had been born by it...

> *'...under a twin black willow*
> *rooted on the west bank of Níⁿshude tʰe...'*

Níⁿshude, the wide muddy river, where her mother clung
to the twisting branches of the twin black willow who helped
her to give birth, who gave her name to her.

~

She loved the Earth.
She was lulled by the security of her fingers in the cool dirt.
She loved the days of quiet, in the gardens,
peace from the nights, and their attending nightmares.

These, she shared with no one.

By Grandmother's side in the corn fields,
she was happiest, rapturous.
Sitting on her horse, in the middle of the herd,
or in the rare absence of wind -and No Voices- she relaxed.
She knew to treasure childhood as she lived it.

BEAR MEDICINE
MÁᴺCHU MÁᴺKAᴺ

"What does it mean? To have Bear Medicine?" Water Willow asked one day. Grandmother explained that it was only certain medicine keepers, permitted this honor. To *have* Bear Medicine, came only with permission from the bear. Only with permission, could a partnership be shared. *Bear medicine* came only to those chosen, by the bear.

Furthermore, it was never permitted to use bear medicine without the proper prayers and ways of living required, in offering. If another person came upon a bear in hunting, they were obligated to reserve the fat, oils and claws for their Bear Medicine Man. To make such a gift to him was a great honor for any person.

> "The Bear chose your Grandfather when he was a very young boy, and that is a story only *he* can share with you, and only with his permission can you ever tell another, after his leaving. You see, often the power in a story is held by being careful how you spread it. Such a story as his, expects such care as this."

This of course made Water Willow all the more curious.
So she made certain that she woke next morning long
before her Grandfather, and that she was waiting, standing
by his teepee when he rose. She brought him a basket of
just-picked berries because she knew he loved these.
She thought them a generous waónthe for his secrets.

As he ate them, thoroughly enjoying each and every berry,
Water Willow waited. Finally, she spoke.
> "Grandfather, I am asking you about the
> Bear and how it came to you."

Grandfather shook his shoulders and wrapped his thick
bear robe tight around him. He wagged his finger at her.
> "Oh...no...You are so young... no...no...
> and yet...I look back....I look at you...and
> I remember... I was a winter younger when
> *I lived it* myself!"

Grandfather threw the biggest berry into the fire.
> "And so I ask permission to tell you now,
> since you *are* so seriously listening."

As the plump berry burst and hissed, sweet wild blueberry
filled the air. She inhaled and so Grandfather began.
> "My father and mother were camped, early
> in the Moon of Tender Grass. We were
> journeying between camps, as my mother
> was heavy with her second child and wanted
> to be with her sisters when that time came.
> My mother was building a cook-fire, and warming
> corn soup, while my father was off hunting.
> Mother complained of tugging in her belly and

asked me to go off in search of raspberries, and if it
was too early, to at least bring back the young silvery
leaves and root bark. I thought this strange. Even as
a small child, I knew it would be another moon
before the fruit came. But I did as she asked,
hurrying away because she told me to return quickly.

I climbed up from the ravine in which she was
hidden. The grassy fields gave way to sloping hills.
I climbed up and down them, scanning from the hilltops,
as the rising sun revealed their undergrowth. The air
warmed and filled with the sweet scent of berries, and
they were not hard to find.

I could not believe my eyes when I climbed a hill
marked by an old twisted cedar tree, dead, bent and
hunched against the winds. Beneath and all around
it were massive bushes, berries hanging heavy with
morning dew.

I forgot the hurry that my mother was in, and started
eating as many berries as I picked. Then I remembered,
and filled a small pouch for her and then started to fill
up my turned-up shirt with all I could carry,

when out of the corner of my eye,
I saw the cedar tree move.
I froze, holding a handful of berries,
and my breath.
It was not a moving tree!
It was a grizzly bear!
An old grandmother bear, who moved slow, ambling
up beside me, reaching her nose out to my trembling
hand. I squeezed those berries in fright, but she just
licked my hand clean and when I let the berries fall
from my tunic to the ground, she just snuffed up
every one of them. Then she did the strangest thing.
She pushed me with her cold nose, as if I were some
stray cub. I think her eyesight was very poor, because
she did not regard me as a boy, but took me in like one
of her own. She nudged me down the slope, directing me.
The Bear showed me many plants it ate in those early
days of spring, Mépahaⁿga. She showed me roots and
young leaves in the deep woods that only she could
stomach. Even so, they sometimes made her wobble.
As a child not much bigger than you, I easily
remembered them. I was low to the ground, and so
the plants were easy for me to find. I dug the roots up
alongside her, but buried them in the pouches at my
waist, rather than eat them – because they made her
mouth froth and stung my tongue when I licked them.

The bear told me all the while what the roots
were meant for- that one for a tooth aching...
the other for grumbling bellies...
this, for pulling out babies.
The bear spoke to me in pictures,
and it is hard to put in words,
but with each new smell and taste
came the full picture in mind of its use.
Grandmother Bear slipped her paw under
loose leaf litter. Wrapped a claw under,
and pulled up an old root.
She chewed on it before giving it over to me.
A long, fringed root- its pungent smell delivered
a vision of yellow moccasin slippers,
the graceful flower that grows from it.
It was one root into guided dreaming,
and one root to help a mother's pain,
a root to help the baby come...
twisting between two worlds.

Then the bear curled up
in one big yawning heap
and fell into a deep sleep
atop a wide fallen log
upon which I sat,
watching.

I smelled the root in hand, licked it again,
and slipped down to the ground, curling
against the warm, thick shoulder of the bear.
Sleepy, I thought of my mother and that I
really should be getting back to her...

Next memory I have, is that of waking by
the warm fire, opening my eyes to meet those
of my mother and the new baby beside her.

I was later told by father, that he found me,
dreaming under a log, talking in my sleep,
my lips and hands stained with berry juice.
He shouldered me and carried me back to camp.
I was in a delirious state, but as they listened
to my rambling, they heard tell the secrets of
the root that I still gripped in hand.

And so mother simmered a tea, and soon after
drinking it, the baby that had been pulling the
wrong way in her belly, easily turned,
and came into the world.

And so she was named, Mánkaⁿ Híⁿbe-zha,
in honor of the Moccasin Flower root
that delivered her."

Water Willow smiled at this happy ending of the story and was glad she had been brave enough to ask Mánchu Mánkan.

FIRST HUNTER
PAHÓᴺGA ÁBAÌ

Water Willow was invisible in the tall grass
when hunting rabbits and birds.
She melted into the shadows of dusk,
to track deer in the woods.

Kíka Toⁿgà, Chief Shúde Gáxe's youngest son,
and her promised ally in hunting,
stalked the thickets alongside her.
They pretended they never missed
with their blunt, green sticks.

She cherished her first bow.
She slept with it beside her,
near her birth-cord turtle charm,
and her beaded hide-scrap pony.

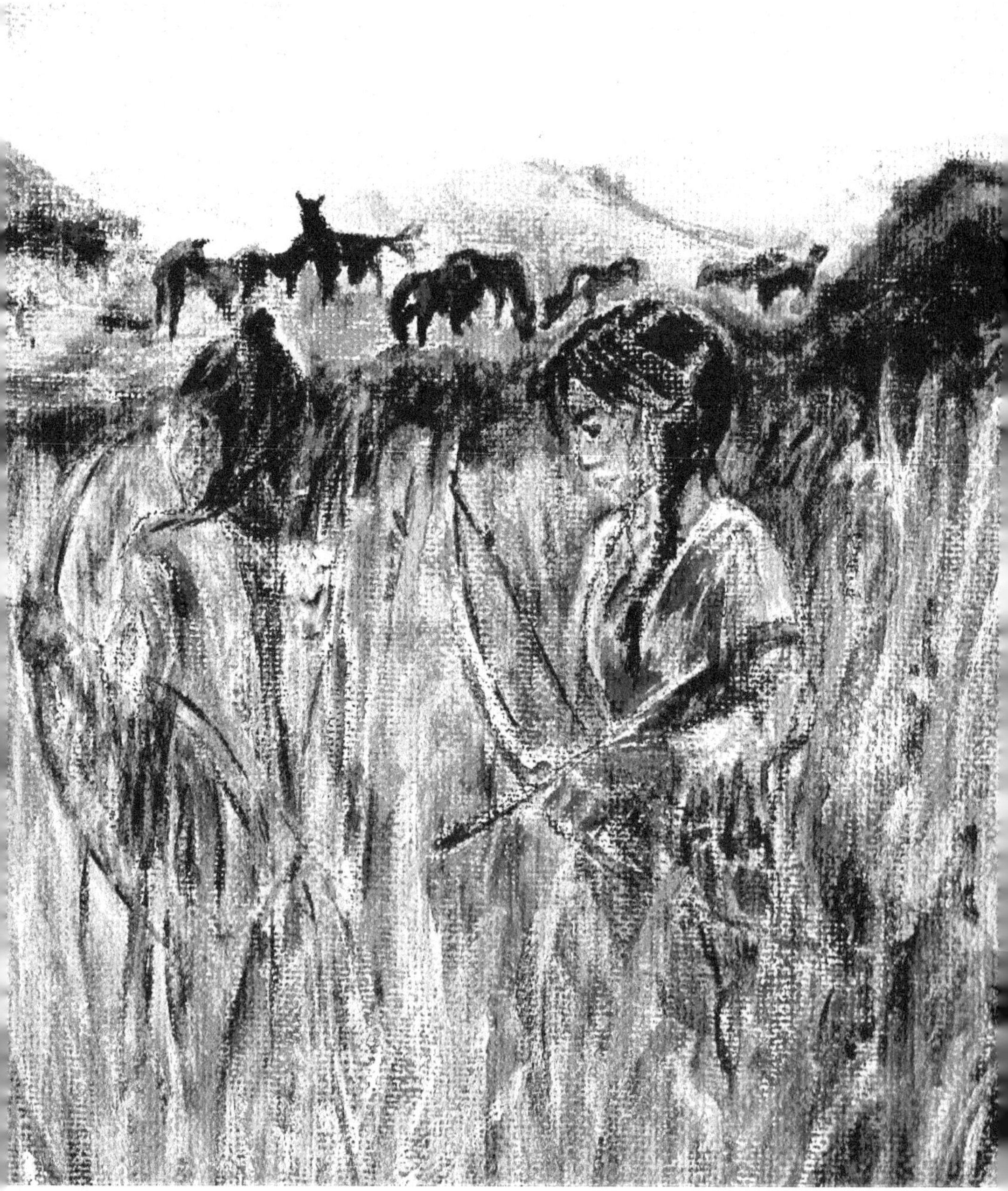

Many people made gifts to her elders, in gratitude for Water Willow's dreams and for the lives that were spared in heeding them. She was given her own horse, a fine Palouse, with a beautiful red and white spotted rump, and already thick winter coat.
When the time came, she was taken by her mother's brother to further her skills and ways of weapon-making, to find and flake her own arrow tips, to make and use her first real hunting bow.
Her uncle took them far into forests that spoke in deep voices.
She stalked animals that froze and looked her in the eye.
These, she could not kill. She had to be taught.

So Uncle told the Story of First Hunter, PaHóⁿga ábai who had long ago come from woodlands of the eastern door.

PaHóⁿga ábai walked on cold and naked feet
and he was starving.
His belly gnawed against his ribs.
He fainted from hunger
and dreamt an Elk
dragging one rear foot
hiding in thick trees.
The Elk spoke to him,
saying he would give his own life, to First Hunter,
<u>if</u> he would forever keep a Promise...

The Promise

My life will soon be yours, if you follow my trail
Of steps to the grove of dogwood saplings.
Choose the sapling that will give itself to your bow
Choose one that will offer its arms for arrows
Fine branches that will best pierce the sky
Offer to it, many prayers and thanks
For giving its life so that you may live.
Promise, once you have chosen to take a life
To use every part of it, let none be wasted.
Follow my trail into the deepest woods,
To find the black stone that can be carved to fine sharpness.
Make it beautiful and narrow, with your carving, your thoughts.
Chip and carve the tips, with the full power of your hunger.
Form the bow, form the arrows, with the power of your prayers.
Then Follow my steps back to these foot hills
where I will be waiting for your arrow
to release the pain of my broken leg

<<<< -- *The Promise, you must forever keep* ----- <<<

That you take only what you need,
Only with thanks and proper offerings
And to make good use, let none be wasted.
Remember, we <u>give</u> our lives to you
so that you may live and so that
We may live in you.
You cannot <u>take</u> life
or break the Promise.
If this Promise is forgotten,
Honor and Balance is forgotten
and You, Your children,
All Your Grand children
will suffer the fate
of starvation...

When he awoke, the weak hunter knew he'd soon be eating and this gave him strength. He crept ahead into the cold forest.

In a shadowy clearing, his eyes fell upon the recent trail of a large Elk. Three hooves sank deep into the earth and the fourth scraped along behind.

He followed the tracks to a circle of saplings. One sapling had long been pinned to the ground by a heavy fallen limb. It was bowed over, growing in an arch, its branches shooting straight up to the sky in search of light.

He thanked the tree and its family. Sat talking with them while he untied the long cord wraps from his hair. He cut off one long braid and hung it from the sapling's mother tree, with a prayer of thanks.

He would use every part, root, twigs, branches and bark. He cut the first branch. The sap smelled bitter sweet. First Hunter licked the bud, chewed on it, sucked its bitter nourishment. He trimmed off the tender twigs, to use for tea. Stacked these in bundles.

Next he cut straight branches. Sorted through them for arrows and praised their perfect growth. He thanked the thicker, sturdy branches on the lower trunk, saving these for the Grandmothers, to make root digger sticks.

All that was remaining was the thin arched trunk of the sapling, which spoke to him, suggesting how best to shape the bow into his hand. He worked long, the voice telling, how to shape a perfect bow, and carve a straight, swift arrow.

In the end, he hauled up the roots that held the leaning tree in the earth. He cut a length of root to small pieces, and shook them free of dirt, to bag and keep for later use. Elk Hunter left the upturned root clump for the forest animals to finish off. The bitter roots would help some survive the coming winter.

Carrying the Zhon-zi-zhu[5] bow, First Hunter followed the elk trail, past a dark rock hollow. He found flint there; sharp rocks which he chipped and shaped into arrow tips. He fastened these to split ended shafts.

When all was ready, he followed the Elk trail to the nearby
foothills. Step, step, step, scrape...

Came upon the wounded buck, at rest in a grass clearing,
curled in tall grass, slowly chewing.
Its eyes were glazed, its nose was dry.
It stood, but did not try to run.

When their eyes met,
the Promise was kept   >>>------------>

FIRST DOE
TÁXTI MÍGA PAHÓⁿGA

Water Willow stalked her first doe for three days. This doe was smaller than the others. Her trails changed erratically, often separating from her group, as if searching for something.

Water Willow hid behind a fallen log that crossed the doe's morning trail, and waited. But she was not the only hunter out this morning.

In the distance she heard the distinct crack of a white gun. The deer came running, leaping clear towards her.

Water Willow aimed an arrow at her chest,
let it go straight to her heart.
It struck the doe as her feet touched the ground
and once more she leapt
briefly flew, before her front legs buckled under,
her chest collapsing to the ground.
The doe cried as it crumpled to its side.
Water Willow approached her, bent low.
She should have been quick then,
to end the suffering.
But her body was frozen helpless,
only her eyes and lips could move.

"Tstststs tsts   tsss...." she whispered.
"SHHHhhhhhh... shhh sssshhhhhhhhh..."
she had no words.

Only the comforting death song started tumbling itself out,
already knowing, she had killed it.
>"E ah tha ha ah e
>tha hae ah hah ha ah
>hae ah ah ah
>e tha ah ah ee."

The doe lifted her head to listen,
but her neck buckled to the earth
heavy with death.
Sunk into the grass.
Stilled her heaving ribs.
Water Willow wept as the veil came quick
over the doe eyes.
So it was, weeping Water Willow
that brought down her first deer.

CORN FIELDS
WÁHABA WA ÁITE

KóⁿdehiWiⁿ's voice was newly accompanied by the gurgling baby on her back, Water Willow's first brother, who mostly slept and nursed, humming like a bird. When Water Willow held him, or rocked him to stop his crying, she sang planting songs to him and sometimes she made up new ones...

"Green corn, green trees,
Yellow corn, yellow leaves
Brown stalks, bare branches,
Corn powder, snow showers"

She often watched him while sitting up on the corn stand. She liked singing the corn to grow while her mother hoed the rows below them. She liked hearing the wind and the corn and her mother singing. She liked the feeling of roots pushing down through earth, of corn leaves rustling up. She liked to chase the crows with her flapping blanket, and to outsmart them.

But she did not care for the flies, or gnats that ravaged them. So she swatted and swung until she could not bear it.

If the baby was not in her care, she often abruptly deserted the corn-field platform, to head for the nearest cool water. She'd leave her blanket and moccasins hanging on a platform post, blowing in the breeze, to fool the crows and any rodents who thought of stealing. Her deceptions did not go unnoticed by KóⁿdehiWiⁿ …

> "Most crows are napping in the heat of the
> day but when they catch us napping, when
> our backs are turned, those smart birds take
> this time for thievery.
> That's why you must stay on the platform
> by day or some cunning birds will pick
> your fields clean."

BUFFALO RING   Late September 1843
TÉ'ÁMA UTHISHÓN AYÁTHAI

Looking over the hill below,
she saw a massive buffalo ring,
It was a long ride wide.
The ring was formed by countless buffalo bulls
protecting the cows and calves
within their circle.
Behind the bulls, the cows
formed a thick inner wall,
a wall of protection for their young.
Inside that, the young cried.
The buffalo had circled up
against a pack of circling wolves,
snarling, closing in
the hungry packs coming at them
from all directions
yellow, white, black and red, hair bristling.
The wolves trotted, circling tighter,
tongues hanging, waiting for a gap,
patient for a weakness.
The buffalo did not retreat.
The bulls did not falter.
They stood their ground
churning their circle of earth to dust
until one young cow panicked,
she and her young calf darting outside the ring.

The ground shook as young bulls
stampeded to claim her
and wolves tore past them.
The cow charged on
as her calf straggled behind her.
Water Willow watched the cow,
running blind
straight into their buffalo corral
when a scout ran his horse to the gate
and dropped the latch.
It shut tight against the wolves at his back
and his horse ran forward,
hard away from there
as he turned, shooting arrows behind.

The panting cow turned and bellowed
at the solid gate wall,
at the feasting wolves outside-
frantic when she heard her calf scream
in their mouths.

Water Willow watched the carnage.
Gorging wolves covered the cliff side,
taking down young bulls, tearing at carcasses.
Water Willow galloped her fast pony
for the hills to tell the others.
Bulls and wolves stampeded below her.

Then she saw the buffalo hunters,
led by sharp toothed buffalo dogs,
coming up fast on the broken circle of buffalo.
The dogs and riders funneled the buffalo
towards the corral.
Buffalo fell to arrows.
The rest, trapped in the corral.
Water Willow saw through clouds of dust.
A grey wolf with yellow eyes looked up.
> *"Dreamer...see the buffalo come...*
> *running from wolves from all directions.*
> *Dogs will help you stalk them..."*

*The wolf turned on his heels
trotted over the hill,
loped away into the distance,
his gorged belly swinging,
disappeared into the dust cloud
where the buffalo circle had been.*

*A ring of tall buffalo grass
had already sprung up,
thriving in the circle of churned earth
and buffalo dung, where the herd
had only just been.*

Upon awakening, Water Willow knew her people should look for the buffalo grass ring, and use the buffalo dogs to stalk and close in on them.

She shared her vision with her Father, who offered the proper gifts to the Chiefs, offered himself again, as wátho[n], to lead the buffalo hunt. He would conduct the hunt with respect to details of Water Willow's vision. The council agreed and camp made ready to herd in the buffalo.

~

The fire was big in the center of the camp circle. Water Willow sat with her grandmother, burning zhabátazhon, beaver wood, bark down to charcoal, with which to mix bowls of black paint for the hunters.

Hunters bathed in sage and cedar smoke - purified their weapons and their horses. They lit their pipes to the buffalo. They sent smoke to the sky, as red dawn broke over the horizon. They smoked east to the sun and its fire. They smoked south to the water, west to the hills. To the north they blew their smoke to open plains, to the buffalo that lived there, touching earth and sky. When they rode off, the horizon was a thin line of black against the first red light.

At sun rise, Water Willow practiced with her new bow,
balancing arrows, left side of the string, looking down their
grooved shafts, straight into the heart of her target.
She shot at a hill of red mud piled high on the shore.
The arrows burrowed into the hill, and the mud oozed
from the carved grooves, like thick brown blood.

A scout soon reported back. A buffalo grass ring had been
found to the east. The people rode out of the valley in
silence, cutting across the slope of Water Willow's dream,
towards where she had seen the buffalo ring.

Water Willow watched them go, saw them line the slope,
hiding behind trees and boulders, waiting to surprise the
approaching buffalo and funnel them towards the corral.
Water Willow shivered, remembering the stampede that
was to come and thought, only just then,
of the single cow crying from the corral,
at her calf, being torn through.

She wondered why she had forgotten to tell about that.

CALICO RAG
WAXÍᴺHA

Udaⁿ! The noise rose up! The returning hunters were near. The camp was strung with readiness. The people lined the incoming valley, holding their blankets, dogs and rattles, their skinning knives sharp and ready at their hips.

A whoop came sounding from the eastern hills and two scouts galloped down, paths crossing, signifying that buffalo were coming straight at them. They flew down the hill, soon followed by the stampede and then the rush of mounted men driving behind them.

The camp moved as one huge river, waving blankets in a colorful current that funneled the herd between piled brush and boulders, towards the corral. Pushing, pounding, churning, hungry dogs chasing their heels. Arrows flew. Buffalo fell along the swath of the hunt.

Water Willow chose a limestone cliff on which to perch her sure-footed pony. The valley below was cloaked in the buffalo cloud, obliterating vision until they had passed – most of them straight into the corral.

Buffalo rammed the trunks of the pole circle which held them. Hunters climbed the surrounding cliff sides and aimed for their chosen kills. Arrows sank into hearts, lungs, ribs and shoulders.

The arrows marked them; some by the feather signature of the arrow's maker. Others were claimed with torn pieces and strips of painted hide or trade-cloth, tied to the buffalo horns.

As the dust settled, Water Willow watched scraps and ribbons of colorful cloth flutter in the wind. She talked her pony down the dusty cliff side for a closer look.

Water Willow approached a dying bull, a strip of red calico fluttering from his horn. She circled with her pony, to get a good look. When she saw his breath subside, she slid down and walked slowly towards him. She held her breath, reached for the cloth, snatched it away and stood at a distance.

Her pony quivering, she held its rope firm with one hand and held the cloth tight in the other. She had never seen such a fine cloth.... had never seen a pattern so delicate, so perfectly woven, so precisely repeated, row upon row of rosebuds, perfect and alike... never ending blossoms. She smelled it, half expecting the scent of roses. She turned it, over and over in her hands, rubbed it between her thumb and fingers.

She thought of the time it took her to bead one floral design.
Wondered *Who on this earth could weave flowers so small?*

Then the bull heaved a deep and final breath,
shook Water Willow where she stood.
She froze near his open staring eye and
felt smaller than she ever had before.

She felt his life leave in the breath
that wet her shivering legs.
Washábe' Té-nuga
the spirit bull passed through her
buckled her knees.
Pinned her to the ground
with cold breath, dead stare.
She could not move,
no matter her thoughts.
Her eyes, dark.
Her body
fainting
away.

~

67

When the Palouse Pony returned to camp without her,
Kímonhon led the search.
He found Water Willow laid out on the ground beside a
bull, a grey buffalo dog standing guard over her. The dog
snarled at his approach. Kímonhon snarled back and chased
the dog off.

Kímonhon picked up his daughter and carried her,
still clutching the flower cloth, back to camp.
The grey dog followed, yellow eyes fixed, growling low,
keeping just out of reach of Kímonhon's kick.

When they reached Grandmother's lodge, Kímonhon
threw the loyal dog a fresh rib, hanging with raw meat.
KóndehiWin was called in from the skinning fields to tend
to her daughter.

Nónzhin Mónthin set pots to boil and gathered fever
medicines, but felt a powerful chill creep up her spine, and
already knew that powers greater than hers had slipped in.

They all listened to Water Willow's garbled speech
as she fought the small pox fever
carried by the spotted calico cloth and blankets,
from a Trader's camp, to theirs.

>>>--<<<

Some whispered outside Grandmother's lodge.

There were some who said
  'they would never <u>have</u> the fever'

        'if Water Willow never dreamed
        to send the hunters out ...'

'What of the hunters who stopped - to trade for guns
              and feed on tender white calf ...
              when they crossed a Trader's camp?'

'Though the Trader Camp was not part of her vision...
            It happened.'
There were some who said it was
      'the taboo against eating calf'.

Some who said
    'It was the Cloth...
          that brought it to them'
and so
    all the 'White Cloth'
          was burned.

Waxíⁿha	*The White Cloth*
Péde oⁿgáxe	*They burned*
Waíⁿ ska	*The thin skin calico*
Péde oⁿgáxe	*They burned*
Waxíⁿha	*The White Cloth*
Na xúde, oⁿwàgaxe	*Burnt all*
Waíⁿ ska	*The calico.*
Na xúde, oⁿwàgaxe	*Burnt all*

NETTLES
MANÓNZHINHA-HI

Everyone was asleep in the lodge circle,
feet facing the fire in the middle.
The sound of her own labored breathing
scraped against her ears.
Water Willow's head was so heavy
she could not lift it.
It hurt to open her eyes. The pain throbbed.
She dragged her tangled, smothered limbs,
out of the twisted robe covers.
She crawled, stumbling by the flames.
She was so hot, fire did not scare her.
She was already on fire.
She tried to scream... but no sound
no scream would come, so she *knew*
she must be dreaming...
Her tongue, so dry and swollen
choked her breath.
Gasping, rasping, '*Ni... Ni... Ni...*'
Begging for... *Water...water...water...*
Her steaming face, like broth
she stood, her legs like soup
scuffing bare feet out the door
crackling fire behind her...

hissing... *Water...water...water...*
Outside, cold air tickling
and she heard *giggling*
Heard the bubbling stream... *Water... water... water...*
its bright surface, sparkling against black depths...
She ran with every drop of strength the cool air offered.
The giggling surrounding her...but she saw no one.
Did not see the stalks bent towards her
or the shoots covering shore
or the potent roots
breaking through eroded earth
running across
the sandy surface
spreading, sprawling, fiery brush
but she ran through it
until all at once her ankles *burned.*
Her legs, her fingers, wrists, arms
stinging...stinging...
on fire with needles!
Tripping in the dark
she fell flat
her face pressed
with potent quills and barbs.

Her nose and cheeks blistered.
Her brambled eyelids swelled shut.
Covered with welts
that stung like sparks
she rolled downhill...
toward the cool *water*...
into the smooth *water*...
rolled under deep *water*...
Stroked her heavy arms against the fever
the burning, the stinging.
Her head submerged, her face immersed.
Her feet no longer touching sandy bottom.
The burning stopped
in the black cold rolling water...
She thrashed back up only
in need of *Air!*
She sucked in, heaving, inhaling.
In and out of the cool rushing water...
her body rolled...into the dark, gasping
until she was pulled
by strong arms
Out.

~

Thédewathatha carried her across the bank.
Running up the hill, he did not feel
the nasty stinging at his ankles
up to his knees.
Until later.
Sobbing, eyes swelled shut, she could not see
but felt Grandmother's hand,
heard her hushing *"Shhhh... Shhhh... Shhhh..."*
and still she fought, arms swinging, nails scratching
wanting to go *back*... to the *"Water...water...water..."*
Shaking, cramping cold, turning blue, blacking out.

~

Nóⁿzhiⁿ Móⁿthiⁿ did not know the rash, until Thédewathatha showed the welts burning up his own legs, and so he brought them to the place where he'd found Water Willow and carried her uphill. The path was clear.

Under the light of torch fire, they found the sprawling plant, touched its leaves with care. After one touch, one sting, they all became respectful of its strength and poison. The plants were covered in potent stinging hairs! One brush against them brought the burning rash to even the toughest skin.

But now Nónzhiⁿ Mónthiⁿ discovered that if she held the stem carefully, with its hairs pointing up, flattened against its square stem, the barbs held their sting at bay. And if she poured hot water on them, the stinging hairs dissolved to harmless.

But the stinging plant seemed to be laughing, every time it got her! Soon her finger tips tingled up through her wrists. As she felt the burn move, heating up her skin, she thought
>*This is a plant to set fire to fevers*
>*and move them out quicker...*
>*Their power to burn will drive out the fever*
>*their poison barbs will chase it out fast...*

Nónzhiⁿ Mónthiⁿ boiled some fresh crushed nettle. Watched the water turn gold, then green, then almost black, a shiny scum rise to the top. She tasted the medicine and let it soak in, warm her throat. She filled a bladder flask with the nettle medicine, for Water Willow to drink from.

Water Willow whispered as she drank,
>*"Nettie! Nettie Stinging! Manóⁿzhiⁿhahi!"*

Rain Walking leaned over, listening, learned the name.
>*"Nettie?... Manóⁿzhiⁿhahi! Standing hairs!?!"*

~

With thankful prayers, Rain Walking gathered more at first light. With KóndehiWin's help, they soon filled a blanket with pinched shoots and long stems and delivered some to the lodge of every person who showed signs of the sickness- with instructions – how long to boil it, how to use it to fight the spotted fever.

KóndehiWin wrapped Water Willow's hands to keep her from scratching the pox welts and pustules that covered her skin.

Nónzhin Mónthin was certain that the sickness was carried in those spots, that the oozing crust was what spread it. She said the less a victim touched, picked the oozing scabs, the less chance of spreading the sickness. She knew the illness was carried in their blackness.

LODGE
Í'UPE

Stone-people lodge; Sweat lodge

The family prepared a stone people lodge, gathering smooth stones from the river, heating them, deep within the sacred fire.

Grandmother made a strong pot of coneflower-root medicine. This they drank, and washed over their skin, to help them bear the intense heat. She washed Water Willow's skin in the decoction, before laying her on a clean buffalo hide.

Kímonhon carried Water Willow to the lodge and laid her down in the east, where the heat would be most intense. Then he took his place outside, as fire-keeper.
Mánchu Mánkan arrived with his strong Bear Medicine. They burned sage and bathed themselves in its smoke, and offered tobacco prayers to the fire, before opening the sacred lodge door. One by one they crawled in, then closed the lodge and sealed Water Willow in it with them.
Nónzhin Mónthin sprinkled fresh cut cedar on the red hot stones. Thick cedar smoke and vapor filled the air, burned their eyes and throats.
KóndehiWin led their prayer songs, beating on a small drum, calling in all directions.

Kímonhon used deer antlers to carry in the hot stones.
He slid them steady through the door flap, kept the hot
stones coming, though he himself felt weak. The heat slowly
stole into him. He fought it off, thinking of his daughter's
shallow breath, and how she needed him, how this lodge
would give her strength, and so he gave his.

Mánchu Mánkan poured water on the hot stones.
It came up steaming, filling the lodge with strong heat.
They sang for Water Willow. Watched her shivering lips
as she struggled to draw breath, bound in cloth, cocoon
tight.

Grandmother loosened Water Willow's cloth robe.
Uncovered her feet and unwrapped her hands, which were
bandaged and tied at the wrists.
> "She is so weak, we won't worry that she'll
> scratch now. Leave her hands free for a while."

Grandmother chewed on juniper[6] berries, breathing its
juices onto Water Willow's face. The juniper berries were
a barrier to the fever's spell. Grandmother spit the well-
chewed berries into her hands, rubbing their oil onto her
own hands and forearms, so the fever could not move in
to her. She rubbed the berries briskly into Water Willow's
hands and feet. Water Willow was limp to every touch, and
her eyelids never twitched. Her legs were logs and she floated
so far away.

Even so, Grandmother had KóⁿdehiWiⁿ hold Water Willow, to restrain her during the nettle lashes that were coming. Grandmother removed the cloth robe and poured warm water over her, then thrashed her spotted skin with stinging nettles. Like a broom she swept her granddaughter's body of every sick spirit. She lashed out at the sickness and color rose in Water Willow's skin.

> *Water Willow was unconscious*
> *but she screamed inside her*
> *as blood rushed to the surface*
> *of her welting skin*
> *she tried to scratch and claw the animals biting*
> *the wasps stinging all over her!*

Grandmother felt the nettle medicine work into her own hands, felt their tingling vibration, their intense and tangible spirit.

Finally, she spread a paste of windflower root over the nettle- reddened skin. This fresh salve would draw out the sickness, as it soothed her welting skin. Water Willow vaporized the juniper oil, wind flower paste and nettle steam, in the rising heat of her body.
Her skin opened wide, drinking in the medicines, sweating out the poisons, bathing in the smoke and steam.
They watched it rise from her. Listened to her breathing.
They let no one in or out, but for the incoming hot rocks.

Again the door closed, water poured, steam rose.
They went on, drumming songs, carrying her along,
sending prayers up, pleading.
Mánchu Mánkan shook his gourd rattle,
waking the pulse and flow of Water Willow's blood,
the drum beating with her heart,
breaking the fever in her body.
He used his eagle bone straw to suck the fever from her chest.
He trembled with a deep chill
that passed from her,
rattled his old bones.
He soaked in the vapor.
Breathed in the heat.
Yet still he shivered.
He called for more hot stones.
Generously splashed the water onto them.
The lodge filled with seething steam.
Everyone gasped for breath.
Grandmother lowered her forehead to the cool earth.
Mánchu Mánkan watched Water Willow's breath quiver,
until shaking, chin to toe, she drew in deep breaths,
her limbs relaxed, and her breath evened out,
drawn deep and steady now.
KóndehiWin sang strong, their final song,
drummed the spirits back on their paths.

Mánchu Mánkaⁿ called for Kímoⁿhoⁿ to open the door.

Kímoⁿhoⁿ was slow to answer, slow to move.
Bear Medicine called.
When Kímoⁿhoⁿ came and finally lifted the door
the cool night air seeped in as steam rolled out
and the fevered spirits rushed right through him.

As Water Willow was carried from the sweat lodge,
back to the earth lodge, they *all* heard the giggling nettle
on the nearby slope, steam and spirits floating over them.

~

Next day, Grandmother stirred more crushed nettle shoots
into a bowl of steaming water. As she stirred, their smell was
so distinctly pungent that Water Willow, nearly conscious,
could almost taste them. Grandmother held the brew to
Water Willow's lips until the bowl was empty.
The fever declined as the nettles cooled her exhausted body.
They removed the cloth and buffalo robe. Grandmother
and KóⁿdehiWiⁿ rubbed her legs with arnica and bear grease,
to bring life back in them.
As Grandmother stroked her arms from shoulders to wrist,
Water Willow's hand fell free, its tight clutch unfurling.

Steamed nettles uncurled from the moist palm of her hand. They were black and limp, cooked there, inside her small hand. Before drifting back to incoherent dreams, a song slipped from Water Willow's lips and they all listened...

    "Run through me, I scratch and sting.

    Touch me sweet, I will not prick.

    Soak and twist my fibers,

    to rope and weave.

    Pinch my leaves, for soups and teas.

    If you dare, with great care,

    use my roots and seeds.

    I'll creep under your skin,

    rush into your blood,

    green strong medicine."

Mánchu Mánkaⁿ, Nónzhiⁿ Mónthiⁿ, KóⁿdehiWiⁿ, Kímoⁿhoⁿ, all listened. They all leaned closer towards the girl. Whispered when they thought Water Willow deep asleep,

    "Where did Water Willow learn that song?"

    "Is that... her Dreaming?"

    "Such voices and songs come to born healers, Wazéthe-ma."

    "We must watch closer, protect her further."

These, their last words, before deep sleep.

As Water Willow slept, Grandmother gently sloughed her
dead skin with dried squash stems and bristled leaves.
Their hairy surface removed dead and dying skin, made her
skin pink. She cooled her with a wash of sage tea.
Continued to spoon meat broths into her mouth.
Burn sage and cedar in their lodge.

Finally, Grandmother removed the bedding from under
Water Willow, and threw it on the outside fire.
She burned the buffalo hide and robes, the blankets,
cloths, buckskin clothes, bandage mittens
and all the scabs within them.
The dread disease went up in smoke
but not soon enough.

In the next days
the fever widened its reach and grip.
While Thíxu wiⁿ recovered,
KóⁿdehiWiⁿ, her mother
Kímoⁿhoⁿ, her father
Máⁿchu Máⁿkaⁿ, Grandfather,
and her new Baby Brother,
were taken.
Nóⁿzhiⁿ Móⁿthiⁿ alone
remained with her.

FUNERAL PYRE
P'ÉDE WÁT'E[N]

September 1843

Water Willow saw her father,
mouth agape like a grounded fish,
her mother's body wrapped
around her little brother,
cradleboard dangling
from her charred arms.
She saw the flames eat their bodies
like sticks of tinder.
She smelled their burning flesh
and stinking hair.
The smell...
of funeral fires
is what woke her, floating.
She saw The Dead inside their homes,
weapons, clothes, their sacred things.
Tobacco and medicine bundles
went up in great clouds of smoke.
They burned the dead and all they touched.
Mourning cries, a ceaseless wailing,
rose with the flames, piercing.
Dogs howled and roamed the camp, rib hungry.
Those remaining standing moved on.

Water Willow saw Ears Up, skinny, dragging
few possessions on a small travois alongside her.
She saw her Self, a swaddled sack, bundled down there,
packed onto travois dragged by Red Pony.

So alone, Nónzhiⁿ Mónthiⁿ carried them all
on the Trail Away.
Nónzhiⁿ Mónthiⁿ did all she could
to remain standing.

Water Willow's dreaming eyes shut tight.

Along the Trail Away, Grandmother fed her teas of sage
and cedar. Rubbed wild onions into her feet. Poured
coneflower concoctions and bee balm tea, into her
parched throat. Thrashed her more with stinging nettie to
bring the blood rushing up, to keep her skin.

She felt none of it, tasted nothing, saw no time passing,
merely saw her body there, Grandmother tending it,
remembered dreaming ~

Great crowds faces empty
but for black hole mouths gasping
Walking, crawling, writhing
as if air was water
could not satisfy their breath
Faceless mouths sucking the air dry
hot and burning, hissing
grappling with each other
faces drowning in fire
that turned to red water
Deep swallowing water
She decided she could not breathe
but she could swim... up for air...
She could swim... this wide water
back to her People...
Tuck her arms, when waves pulled under
She Saw rolling wheels churn all around her
scraping sand against her burning skin
until something in the dark
pulled her Out
and squeezed
Breath In ~

Water Willow woke in the new camp

Not knowing how she got there

Not remembering anything

but fear and fire and water

Not remembering

Crowds drowning

Wheels turning

Her People dying.

Here she was

still alive.

RAIN WALKING
NÓⁿZHIⁿ MÓⁿTHIⁿ

Grandmother could hear Granddaughter from near or far, and did not always need to hear Water Willow's voice to know her thoughts.

It was this way with some families, with some people. Sometimes a wife could hear her husband, returning from hunt, before even camp dogs smelled the meat.
Some mothers knew, before told, of their wounded child. And always, Grandmother knew when Water Willow wandered off, and when she was on her way home.

Water Willow's mother, KóⁿdehiWiⁿ, had always worried more. She was one to lose her senses and her sleep, who sometimes shed quick tears of fear, when her daughter disappeared. Only over time did KóⁿdehiWiⁿ grow comforted knowing that Rain Walking felt no apprehension during Water Willow's wanderings.

Only when this Spotted Death, this Small Pox Fever, struck the village, did such a fear bring a well of tears from Rain Walking.

The Baby. KóⁿdehiWiⁿ. Kímoⁿhoⁿ. Máⁿchu Máⁿkaⁿ. Gone.

So many, many, lost.

Later, when the tears dried, Nóⁿzhiⁿ Móⁿthiⁿ told Water Willow that her tears were not only for the dead, but for herself. The self-pity of not *knowing*... not *knowing* Death was on its way.
For not *fore-SEEING*.

She asked Water Willow,
    "Did you dream, Granddaughter?
    Did you *see it* coming?
    Did you know?"

Water Willow answered her with a depth measured well beyond her years.
    "Grandmother, it is true.
    I do .... sometimes see and hear
    things long before they are visible.
    But when it's those things,
    those bad dreams,
    those I keep inside.
    Asíthe káⁿbthamaⁿzhi, asíthe naⁿmáⁿ.
    Things I don't want to remember, I always remember.

"I Fear the People would not live
even knowing Death will strike.
It is torture to know a thing
you cannot stop
you cannot believe
till it comes real.
And you live it, again.
Do not cry for not knowing, Grandmother.
You were *spared this bad vision.*"

SHE HAS CHANGED
WA'U THIK^HÉ THIÁZHI

For many mornings after, Water Willow woke groggy and
quiet, no courage to speak. She wandered through camp,
listless.

But she would often jump or startle, look back,
over her shoulder, as if she feared something following.
She told no one, what she had seen coming.
So afraid was she, but of *what*, she could not quite remember.
Something churning. It took years. Years stretched out in
fear. Water Willow healed from the smallpox fever,
but the drowning feeling inside never completely left her.
Grandmother could not uncover it.
Could not put her finger on it.
Water Willow was changed.
The People were changed.
They lived with an invisible undercurrent.
Bracing against waves.
But still, it came.
The flood of wagons.
Wheels turning...
the flood of memories,
finally unleashed...
and now real.

MORE MEN   Mormon Camp, Winter 1846
NÍASHIⁿGA-MA AHÍGE
Men, more

These blue people with their blue books, black hats, black bonnets. Grey, quiet faces. Ghosts trailing beside them.

More men and more women, English speaking.
The Strangers that accepted Ponca hospitality,
called themselves Friends, and stayed all winter.
They were watchful, thin lipped men and women.
Staring, shy children.

Water Willow saw they were the ghouls she had seen in her dreams. The same faces without mouths that woke her shivering from deep sleep. When their wagons rolled into camp, she hid inside, trying to think her way out of drowning. Ears Up whined outside, forgotten.

Since their arrival, Grandma could not coax her out the door in daylight.

    "No Wikóⁿ! *No!*" Water Willow cried.

    "They will *see* me!"

    "Of course they will see you. They have eyes, the same as us." Grandma answered calmly, knowing Water Willow referred to the long wagon train - over 400 More men Whites that set up camp along the Niobrara, a mile west of their village.

"*No* Grandma, *no! Not* eyes... *Holes!*"

Grandma tilted her head, trying to understand what her granddaughter had just said... *"Holes,* witúshpa?"

Water willow formed her fingers in round circles over her eyes.
> "Their *eyes* Grandma...
> are like gaping holes in their heads...
> There...in my dreams...
> *Holes! Where their eyes should have been!"*

Grandma nodded. "I see."

> "I cannot go *out there* Grandma...
> when their eyes are *open!"*

> "Hmmm...You are safer by night than by daylight?" asked Grandma, thoughtfully.

> "If they cannot *see* me,
> they cannot *suck* me in!"

Water Willow gestured emphatically, her hands acting it out, being sucked up from existence by a great spinning twister.

Grandma raised her head, raised her eyebrows. It seemed these white people held strong power over her granddaughter in dreams.

She waited for further explanation.

"They frighten me, they are so *hungry*...

for *some*thing... we cannot give them."

Water Willow answered, then turned her back to the door and went back to grinding corn like it was the most important chore on earth.

Grandma watched her - saw that her hands trembled with real fear, and that whatever her granddaughter saw, was indeed real.

~

Soon after, a chilly predawn came when Rain Walking let the fire go out in the night, then buried it.
She woke Water Willow and whispered instructions to her. As her eyes adjusted to the dark, Water Willow saw that Grandmother had packed full saddlebags and parflêches, and that now she bustled out, loading up Red Pony and Water Willow's Palouse mare. Together they rolled their lodge and packed the travois. Still dark, they quietly moved away from camp.

Water Willow did not ask where they were going.
She was still yawning as the sun came up over a faraway hill.

Grandmother answered Water Willow's silent questions nonetheless, by talking aloud, telling Red Pony where they were headed, just so the horse could get the picture and aim for it...

> "Water Willow will feel safer, at a distance
> from this crowd. Safely out of sight."
> "Yes," she went on, "Ponca have welcomed
> the strangers, but Granddaughter must
> avoid them.
> So we travel north to the Three Maidens.
> The people are in need of pipe stone.
> This won't be the last passing crowd.
> There will soon come need for more
> council, more talk, stronger prayers.
> One step ahead, we must remain."

~

In Minnesota, Rain Walking cared well for them. Rationed their food so Water Willow was never long hungry, always fed her something warm when she woke. When early snow covered the ground and their lodge door was shut against it, Grandmother filled the hours with carving, beading, stories and lessons.

Always some berry or leaf tea, some bark, twig or seed, that she told about in stories as she prepared it. When clear skies came, they stored game enough and hunkered down for winter.

Water Willow knew Grandmother was her best protection.
Grandma Rain Walking always took her serious,
especially when she was most scared.
Grandma made her feel strong on her feet,
instead of weak to her stomach.
With Grandmother's tall back standing up for her,
her eyes watching out for her,
her voice speaking up for her,
guiding her, Water Willow felt her own strength
grow back inside her.

~

Tender Grass came thick, and Grandmother knew the White wagons had surely moved on now, with plenty of forage. So they returned to their People. The other women welcomed their return, set their tipi up where it belonged in the camp circle.

SACRED
XÚBE

When her belly grew hungry, voices gave direction.
When lost, voices guided her.
She felt something, and voices told what was coming.
Her head was filled from waking to waking.
This was not magic, yet the People called it such.
Xúbe they called her.

She remembered the day her brother asked,
    'What **do** your Voices sound like?'
Young Elk, her father's brother's son, grew fast,
like a weed beside her and looked up to her.

She asked in return,

> 'What do *your* own voices
> sound like, ékithe?
> How do you know it *is* yours
> and not someone else's?
> Is it ever someone you love
> or who angers you?
> Someone who spoke long ago?
> Echoing around?
> Do you hear their voices clearly?
> Or does it sound like some whisper
> from far, muffled in the bushes,
> scratching at you from some distance,
> pulling from a dream, half remembered?
> Ónpon Zhínga,
> what do *your* voices sound like?'

Yes, she heard voices,
but could not know how they were different.

Most People knew to let her alone,
so she could listen.

BLOOD   Spring 1847

WÁ MI

When Water Willow began to bleed, she told Grandmother.
She held out her hand, showing the patch of moss,
now stained with use.

> "I am bleeding, Grandmother.
> Grandmother, we all know this comes,
> yet to me it seems so strange,
> to have blood flowing from within,
> yet no flesh has been pierced,
> no wound visible,
> but it is felt. My belly aches.
> My body wants only sleep.
> I sat under the pines all morning,
> staring at the sky... and bleeding.
> The moving clouds made me dizzy."

She curled up by the fire, even though it was a warm day.
She stared into the embers, watching burning black edges
of bark, peeling, shriveling red, from wood to ash. She
listened to the fire. Smelled its smoke, felt its pulsing heat,
released in its own death.

Water Willow is dying
she told herself.
Just like that branch.
Water Willow is turning from green to red.
Her sap is finally running
and they say she is blossoming.
But she does not easily accept
this fruiting and bearing.
She does not welcome this blood running
this ancient flow of life.
Being a boy seems easier.
Water Willow is a girl. A Woman now.
Water Willow wants to be
a tall boy with fast feet
and strong hands
and no need to bleed.
But boys bleed...
her self said.
They go looking for reasons...
Perhaps somewhere deep,
they are jealous of ours...
And so in vicious cycles,
they wound each other...
Perhaps, the need to bleed is universal...

Even still, she resisted.
Such ridiculous thoughts rambled through her foggy head as she drifted, staring at the fire.

PREPARATIONS
WÓⁿGITHE WAÍ'K'IGTHÍSHTOⁿ
Everyone, Pack, Be ready

Nóⁿzhiⁿ Móⁿthiⁿ felt suddenly younger, light in her moccasins. She slipped outside, to gather a supply of moss and make necessary preparations. In the cool shadows of the creek, Nóⁿzhiⁿ Móⁿthiⁿ bent to touch the carpet of thick moss, where lush, deep patches covered the stones. She pushed her palms into the softness, thankful for it. Here was something that a woman always carried in her pouch, a necessary item. She sprinkled a corn meal offering, before peeling off a thick edge of moss.

Water Willow was still sleeping when Nóⁿzhiⁿ Móⁿthiⁿ returned to their lodge, and went ferreting out preparations she had made over time; foraging around for secrets she had hidden away, in expectation of this day. She slipped the ermine bundle out from its hiding place and lay it on the half-moon altar by the fire. She offered small squares of dry meat to the ermine's mouth. She arranged fresh lupine and horsemint blossoms beside it.

Finally, she lit a sage bundle- calling spirit into the circle. Nóⁿzhiⁿ Móⁿthiⁿ watched Water Willow sleeping by the fire, her eyelids fluttering, sifting out tangles from the soft bed of her dreams. She watched her gentle breathing, her shining hair. She measured Water Willow from toe to chin with her eyes.

It was clear she was no longer a child. Water Willow was slender and fluid, in sleep, a peaceful beauty. Nóⁿzhiⁿ Móⁿthiⁿ glowed with deep satisfaction. Yes, Water Willow was something to watch.

Sometimes it seemed to Rain Walking that the men had forgotten the true beauty of their women. They had gorged in recent years, with their proud hunts and fast pony races, their games of pride and glory. Men could fight, hunt, raid, trade, more than ever, because of the horses. They seemed to have forgotten the beauty of knowing something slowly, intimately. These thoughts led her down a trail of memories.

Because now, everyone could go everywhere, and the Ponca were being pushed from all sides. It was always more of the same. Eastern prairie and woodland tribes crossing the Niⁿshude, pressing west, themselves being pushed by the white wave beyond. The Real Sioux to the east and north, the long haired Crow from northwest, the Sicaⁿgu west, and unpredictable Pawnee from the south, all pushing borders, crossing hunting grounds.

At the heart of all this, these Ponca homelands.

Now, thinking of all the stinking, bearded White Traders. They, the smallest band of people she'd ever seen or heard of, traded for more robes and skins than they could ever use in their lifetimes. Nóⁿzhiⁿ Móⁿthiⁿ gathered her thoughts together and began to add it up. Concluded that they traded for some distant hungry crowd. Their large boats delivered to their People beyond the Muddy River. People who never seemed satisfied with the heaps of robes and mountains of well-tanned hides.

Over time, Nóⁿzhiⁿ Móⁿthiⁿ also saw how each time their men left with *more* to trade and came back with *less* for it, forced to settle for prices whittled down by the whites. Rain Walking did not like this and saw little sense in more trading. She'd waited for the right time and right person to share her realization.

~

> Over their next meal, she mentioned the First Hunter story to Water Willow and their guest, Kíka Toⁿgà, first son of Chief Shúde Gáxe. They were both quiet with chewing, when Grandmother turned to Kíka Toⁿgà and asked him to do the telling.
>> "Tell it to me again, Kíka Toⁿgà. Our old mind has grown dark in forgotten parts. Tell again, about First Hunter. Let us hear it, while the crows are napping."
>
> And so Kíka Toⁿgà swallowed, cleared his throat, and began the tale of First Hunter. Repeated again, The Promise made.

*"PaHónga Abáe walked
with cold, naked feet
and he was starving.
His belly gnawed
against his ribs.
He fainted from hunger
and dreamt an Elk
hiding in thick trees.
The Elk spoke to him
saying he would give
his own life, If First Hunter
would forever keep a Promise...*

<<<< *The Promise, you must forever keep* ------- <<<

*That you take only what you need
With thanks and proper offerings
To make good use, let none be wasted.
Remember, we give our lives to you
so that you may live and
We may live in you.
You can not take life,
or break the Promise.
If this Promise is forgotten,
Balance is forgotten,
and You, Your children,
All Your Grandchildren,
will suffer the fate."*

Water Willow asked,
> "What are you thinking Grandmother?

> Why did you want this story today?"

Grandmother answered,
> "I think the *women* and *children*

> of these bearded Trader men are very cold.

> and that is because they must all be very skinny.

> They ask for more skins,

> more robes, but they never ask for meat.

> Our meat is good. T'agát'ubè and fat

> keep us alive all through the cold times.

> Yet, *they* never ask for the buffalo meat.

> I think we kill too much for them.

> I think we are killing more than is needed.

> I fear we will all be dealt the fate

> of the broken Promise."

Kíka Toⁿgà was curious now, and a little bit afraid,
but tried to hide it in his voice.
> "Grandmother, what *is* the fate of that
> broken promise?"

Grandmother answered him with yet another question.
> "What does it mean to upset the balance?
> Who measures?
> Who knows, what is more than needed?
> What *is* enough?"

Kíka Toⁿgà answered smartly,
> "We all know the earth around us.
> We have hunted these lands for many years.
> We know the rise and fall of the four legged
> as the herds come and go, and these hills
> have fed us for as long as we can remember.
> It is only *now* that the hunt is harder.
> If it were not for the *other* tribes.
> pushing us around, squeezing us a little here,
> a little there, I am sure that the balance
> would remain... and we would still have enough
> to trade with the bearded."

Nóⁿzhiⁿ Móⁿthiⁿ was silent, looking, before finally answering.
> "You are quick to blame the other tribes.
> It is easy to think...

*'Oh if my neighbor were just a little quieter,
we could all sleep well at night.'*
But often, it is that *they* are being pushed,
from *their* neighbor, and they from *theirs*.
That makes it seem that the person *next* to
you is gnawing away at your peace,
when truly it is someone you will probably
never meet, or *ever* see.
Kíka Toⁿgà, the impatience,
the thirst for more,
the need to always be at war,
over hunting grounds, over horses.
This is not what I remember of our People.
If this senseless Trading continues,
the Women will *not* tan the hides.
Tell your Father this.
That is all I have to say.
Shóⁿ."

Grandmother reached for her corn-cob pipe and
Kíka Toⁿgà knew it was time for him to leave.
He rose, nodding to Rain Walking and Water Willow.
Rode a slow horse back to his father's camp.

BLOOD ROBE
WAÍⁿ WAMÍ

When Water Willow woke, the fire coals still glowed. Looking up through the smoke hole at the dusky sky, she came back to her body. Her moss was soaked again. The skin of her thighs stuck together when she tried to sit up. She was glad for the warm, sage-soaked doeskin scraps Grandmother handed her. She wiped herself, then lifted her sweaty tunic over her head.

She had been carefully prepared for this day. Grandmother and all of her aunties were recently telling, advising, warning, guiding.
Yet despite all she had heard, her present body seemed foreign to her. No talking, stories, or telling, could be the same as *bleeding*.

Though Grandmother's voice was comforting, Water Willow couldn't help but feel that until she accepted *this*, she would be quite useless, to anyone or herself. She stared at the blood on the doeskin. She stared at herself. She stared at her grandmother and without knowing why, she started to cry.

Grandmother started a song and sprinkled cedar on the fire. The smell filled their nostrils. Grandmother washed Granddaughter's face with the warm sage tea, untied Water Willow's braid and combed her hair free. Rubbed fresh red grease and horsemint perfume over her hair and limbs.

All the while she was singing, words and rhythm that helped Water Willow breathe.

> "Small and round, we are born,
> growing taller, taking form,
> rooting down, branching out,
> until running with red blood,
> we are finally blossoming,
> Every moon, every circle,
> the flower, the fruit, the seed,
> small and round, we are born."

Grandmother gave Water Willow a wide soft belt with a snake beaded on. Red spirals curled from tail and tongue. She wrapped and fastened it around Water Willow's waist. From this belt, Water Willow hung the breech cloth and moss, adjusting it to herself.

Grandmother then presented the ermine bundle, which protected the finest buckskin dress ever made by Water Willow's mother. It was the one piece of her they had kept.

Grandmother helped Water Willow change. Once the dress hung square on her shoulders, beaded roses, stars, patterns, and bold colors, intertwined over her breasts and down her back. Water Willow felt the power in the dress as soon as it hugged her. She wiped her quiet tears and looked up from the fine beading.

> "Thank you, Wikóⁿ. I am ready now."

They walked through the settling evening, dinner smoke
rising from the fires. Horses stretched their necks to
forage moist evening grass. A thick trill of insects filled
the night air.

Water Willow walked with Grandmother,
towards the Niobrara.

Kíka Toⁿgà saw them go and felt a strange pull
towards Water Willow that he had not felt before.
He watched her feet fall.
He watched her shining hair.
He smelled her perfumed wrists as she passed.

The girl that passed in the beaded dress was not the same
one who had hunted with him until they were twelve.
Not the same that had shared her corn drink and laughter
in the fields. Not the Water Willow that kept up, racing
ponies, stride for stride, on the hills.

No. This Water Willow would not be back.
This he knew as she slipped away.

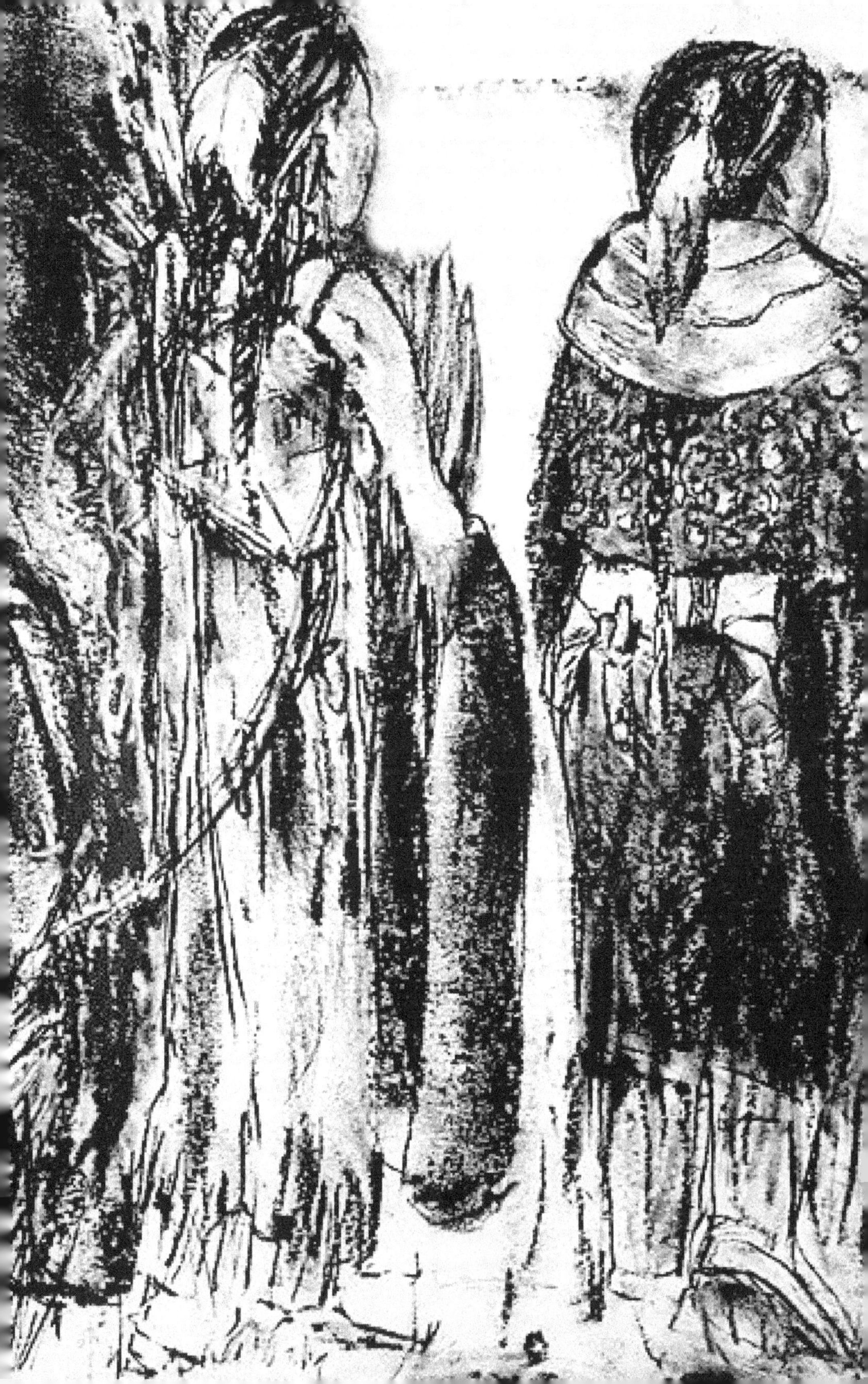

MOON LODGE
TÍBUTA WA-MÍ

The Willow lodge waited for her, a way from camp and its surrounding trails, snugly woven into the shallow shoreline, on a dry sunlit bank. Inside, a bed of buffalo robes, over layers of sweetgrass, were spread out on the earth in the west. A sandy fire pit, recently dug, was at the center of it.

A small groove was carved in the ground in the south, over which Water Willow was told to sit when awake, so that her blood could mingle with and feed the earth. She sat, lifting her dress, and removed her moss breech. Facing north, she saw the lodge empty there, open to receive spirits and visions. Water Willow closed her eyes, soaking in the warmth, feeling safe.

Aunties and grandmothers gathered at shore to light the sacred moon fire and keep it going, to help Grandmother and Water Willow. They stacked driftwood and small branches outside the lodge door, enough so Water Willow could keep a fire inside, enough to last four days.

Now, the center fire pit was empty, waiting on the smooth river stones, heating in the moon fire. Grandmother lit sage, then sweet grass, as the first stones were carried in, then sprinkled cedar onto the hot rocks, filling the willow lodge with purifying vapors.

Once they'd brought in the last of the hot rocks,
Grandmother gave Water Willow blessings and prayers,
then left the willow lodge and joined the others. They
raked the outside fire to coals and buried the red embers.

They would check on her in turn,
but Granddaughter would mostly be alone now.
With only water.
No other provisions.
Food interfered with visions.

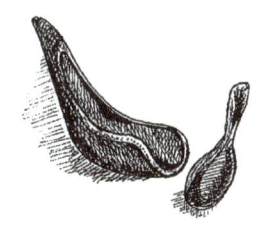

SORE EYES SUN RIVER
Í^NSHTA NÍYE NI^N MÍ

Eyes, sore   River Sun

On the third night, Grandmother returned to Water
Willow's moon lodge with black broth in a turtle shell
bowl. She brought it to Water Willow's dry lips and let her
slowly sip the liquid. Banked the fire and added some thick
sticks.

Nóⁿzhiⁿ Móⁿthiⁿ sang for visions
that would reveal this young woman
to her Self, to her clan, to her People.
She sang that she be revealed, be welcomed.
She sang for her spirit, her animal,
her source of power and protection.
She sang to the trees and stones to keep her.
She sang to the sky to take pity on her.
To forgive her for any forgetting.
To guide her in remembering.

Then Grandmother left the moon lodge
and darkness settled in.

~

Water Willow sat in the last light that seeped through the cracks of the willow lodge. She felt drowsy. She felt alone. She curled up in a ball by the fire.
So heavy her heart.
So heavy her tongue.
So heavy her eyes.
So heavy her head.
She did not remember falling far
but she did.

~

    The sun was mid-day high in the sky when she woke. It burned straight through the narrow smoke hole. She opened her eyes to the glaring shaft of light. She stretched out from a stiff rigid knot.
    Her body ached. Cold to the bone.
    The fire! She had not kept it!
    It had gone out.
    But why was it *so*
    teeth chattering *cold?!*

    She went outside to sit and warm in the sun and found it reflecting on *new fallen snow!*
    She was suddenly aware that a very wide divide of time and space had passed…

The ground was frozen, hard and cold.
She stood in the sunlight
feet in the snow
shivering
weeping.
She saw her tears fall.
Melt the snow.
There was no color.

Where was Grandmother?
Had everyone forgotten her?

The river was quiet.
The camp, silent.
She wished for a friend.
She wished for someone,
something to lay her head on,
to just hold her.
So tired.

She wished for her Mother's touch,
her way of stroking her eyebrows like birds,
of stroking sadness out from the roots of her scalp.

Her wish was heard,
and answered by nearby willows
as a sudden wind bent their branches,
combing through her tangled hair.

She smiled at the tree,
looking straight up through the branches,
into the clouded Sun,
diluted light soaking deep
into her black eyes.
When she gazed back to the horizon,
a fiery afterglow fringed the trees.
Like prairie-fire skeletons,
the tree line burned
on the horizon of her vision.
Then, the Sun spoke.
> *"Are you finished crying yet?"*

She knew such lamenting to the skies, to the spirits,
was only proper, her tears not shameful.
But in that moment, she felt embarrassed,
quite small, harshly judged.
Tears, tracking down her face.
She could not stop them.
They pushed on into sobs.
Tears went on streaming. A great flood.
Grand Father Sun *was* watching,
and drying the tears that ran
down her upturned face.
No. She was not finished crying
and did not know when she would be.
She seemed so full of tears,
all she could do was empty them.

She wanted to go back, to the tight circle of camp.
To Grandmother and the stories and even the careful slow
beading and tedium of skinning and scraping.
If only she could walk. Her legs rooted, so heavy, numb.

She looked straight into the sun, cloud covered.
But clouds moved on and so the naked sun
burned into her eyes.

She glanced away, now seeing more ghost skeleton trees,
and the burning bodies of her mother, her father,
smoking silhouettes glowing in the setting sky,
so horrid. So vivid.
She could not wipe the sight away.

Cried more
for the loss of them.

So many years
only gave her
more time
to miss them.

Then, again,
the voice...
    "Are you finished crying yet?"

This time she answered.

> *"There are times my eyes fill up*
> *and it seems they'll never stop.*
> *These are times I wish I did not have feelings!*
> *I wish that memories and dreams*
> *did not stay with me!*
> *Haunt, swallow, devour me!*
> *I wish I was good at*
> *Forgetting-*
> *That I could forget the things I see*
> *before I have to live them,*
> *live with them, carry them*
> *forever and never forget.*
> *Because I CAN'T just SEE them.*
> *My eyes FEEL them.*
> *Feelings I am helpless to change.*
> *Gut churning. Compassion. Rage.*
> *Storms always building.*
> *Deep waters threatening to drown me.*
> *Fires that burn from inside.*
> *A heart so big to burst.*
> *It's all too much and yet the very thing*
> *which gives me freedom.*
> *Because I can FEEL in every part of me*
> *what is coming...*
> *instinctively....*

I feel danger, and move far from it.
I feel approaching frost, or thaw
and I am ready to harvest, or plant.
Like the deer beside me,
know when it's safe
to browse an open field
or when to hold my breath
and freeze in shadows.
My skin feels it.
My hair feels it.
Before I see it.
Yet, when it's my feelings
that overcome me,
I am most weak,
I am most threatened.
My feelings, I most fear
because I cannot escape them."

She thought if she kept crying, the floods would come,
the corn would sprout at her very toes,
where her tears were melting away the snow.
She wondered if blood brought tears.
Why she felt everything stronger, deeper, quicker.

"Are you finished crying yet?"

Again the question came
this time with its own answer.
> *"You're finished now.*
> *Time to look ahead and not behind.*
> *Look down at your feet."*

The snow was gone! The river tide was slipping in
over banks that shined with streaks of cool green clay,
silt and sand.
> *"Use the green clay to sooth your brow."*

She remembered then,
the tradition –
To honor the diving animals
who created the earth from
lake bottom mud.
To honor them, she dug into the green clay
with her fingers, spread it cool across her forehead...
and yes, it soothed her brow, calmed her...
cleared her eyes

She saw the sun glow red in the river raging towards her.
Let the Voice coax her along...

> *"Close your eyes*
> *watch the River.*
> *Flow with it, round its bends."*

She saw the floods coming, boiling up
changing course
washing over banks
making lowlands soft for digging
rich for planting.
The light on the river snaked and rippled
away from the blood lodge
swollen and rolling east.
Willow branches hung low
dipping into foaming waters
like women bent, washing hair.
The river flowed, turning
and twisting into white falls.
The current churning
yellow, muddy depths,
deep silt, the river bottom black.
Catfish alongside her, she crawled,
until sucked up, into the hollow tunnel
of a long-fallen wide willow trunk.

As she came through
the tunnel widened, spilling out
a network of roots
snagging her in a web
of Root Voices
speaking
of healing powers
linked underground
Root Voices came alive
in the dark
tangling inside her
weaving secrets
connected... woven...
relations... pulling
back to the river,
breathless
until she rose
from the undertow
of strong currents
and saw them!

Big Horses!

Enormous horses!
Dappled grey, and black
flanks churning through waves.

Tied up in lines, hooves pumping, circling,
nostrils flaring, and rolling whites of their eyes,
until lines snapped

                                            free

from the dragging depths
and they barreled downriver
swimming hard away
Her... climbing...too
stumbling, hugging the shore.
Somehow, she crawled
up to them
reached her hand out, unbelieving
even with all fingers spread full wide
her hand could not cover a single track,
the sole of one hoof so wide and deep.
Such hooves, enormous.
And only then did it occur to her
That she might be Dreaming…
"Horses
are not
this big."

    Her self said
and woke up…

Soaked, covered in sweat,
her beaded buckskin dress clinging to her,
her hair a matted nest, her cheeks flat against dirt,
her fingers dug deep, in sand.
Her mouth and throat, so dry.
Every rock in the fire pit, stone cold.
Some wood, unused, still stacked.
The fire *had* gone out.
That much was real.
The brown color of her moss—
she was no longer bleeding red.

She rose and washed herself in the cool sage water,
left by the door for her.
Wrapped herself in the dry blanket folded beside it.
Even with the blanket thick around her,
she shivered long and hard before she was warm.

Her moon lodge was completed.

When she felt ready, crouching low at the door,
she kissed the earth, and returned to the world.

~

The river's quiet surface reflected a warm sun.
The willows were gold.
There was no snow.

Water Willow saw Grandmother
sitting on a distant river rock
bent and squinting over quillwork.

Grandmother felt Water Willow's stare,
looked up and turned to her.
A quick smile washed over her face
as she stood to welcome her.

~

On the return trail to camp
the trees bent low,
comforting Water Willow
with familiar whispering.

JOURNEY
ÚGA SHÓⁿ

April 1847

Water Willow sat with Elders, who listened as she told
what she remembered of dreams and visions.
She told about the snow, melted by her tears,
revealing green clay to brush on her forehead.
How the Sun guided her downriver through her vision.
She described white waves and yellow mud
and the churning flood that pulled her
to the muddy river's bottom, and the catfish,
the hollow tree journey and many root voices.
Then she told about the *giant* horses.
Their *monstrous* hooves.

They told her that Voices could not be ignored.
That Visions would come clear.
That she must pay close attention
to recognize those places when she saw them.
To remember those voices if she heard them.
To recognize moments when they came again.

The swimming horses were her sign to follow.
Her guiding spirit.

She was instructed to follow the Niobrara, bending north
towards the wide mouth where it joined the Nínshude.
When the heavy rains came, and despite the floods,
she was to go alone. She would be protected,
if she did these things, and in time,
the horses would come to her.

Water Willow thought about these things, as she collected
zhón hozhe wázhide, buffalo berries, for the feast that would
be held next day, in her honor.

People would gather in good spirits, and welcome her as a
woman. But all she could think of, were the monster horses.

~

When heavy rains came, she walked east then north,
for days, with only a dog at her side, so they say.

Ears Up, the yellow eyed dog from the buffalo hunt, had
stayed by Water Willow, protecting her, from that day
to this, always on guard. He greeted her each morning
with bright eyes and a fat field mouse, the daily gift held
delicately between his sharp teeth.

She was well equipped for her journey- bow and quiver, sharpened arrows, her ash root-digger, spare moccasins, and the many bags and pouches she would use for gathering. Some were full now of trail foods and t'agát'ubè, her basic sustenance.

She followed the Niobrara, and answered to the plants that called out to her. She was often drawn to unknown roots, shoots, berries. The further east they traveled, flowers caught her eye that she had never seen.

It was on this journey that she came to trust the plants,
to hear their lessons clear, without Grandmother's telling.
She gathered some of every new one, to take back to her People,
so that they too would know them. She learned their new names,
heard different songs.

Níta Ánoⁿzhiⁿ - Ears Up - heard voices too, alerting her
when there was game to chase
or winds coming
when he heard distant cries
distinct calls
or the sound of thunder
bringing sudden flooding.

DROWNING COLT 1847
SHÓⁿGE ZHIⁿGÀ NIÚT'Èⁿ ÁⁿTHIⁿÀⁿ
Horse,   Little,   Drowning, Almost

The floods came, swelling the Níⁿshude, washing out
whole trees, cutting banks. It rained for days, relentlessly
washing earth away, shifting the river, crowding it thick
with mud. Stones rumbled and rocks piled high where the
river pushed.

Water Willow was hunkered high up, in a limestone cave
on the white cliffs, sheltered from the storm. Looking
down river, she thought of the rich, brown soil the river
would leave in its wake. Her eyes scanned below for foods
and medicines, tender leaves and swollen tubers. She knew
the banks would be brimming with wild foods in a moon.
She imagined arrowhead, sweet-flag, cattail.
She measured in her mind how many days it would be until
the women rolled their robes and pack baskets to go out
and dig tipsin, núgthe and camus, the ground rich with the
crisp bulbs that brought them new strength.

As she was dreaming, Ears Up came around sudden with a
wet nose in her face, licked her cheeks and tugged her sleeve.

She stood to follow, and leaving the shelter of the limestone,
heard a high cry in the distance.
The sound...from far up river.

The river roared below the cliff.
Above its steady push, she heard the squealing cry
and turned to see an animal upriver, slashing through the
water, bleating a boiling cry for its mother.
Its slick, dark flanks bobbed closer to the ridge.
Ears Up zipped down to the river's edge and
Water Willow leapt down the bank, running to shore,
as the animal was propelled towards her.
Its front hooves flailed the current
and she realized it was a *pony!*
She dove into the icy water,
which pulled faster than she could swim.
She held her head up and twisted round
till she caught sight of the pony again,
realized it was up to her to save them.
She swam against towing waves of undercurrent
to intersect the pony's path.
Ears Up watched, barking from the shore,
running alongside the rushing river to keep up.
He trailed behind, as they cut out of sight.
The sharp hooves hammered desperately at the river,
lashing a hind hoof out, squarely kicking her thigh.
Her cold blue hands came within reach of its stubby tail
and she stretched to catch it, heaving its rump up
with all her strength.
Losing momentum, the pony's head slipped under.
When it came up again,
she had her arms hung round its neck,

her legs wrapped round its back,

toes curved up under its slick belly.

They swam hard to the river bend

where they clawed, six legs up, onto a sandbar.

Once there, her arms went limp

she lost her grip

slid off his neck.

Let him go.

The pony scrambled

bucking up, lashing hooves in all directions.

He slipped through deep mud.

Struggled up the slick bank.

Her body collapsed.

A dizzy ringing filled her ears.

She watched the pony trot away.

Water Willow wrung the water from her moccasins and dress.
She watched the horse, head lowered, coughing, grunting,
its legs stretched out.
She noticed how different this pony was
than *any* she had ever seen.
Its legs seemed twice the length of its body.
It wobbled as much as it trotted.
Its head was much too large.
Its cry was weak and scrawny.
Its tail, short and stubby, hung like a weed,
still dripping the river from it.
She watched it go a ways, and then followed.
The pony slowed and dropped to its knees,
rolled in the sand, back and forth, from back to belly.
It stood up. Shivered all over like a cottonwood tree,
to shake itself off.
She watched it sneeze into the grass,
wobble to one side
and fall over.
The pony lay there, tangled in itself.
Panting hard.
She could count every one of its long ribs,
heaving so high up on its chest,
that at first she thought it deformed, malnourished.
It turned to her, trembling, as she approached.

Liquid black eyes like the river at night,
thick eyelashes beaded with water.
He blinked, snorted at her,
but did not make another move.
He just lay there, staring,
breathing, with those funny heaving ribs.

Water Willow made herself small and moved in closer.
Squatting, she licked the palms of her hands.
Put them out to ride the current of air that flowed to the pony's nostrils, moving her wrists in a soft wave, like a bird on the wing.
The pony watched her intently, braced, ready to flee.
She whispered soft, made soothing sounds with her tongue.
Breathed a song to the strange little pony, kept on singing until he was familiar with her smell, her face, her voice.
As he relaxed, exhausted, she slowly crept closer.
When within reach, she lay down on the bank beside him, stroked his neck and sang him to sleep.

Water Willow tied knots into a hide strip to make a quick halter. She hummed into his velvety ears and blew warm air at his soaked face. She wrapped her arm round under his neck and scratched his jaw, deftly slipping the halter over his nose. This horse had been handled before. It seemed all familiar. But when she finally touched his muzzle, felt its new softness, she knew this *horse* was in fact just a *baby,* just a *colt.* But a *very large* colt.

> "Little Big Horse," she said,
> "you owe me your life."

SUNFLOWER SEED and BEAR GREASE
ZHÁXTHA WÁMIDE kí WASÁBE WÉGDTHI

Water Willow gathered reeds and grass and made a soft dry bed for the near drowned colt. She brushed his neck and shoulders. Scraped him down with a curved stick, until his short coat was combed slick.

From her medicine bundle, she mixed sunflower seeds and bear grease with fresh pine resin. She rubbed this into his knees and legs, so they would not stiffen.

She fed him armfuls of grass. Wove a large reed matt, to blanket them. She watched his suckling lips as he slept. Water Willow lay beside him, his warm neck propped against her hip. She warmed her cold hands in the steaming breath from his nostrils. She soon fell into a sound sleep beside him, dreaming the same dream.

> *The grey mare with a tangle of forelock*
> *ran alongside, her massive body rippling past.*
> *Hooves the size of gourds*
> *kicked up dirt,*
> *the dusty trail,*
> *over bramble, boulders, snags, stumps*

until the sound of hooves faded
      and the sharp   crack
                              of a
                                    whip

tore through the dream
and
the snap
of a branch
woke them all at once.
A panicked commotion of flying hooves, legs and grass,
and the startled little horse bolted off.

Water Willow eventually caught up to him sideways, calmed him down with common sense, gathered up his short line and took hold of his nose. His body had recuperated some overnight and he was strong, and stubborn. He did not take well to standing still. Once she had the rope secured in hand, he had no choice. They walked together, covering ground like a drummed song. They walked briskly until he grew tired of fighting her weight on his nose and gave in, just a little, slowing.

The colt grazed the tender grass on the bank. He was ravenous. His short, wide neck arched to reach the ground between his too-long legs. She thought perhaps this reaching might force his neck to stretch and lengthen over time. She'd never seen such a wide, short neck. He swished his stubby tail at gnats and black flies.

"Little Horse, *where* did you come from?
Was that spotted grey dream horse your
mother?"

Although the colt owed Water Willow his life, she could not take him from his mother if he was too young. His mother might be anxiously searching for him, heavy with milk. They walked the riverbank, searching for any signs or trails from her. They walked in the sand until Water Willow's legs ached.

They saw no other horse, no tracks, no traces. No signs. The little horse nipped at her, nudged her, tugged her sleeves, wanting a drink. Wanting his mother.

Here they were, at the mouth of Niobrara. As the flood currents died down, Water Willow knew there would be wide banks and sand bars, safe places to cross with the little horse.

But when they approached the river's edge, the little horse stopped, his knees locked, ears pinned back, clearly threatened by the river, and *something* moving fast on the opposite shore.

They watched the grass separate on the distant horizon. Something was coming straight at them!

She forced the pony to the ground and sat on his wide neck, to still him. She reached for her knife and held it ready, watching until she heard the far off whimper and recognized the bushy tail whipping fast above the prairie grass!

Ears Up found them! But stranded on the opposite shore, he could come no closer. He paced back and forth, whining high, his skin crawling up his back to get to them.
Ears Up did not swim wide rivers and so was forced to mirror their movements, on the opposite shore, eager to close the distance between them.
The little horse jumped at the sight of the wolfish dog. Ears Up trotted closer, anxiously looking for a crossing. Water Willow held firm to the line, guiding the pony towards him.

Ears Up waited at the tip of a long sandbar, expecting them to cross there. She edged the colt closer, toward the shallow water, a strong grip on his lead, prodding his hind legs with a long stick in her opposite hand.

The horse would not go, and pushed back at her, hard. She landed in the grass. A second effort was squashed when he just sat on her, refusing to budge. He clearly feared the water and she realized that he would not, willingly, get back in it. And he was stronger and outweighed her. She was in no rush. But she was hungry. She hauled the horse up and they scoured the silty wetlands, until she soon came up

with handfuls of spring lily bulbs.
She eagerly ate them raw, making the colt curious to the crunching sound and fresh smell. Ears Up sat whining, tail sweeping across the sandbar, impatient.

Then she spotted the feathery leaves of young Shóⁿge-máⁿkaⁿ! Pure magic, and exactly the kind she needed! This Horse Medicine would help her get him across! She turned her back on the curious colt and secretly dug up fingers full of the aromatic roots, leaving enough to grow and carry on, deep in the ground. She scraped some of the root so its aroma would be irresistible. She hid the small roots in her waist pouch, and from that moment forward, the colt followed the sweet smell at her hip, his nose stretched out to them.

Water Willow then filled a sack with succulent cattail and bulrush shoots, fronds of sea lettuce and clumps of arrow leaf. On top, she sprinkled bits of the Shóⁿge-máⁿkaⁿ root. He nuzzled up behind her, nosing in on the source. He nibbled greedily, as she coaxed him forward, him pushing his head into the sack, barely aware that he was shadowing her, closer and closer to the water, where she quick pulled the sack over his eyes and head, cinched it tight at his throat, wrapped her arm round his neck, swung one leg over his back, and slapped his rump.

He leapt forward blindfolded, into deep water, and she prodded him on with the stick at his rump. The frantic little horse swam hard, pulling forward to firm ground. Once safe on the opposite shore, she hauled in and circled him to a stop, long enough to pull the sack over his ears. He pulled his head free and shook his neck in revolt, pinned his ears back and galloped fast away from her. Ears Up nipped at his heels, driving him up the bank, herding him south.

They approached a slow curve in the river that ran shallow and calm with fish puddled up in tide pools from the flood. Ears Up pinned them with his paws and gorged himself.

Water Willow scooped up all that she could, gutted and strung them up, slung them over her shoulders. Ears Up cleaned up behind her. Satisfied and full, he lounged on shore licking his coat, grooming his tail, shining with fish oil.

Ears Up greeted Water Willow with a toothy smile.
She scratched his back and told him to gather up the horse.
On this side of the river they knew the trails to follow.
The trio headed south, back to her People.

BIG HORSE WOMAN   1847 through 1852
SHÓNGE TOᴺGÀ WA'U
Horse,   Big,   Woman

The colt ran with other yearlings, bit their rumps and necks, bullied his way to claim the best grazing. The horses that her people rode and traded were sturdy, strong and quick. He was chased off by older mares, colts and stallions, until he matured. He learned horse manners from the Ponca herd.

As the little horse grew, they became strong allies. Water Willow walked by his side for many seasons before she would ride him. Even as tall as he was, she could tell he was too young. He grew strong, and carried her baskets and bundles, dragged her buffalo skin house on her lodge pole travois. She taught him manners at every chance and his natural docility surprised everyone.

Even when he towered above the withers of the tallest stallions, *his* legs were still forming bone and lengthening out. He was awkward and his rear flanks sloped upward to a high, square rump. She waited for him to stop growing and balance out. Eventually, a superbly balanced body of immense and perfect proportion overcame his fledgling awkwardness.

The People watched as the little horse grew, beyond any they had ever seen. One well-aimed hoof could crush a man's skull.

They again concluded that this Granddaughter was acquainted with great powers and had truly found her spirit's medicine.

When he was no longer a colt, she called him Big Horse. The People now called her Big Horse Woman.

Shóⁿge Toⁿgà

Shóⁿge Toⁿgà Wa'u

)))) <:><:><:><:><:>))))

LONER
ESHNÓ[N]

From memory on, she saw, heard and knew things just because, for no good reason, cause or explanation, no telling why- she just *knew*.

In time, as she grew older, there were certain friends and relations who grew jealous of her always *knowing*... never struggling with confusion, or decision-making, never requiring council, or agreement, or assistance in making choices, never quarreling. Never forced to follow another person. She had her own way.

They grew jealous *and* they emulated her. They were proud when her foresight kept them out of reach of horse-raiding and warrior parties, or vicious prairie storms that sometimes came with no prior warning. They would whisper among themselves and, at trade gatherings, boast aloud, of the gift they had in her.

Shó[n]ge To[n]gà Wa'u became a name known beyond the Niobrara River valley. Some were proud to tell any captive audience the story of her Big Horse and how she was named.
Others whispered outside her lodge. Some who said
> *'they would not have had the Fever'*
> *'If Water Willow had never dreamt*
> *to send the hunters out.'*

Some who said

    'It was the 'White Cloth' that brought it…'

Some grew jealous of her freedom to get up any morning,
or in the middle of moonlit nights, and slip away from
them, from daily chores, from gossiping. Some grew jealous
of her ability to go off hunting.

She grew bored of grinding corn meal, pricking her fingers
while beading, and their teasing, but it went on.

They giggled, behind her back, or when she was off day
dreaming. They'd talk about her *selfishness* in whispers. How
she did not follow traditions; gave no particular attention
to customs or hierarchies and approached both chief and
priest with ease. How They Whispered.

They teased all the more because she did not take part in
teasing. She rode away on her high horse and never looked
back to them. Even so, young men followed her like puppies
to milk. Of this, some were the most jealous.

But she did not seem to care who had their eye on her.
She had no need for the skills or charms of young men.
She had skills and charms of her own.

CURLEW May 1852
KÍKA TOᴺGÀ

Kíka Toᴺgà had always been a friend, to her. Spending much of their youth together, she knew him as a brother. As tradition forced, they were no longer companions once she reached her twelfth winter. As she grew older, more a loner, he missed her. When she was old enough, he decided that they should be more.

His attraction to her grew. But the feeling was not the same in her, and this he knew. She did not show any blushing signs, or playful teasing that a young man might expect. She was always serious, pre-occupied with something else.

She rarely lifted her eyes from what she was doing to glance at him. He got the feeling that she had known his face so long, that she had no reason to look at him.

He noticed everything in her, every change and difference, every new feather, every new scent, that became her.

It was a spring fever that made Kíka Toᴺgà decide he needed to prove himself. So he gathered enough warriors to make a raid for horses, on the same band of Crow that had recently run them off their northern hunting grounds.

He told her nothing of his plan, but she heard the rumor
rustling in the corn. She quit her raking and walked to Kíka
Toⁿgà's camp. The young men were gathered in the shade
by the stream, discussing the plan in low voices.

She stood on the outside of them, watching, and did not
say a word.

They saw her standing there. But she would not leave
or answer to them, until Kíka Toⁿgà finally stood and
acknowledged her.

Kíka Toⁿgà walked over to Big Horse Woman and lifted
his blanket around their shoulders, so the others could not
watch their talk.
> *It may occur in public, but it was nobody
> else's business.*

In the blanket's shadow, Big Horse Woman spoke gently
to Kíka Toⁿgà.
> "I have heard. You plan to steal horses...
> to impress a certain girl."

"You have heard true."

> "And if I asked if she once could bend like
> a Willow, would it also be true?"

"It would."

He looked for her to meet his eyes then, just this once, but she would not. She finally spoke.

> "I do not wish to speak before family or
> council and discourage this.
> I know that it would be too great an insult,
> to publicly refuse you.
> Kíka Toⁿgà, you have never treated me
> with anything but care, but I *cannot* encourage you.
> I cannot call out your name.
> Or sing the Waeton waon,
> taking pride in your every action.
> I do not wait for the thrill of you
> bringing horses to Grandmother.
> I *cannot* encourage you Kíka Toⁿgà.
> I have tried my best not to.
> I do not…see it… that way.
> That is all that I can say."

She still would not look at him and she did not see whether it was determination or resignation on his face, when he flatly answered,

> "Perhaps, you cannot see me that way, because you never even look! Perhaps, when we return, you will open your eyes, and like what you see."

She *did* look at him then, at his beautiful, familiar eyes. When tears filled hers, he did not understand why.

She turned away and whispered,
>"You may never know, Kíka Toⁿgà,
>but I *always see you*
>without having to look."

She confused him. Was this an insult?
He did not know what she saw that he did not,
but he lowered the blanket and let her walk away.
He felt all the more that he needed many, many horses,
to reach her.

~

Short of *telling him* she'd seen his death
(visions of which are never spoken. No one had the power
to make such claims, be they coming, or not)
there was nothing more she could say.

But if she *refused* his horses, he would have no *need* to ride
out for them. She would not *have to* wake up tomorrow to
find him *dead.*

For years it was a memory she could not bury...
before it happened.

Up till this very moment, she had tried.

Years before,
she dreamed Kíka Toⁿgà
riding out for horses in her name,
to offer her grandmother, for her.
Years before he *even knew*
he'd fall in love with her,
she'd spent those years pushing him away.
Trying not *to make the dream true.*
Years before, she'd watched,
through a crowded picket of stolen horses,
and saw him pierced by enemy arrows...

No matter what she did, or didn't do,
he sought her out, none-the-less.
And this fateful day came,
when he shared his intentions
to ride out for horses in her name,
thinking that he *needed* them
all the more, to win her over.

PULLING UP THE BLANKET
WAÍᴺ THIDÓᴺ

She could not sleep, but she must have because the grass was thick with dew, the temperature dropped, frost came, and the crisp crunching of footsteps woke her. She heard the hot breath of someone crouching outside. She peeked out from under her blanket and saw Grandmother's back in shadow, heard her deep sleeping breath.
She would not go out to meet him. She heard his footsteps quickening, then stopping by the door flap.

She heard Big Horse, and Grandmother's ponies, snort familiar greetings to Kíka Toᵑgà. Then their excitement grew, and Big Horse whinnied high, bugled, stomped and arched his neck, at the fast approaching, heavy footfall of several horses, coming in from hard running. They warriors and horses pranced around her tent, announced themselves and drove on through camp. Kíka Toᵑgà remained. Grandmother snored.

Big Horse Woman closed her eyes, so he would think her sleeping. Kíka Toᵑgà crept in and waited by the door. Her rhythmic breathing pretended deep sleep, but he knew she could not possibly sleep through such an arrival,
and Big Horse shaking the ground just outside her door.

He whispered, "Willow, I have come to
make known my loyalty to you. I will
offer Grandmother these horses in the
morning... if you will tell me yes, tonight."

She did not move. Even so, he boldly moved the blanket
enough to look upon her face in the dark.

She could have remained, as if sleeping, but she opened her
eyes to reply,
"I *have* a horse, Kíka To^{n}gà.
Grandmother has three.
We need no others, presently.
I am pulling my blanket up, Kíka To^{n}gà.
You call me by my girl name,
and yet you ask for a Woman.
Please, find another. I can *not* become her.
I never wanted to cause embarrassment
and so I will be gone in the morning.
Please- Kíka To^{n}gà, intend these horses
to someone else's Father."

She closed her eyes, and smelled the black-perfume-plant,
its scent heavy on him, meant to charm, but it too, had no
effect on her.
Once again, she slowly pulled the blanket up.
She did not know why she did not want him to share her tipi.
Why she was not stirred that way.

Why she was always pulled in other directions.

She could not see his face, but she knew it.
She heard his shallow breathing and the silence.
He quickly rose towards the flap and went back out under the stars, his footsteps heavy, until he stopped some paces away.

Finally, she heard the sound of his own war horse, dancing circles around him, pulling away from the foul mood that dragged alongside him. Then, the quick gallop of hooves as they raced away from her.

~ ~

))))~   -+-+-+-+-+-+-+-+-+-+-+-+-   ~((((

She knew that she had made him unhappy. Angry.
She felt the burden of it.
But she knew the burden of his death would be greater.

Big Horse Woman was heavy with sadness.
She did not make choices blindly.
Her *hands* made *this* choice for her.
Pulling Up the blanket, *closing* her eyes.
Clearly, this gesture accepted, as *No.*
 The word still screaming inside
Ónk'azhi! Ónk'azhi! Ónk'azhi!
NO! No! No!

VENGEANCE
ÉGOⁿXT'I WÉ'Oⁿ

Big Horse Woman went about gathering her things, aiming to slip away quietly, in the dark. Embers glowed and she stirred them, shedding light on what she most needed. She rolled her blankets and robe. She tied up bundles, and packed saddle bags for Grandmother, too, knowing now, there would be another move forced soon. So she made everything ready.

Finally, she laced her knee high grass boots, her best journey moccasins. These kept her from being scratched by the tall prairie grasses, allowed her to ride fast without cutting up her legs.

But now, the people woke to early warning whoops of scouts before she'd left her tipi. She stood and felt shivers run through her as the camp crier announced that a war party was well on their way, coming to seek revenge, for stolen horses and the fallen Crow warrior, who had failed his guard of them.

Shóⁿge Toⁿgà Wa'u felt the upheaval outside that Kíka Toⁿgà had brought, on her account, even when she had plainly told him that it was not her wish. He would regret this.

Grandmother woke, hardly surprised to see her Grand Daughter standing ready in her high boots. Listened to her tell what happened in the night.

KILLING
WÁT'E^NTHE

Big Horse Woman wanted no part of it, angry that it had led to this. She would not be the blame. She would not encourage battle. She was not going to be cause for revenge.

Not getting what he wants can anger a man, beyond reason. It was something the fire in men caused, that had to be burned off. Some way, some struggle, push or shove, race or fight. It was nothing she paid attention to before, leaving it to others. Something she'd never fully understood, until it happened under her nose. She did not like the smell of it.

She tried to understand the need to create enemies.
She knew the ways of hunters in the surrounding woods and sky. She knew the bear and wolf, the big cat, weasel, hawk and eagle, the snake and fox. She saw mated pairs staking claims, starting new clans of their own. These hunters marked their places with deep gashes in the bark, with musky scents, urine soaks, scat.
They defended their cubs, pups, kits, nestlings.
They sometimes stole each other's kill.
They fought for mates, for hunting grounds, for carcasses.
But she never saw them *kill...* their *own* kind.
She never saw it...

She did not like this in the People. Why killing was necessary.
She wondered why death by war was part of living.
Why since the traders came, it seemed more common.

Grandmother tried to answer this big question. Told how traditions came to be. Told how bands of people had always come together and broken apart, for different reasons over time. In different tribes, clans, families, different manners were acceptable, customary. Traditions kept, which another people might never understand, or allow.

She told of the Hidatsa, who always had a war chief
and a peace chief, who stood for these ideals.
The Kiowa, who would not eat fish,
because their gods resided in them.
The Pawnee, who killed a young maiden every year
as a gift to the corn, by shooting arrows through her heart.
She told of a disloyal woman she had once seen, whose
infidelity was punished by cutting off the tip of her nose.
She said some People would never eat dog.
She told of the lost White Traders, struggling through deep snow, starved and half crazed, begging for horses, because they had killed and eaten their own.

Big Horse Woman begged her to stop.

She felt strings grip hard on her heart.
Nothing was coming clear, but only clouding more.

It was all too much, and the essential question remained.
Why was killing someone else's son accepted? Why was it?

Reasons did not weigh fairly, against the tides of emotion that violent death brought. In her heart it was not in balance. They had seen their tribe sliced through and shredded. Like an over ripened squash dropped to the ground by a winged predator. Half Lost, and the remaining seed, picked over and left to rot.

After the Small Pox Fever, she had seen what was left of the warriors and women, of the children, weeping under cottonwoods, slashing their skin by cold rivers, invisible on lonely hills, cutting their hair, their flesh, offering their blood, faces painted grey, all the while mourning, helpless, with no means of revenge for this Killing Sickness.

> At times she saw them, reduced to vultures, having to eat what scraps they could beg from strangers. She saw how their deep losses cut away at them and made some hunger deep inside for something to tear at, something to sink claws into. To slash. To bleed. To take a fresh scalp lock, wave it high on a green stick. She saw their desperation for *something* to kill their grief and rage, to stop their suffering, to replace it with some measure of strength.

Nóⁿzhiⁿ Móⁿthiⁿ watched her granddaughter sink into silence. She took the lead then, commanding,

"We will go nowhere until we have something warm in our bellies." as she stoked the flames and warmed yesterday's squash stew, added corn and bitter root.

"You will not be leaving, until you are heard."

They ate in silence, as the noise increased outside. Big Horse Woman gave up the idea of slipping away, lifted her eyes and said, "I will need the power of paint."

Grandmother nodded, chewing the last of the bitter root stew, then quickly packed Granddaughter's parflêches thick with journey food, because she knew her granddaughter would soon go her own way.

Big Horse Woman would speak at the Council and so wore her black bear robe over her shoulders, fur side out. She took her bow, and the otter quiver over her shoulder, filled with arrows newly feathered. She carried her medicine and sage bundle under her left arm, her blanket folded over it.

Grandmother burned cedar and sweet grass to welcome the presence of benevolent powers, to summon witnesses and helpers in keeping peace. Then she began to mix the paint.

PAINT
WÉSNATHE

There was a lot to be remembered,
with the colors and their pigments,
the plants and medicines of them,
the power of each color, the meaning
of every mark and line, many details
that mattered each as much.

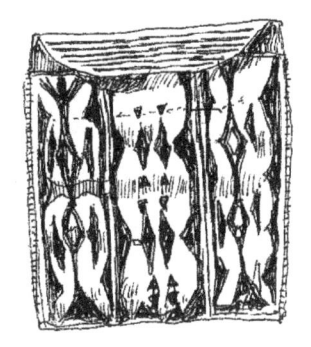

At times a sudden wave of forgetfulness would overcome,
Nónzhin Mónthin's memory failing, and she would think
herself a fool for trying to remember things that could
much more easily be forgotten. But she knew, that though
her blood was growing thin, her pulse slow, and her face
thick with wrinkles; though her mind was like a torn
fishing net, and her eyes often blurred with mist, she knew
that those things infused into her very blood could never
truly be forgotten, as long as she lived. And if she died
without ever having shared them, she knew they would be
born again, in the fruits and flowers that her body fed, and
that the people would know them. And so her arms, hands,
and fingers knew the motions of collecting and preparing
all the pigments she would work her protection with, even
when her mind slipped.

Big Horse Woman sat on her knees, her ankles shifted to
the right. Grandmother began. The songs came as if they
had never left.

The prayer resonated with strength. Her throat was husky with early morning, but her voice delivered itself from deep within and filled the lodge.

She looked at Shóⁿge Toⁿgà Wa'u's skin, at the pitted scars on her cheeks. She looked at her eyelashes, and full upper lids that were rarely raised to wholly opening. This seeming to be the only way her granddaughter could regulate the flow of what went in, or out, of her focused vision. Nóⁿzhiⁿ Móⁿthiⁿ looked into her eyes, as if this were the first time she'd really seen them.

Sometimes Nóⁿzhiⁿ Móⁿthiⁿ thought that *if only* her Grand Daughter could close her eyes and truly rest them, would she be able to live any sort of common life. But it was not in her to be common, this was plain. And so with those heavy eyelids she began.

Grandmother raised the first bowl of color. From it, gold wisped into the air, as Grandmother painted ochre clay above her brows, whispering

>"These grains of gold, the sun flower's glow,
>
>the sun's fire and strength."

Big Horse Woman closed her eyes and Grandmother blew the ochre dust into her face. It covered her round eyelids, golden pigment settling on Big Horse Woman's brow, striping back through her black hair.

She felt it tickle her scalp and earlobes.
She felt it on her lashes, her nostrils, and she sneezed.

Her eyes open now, she saw the red on Grandmother's fingertips, the saturated color of blood, amazed at the shock red always was. Like her own blood, it pulsed into her skin, flushed in stripes straight down her cheeks. She felt sparks, as red was rubbed straight down the part of her hair. Felt vermilion soak strong into her fingertips, circle pulsing around her wrists, as Grandmother stroked it in. She felt the color's heat.

"Your blood, the stream of power
the pulse that guides everything."

Grandmother then lifted cobalt blue, the hue so rare, its origin so secret, most did not know if it were of the earth or sky. None but Nónzhiⁿ Mónthiⁿ knew from where its pigment came. This time, she remembered to tell Shóⁿge Toⁿgà Wa'u the secret of it, to carry on, so they now both knew its source, and the grandmothers to the South who traded in it. Nónzhiⁿ Mónthiⁿ pressed her granddaughter's palms flat into the rich blue paint, then pressed her own hands in.

They walked under the door flap and out to Big Horse. Grandmother raised her blue hands to the sky and sang

"Water and Sky, Moon and Sun
Sky and Water, Sun and Moon
Water and Sky, Moon and Sun
Sky and Water, Sun and Moon"

They placed their palms high up on his shoulders, pressing in the blue strength of wind and water. She painted blue spots on his chest and rump, spots that would bounce arrows off. Streaked her hands through his tail, blue like the wind.

Big Horse Woman painted his face, circling the blue around his eyes to help him see clear, blue over his wide nostrils to help him breathe deep. Into Big Horse's mane, she wove a single crow feather, its tip dipped in red, to honor the Crow warrior that lost his life, for her. She mounted, leaned forward, and told Big Horse

"I hear the pulse of my heart
in my ear like a beating drum
and I am thankful for my life."

Nóⁿzhiⁿ Móⁿthiⁿ secured the bulging parflêches to Big Horse, and walked behind them, *lulu-ing* as they made their way to the center of camp.

A crowd was soon their escort to the circle where the council had gathered. Plenty of people saw them. Plenty of them remember the day Big Horse Woman came all painted, Carrying her Vision to them.

STIRRING
WAZHÍ'ÁSHKA

It was early dawn when Big Horse snorted in all his importance and blew the crowds back. He curled his neck, looked down his nose at them. He danced in wide circles, arching left and right, rolling his eyes back and flexing his shoulders to check what followed behind. His high prance shook the ground beneath them.
Ears Up circled him, keeping children out from under foot. When they arrived at the council fire, a warbling crescendo announced them.

Big Horse Woman felt the people stirring.
Then heard the wails of mourning, for another son lost.
One of Kíka Toⁿgà's comrades had not survived an arrow wound. From the previous night. She felt simmering rage under their skin. But she did not know why *all* they could think of was more fighting. In her heart, she yearned for *quiet.*
It was only there that she ever found answers.
She was not the only one who felt the unbalance,
who knew this was all a great tide and turning,
who knew the earth was shaken,
and that each of their lives had,
since that spotted fever summer,
become twice as valuable.
It was this, Big Horse Woman spoke of.

They all knew, that *they* held the seed of their People.
They all knew, that from here forward, they should take
care in self-preservation. They must save the seeds they
were, for future planting.
She discouraged all cries for further battles.
She encouraged them to stay firm together, *not* separate,
or divide, as waves of change passed through them.
She warned her People of brutal winds and droughts
that would come in the wake of twisting sand storms
and prairie fires. She told them that *when*
they were torn from their ground,
that they should not get ripped apart.
Crowds and fires would try to wipe them from the earth,
she warned them. Instead, she said, they should grow strong
in their roots, cling hard beneath the blowing crust of dust.
Their roots must stretch like runners, so as not to be severed.
Tapping deep, spreading wide, so they could never be
completely pulled up. They must take hold,
creep through dark and under rock.
Though their hearts, in pieces broken,
buried, in their chests,
they must hold with all their will
to the roots of themselves,
born of their Grandmother Earth.
She told them that, only then, would they be safe,
until thunder and steady rain came, falling on dormant
seeds, planted deep, within the womb of earth.

Stretching roots to the past and future, they would be safe.
Like the mole, they would dig, although blind to the way
ahead. They would hide within their own powers.
They would hold onto themselves.
They would become ghosts, unafraid of long silence.

She painted all this and more with her words
until they all saw with their own eyes
that the only way forward was peace,
and only then did she lower her hands.

A WOMAN!
WA'U WÍᴺ NÍ HO!

It was then that Kíka Toⁿgà rose to say things against her
that no one else would have dared.
He was a man of great pride, of great deeds,
who had never tasted defeat,
except in her complete failure to recognize him.

She did not recognize the desire burning in his eyes,
because she would never look into them.

She did not either recognize this side of him he was now showing.
    "You say we should *HIDE!!!???*
    You are a *Woman-* that is clear.
    It is the Woman in you
    who speaks at this council!
    Not the Wise One, Keeper of Bear Medicine,
    the Tracker, the Hunter, the *Seer*!
    It is the Woman,
    who cowers and lurks in shadows,
    who rides off dreaming, head in the stars.
    You, who know, before it happens.
    You cannot know what is in a man's heart,
    when you have never shared one!
    How can you know this surge
    of rage, honor, strength?
    How can you know the sick feeling
    when your bravest, strongest hands
    are not strong enough to change anything?

> We will not sit on our knees, at cook fires,
> digging circles in garden dirt, pretending
> tranquility!
> We will not bow our heads and sing sweet
> lullabies, eat corn cakes, as if nothing is
> happening!
> I am tired of all this sitting.
> *Hiding?* No!
> I am tired of always running!
> This is a time to Stand!
> Only a *coward* would not admit the truth
> in this. *A Woman! Wa'u wíⁿ ní ho!"*

His words reverberated and anxious murmuring circled through them. Some women cast their eyes down, and turned their backs on him. Some people expected a War to start, right there and then.

Big Horse Woman rose.
She did not speak until her stand was met with silence. When she did, her words, accompanied by her hands, struck everyone.

> "Look at me. Look deep into my dark eyes.
> Look closely at my long, painted hands,
> my strong feet. Look at my breasts.
> Look at my shining hair,
> so beautifully braided by Grandmother.
> Look at my scarred and pitted skin.

See the flesh wounds -
for my Mother and my Father.
And these - that mark offerings
to all those lost from us.
All these marks tell you
something about me.
Some things tell you that I am not,
could never be,
the same as You.
They tell you I am different.
I *am* a Woman.
I am not You.
And it is not with eyes
that you will ever see,
what lives inside of me.
It may be with hands
that you could feel,
what is inside of me.
It may be by joining me
that you would sense,
or taste or smell, of what I am made.
It may be in molding a child,
that you would become part of me.
But you will never know in your body,
what it is to be in mine.
You will never feel
what I know,
inside me."

She pointed to her belly, and circled her womb
with the palm of her blue hand.
> "You may never know it, never feel it,
> never see what I see. And all I have to say
> is that it would be denying
> that flowers will bloom,
> that the sun will warm us,
> that birds fly and fish swim.
> That what I say is more than my own
> feeling, thought, need.
> That what I say is as real and true
> as a fertile seed.
> If you could close your eyes to the mouth
> that is speaking,
> and the body it comes from.
> If you could hear the words as loudly
> as those spinning tight in your own head.
> If you could own the words, not doubt them,
> as you do yourself,
> then you would know them to be true
> and let these words become your own.
> We will not grow tall corn or live long,
> if war is what we seek.
> We will not live to bear our children,
> onto this sweet earth.
> If we go forward with hateful hunger,
> attacking the crest of each vengeful wave
> we will never see the raging river that fuels it,

but only catch a terrified glimpse
as the current sweeps over us,
crashing us to splinters.
We will *live,* by being invisible and silent,
on higher ground,
until the waves stop crashing
and the tide turns."

She looked at him, her voice quieter
"If these words cannot seep,
deep and true into your heart,
then I may never see you.
I give you all the strength of my heart,
as you've *always* had from me,
to take on your journey.
I will not see you again
and you will not see me,
if you choose to ride today.

That is all I want to say.
Shéno[n]."

She stared at her feet, willing them to move.
Then without further formality or warning, she departed.

)))))))))   )   )   )   ))   ))

)))))))))   )   )   )   ))   ))

PLENTY OF PEOPLE
NIASHÍᴺGA AHÍGI
People,   Many

Kíka Toⁿgà wanted to stay angry, wanted to go on riding
the wave of rage that welled up in him. But he was choked
by the idea of never again seeing Shóⁿge Toⁿgà Wa'u.

He knew that his words had hurt her, it carried in her voice.
He felt something besides his own anger stirring up inside
him. He felt the overwhelming love she had always had for
him, but kept to herself.

The others at the council fire were mournfully silent as
they stared ahead, into their own thoughts of what *could*
happen next.

Big Horse Woman rode Big Horse away.
Grandmother watched her go, knew to let her.

Plenty of people saw her ride away that day.
Plenty of people saw them. Plenty of them remember
the day that Big Horse Woman left all painted,
Carrying her Vision and them.

SEEING
NÓᴺZHIᴺ ZHÓᴺ ÉTAI
Standing, sleeping, while

She had been born into dreaming on the night the stars fell to earth with her. Her dreaming was influenced by where she slept. Wherever, the roots and stones beneath her always whispered. What was coming, What had been.

The visions of the future that her dreams often were, perplexed her, until they actually occurred and only then, made sense. Broken images she dreamt by night, were made complete by day's light. She watched matter and fates twist their way firm into the real world.

She struggled with a sick stomach when she witnessed horrors *she could not stop.*

She could not stop the memories, recently erupting, as she rode away from what she could not change.

She looked back at the stream of such occurrences in her life, and saw memory of the Black Bear rise up...

BLACK BEAR
WASÁBE

While out hunting, her
Father's favorite buffalo horse
ran away, sudden, spooked,
leaving
Kímonhon and Water Willow stranded in a dark ravine.
Once they'd climbed out, Water Willow jogged behind
Kímonhon, tracking the swift horse. They soon came to
overlapping tracks of a bear.

The bear had no wind of them, lumbering ahead, fat with
the late season, his tracks lazy in the soft earth. But then
his tracks sped up, sinking deeper and so they ran faster.

They came off the hill and into a clearing when
Water Willow shivered and felt her skin crawl.

> *The horse flashed into mind.*
> *She heard its panicked snorting,*
> *though it was not in sight.*
> *She ran as hard as she could*
> *towards where she saw*
> *the horse tangled, struggling.*
> *Heard his cries, saw his frantic eyes.*
> *Saw the old black bear, standing tall.*
> *Saw muddy hooves thrash the air.*

Paw swinging, cracked nails, catching
flaked bark, the smell of cedar
his nails tearing,
she felt claws,
bring her to her knees.

She saw this, before they were in sight,
heard before hearing, smelled before smelling.
Her legs caved, as she had seen them.
She could not catch a breath.
She willed her legs to continue, stumbling,
but her effort was not enough to bridge the gap
between them and the horse.

They saw the bear, its claws now deep in the horse's neck.
Felt the blow of being so close, yet so out of reach.

Kímonhon eclipsed her and raised his bow.
His arrow sank into the standing bear, bringing blood.
Too late.
The horse fell in a heap, its legs folding.
The bear crashed down to all fours and turned in fury,
charging straight towards Water Willow.
There was no fear, only her body, trembling uncontrollably.
Because she already saw that she did not need to move.
That Death had not come for her.
Kímonhon's flurry of arrows brought the bear down,
as dead as the horse.

The bear was skinned, his black hide scraped and cleaned
for Mánchu Mánkaⁿ, who presented it in turn to Water
Willow, to reward her Vision and bravery.

Later, when her fingers stroked the black bear hide,
she counted the arrow holes with her fingers.
She wrapped it around her, in less than comfort.

She whispered softly
to the gone horse,
to the fire,
to the Voices,
to the Visions,
that she would rather not know *at all*
if she was going to be
so powerless to change it.

VISION
NOⁿZHÍⁿZHÓⁿ ANÍ

Her path, lately colored by the dark of the previous night,
was uneasy. By night she intimately knew changes ultimately
coming. For her, What Would Soon Be, *already happened.*
For her, This is how it was.

Kíka Toⁿgà's words still burned.
She was not a Coward.
She was not Selfish.
She did not take anything but time to be alone,
so she could see.
'Always dreaming' was not easy.
Sometimes she was afraid to close her eyes,
where the future tortured her.
Sometimes it forced her into hiding.
She had not meant to, but she had shown them all.
The future.
And she knew that now, they too would suffer
the raw consequence of *Seeing.*
Now, they knew the pain of death's approach
before it showed its hand.

Now, they all saw the spirits floating down river, the tips of sycamore trees turning pure white when these ghosts were snagged. Frozen in their branches, pointing bony wooden fingers to remind the people of their passing over, of their loss.

Now they saw the dead turn to angry dust, churn up sandstorms and twisters and clouds of insects.
They saw buffalo bones piled high on empty plains.
No people.
Just carcasses, bloated, rotting.
Clouds of flies, maggots hatching.
This is what she left them with.

Vision.

Big Horse Woman knew that what the People
felt, what they sensed, what they imagined,
could stun them into utter helplessness.
Even the bravest brave amongst them would reconsider offering his own death, knowing none may remain to avenge him, no one left to carry on, and *theirs* no longer a drop in earth's blood.

Though she had lived with the burden of such Vision all her life, she realized that this sudden show of it could cause real shock and damage to those who had no learned sense of how to carry it.

They would wake from the bad dream, but know it real.
There would be nothing they could do,
but shake their heads.
This was the helpless sense
she had just shared with them.
The warning of Death, now let loose on them.
There would be nothing they could *do*...
except listen to the *warning*...

...Except *listen to the warning!*
and *not* engage in the prophecy.
Not be there when it happened.
Not be a part in it.
They *could!*

They could...
They could *turn from it...*
Go another direction.
Close their eyes again
and *together dream it different.*
They *could* be ready,
when they opened their eyes again.
They *could* be gone,
before Crow came.
Together, by choice, they could *dream it different!*

They could now see over the horizon,
and with eyes wide open,
they *could* look towards another direction.
They *could* work together to avert it.

They could see it all coming
and turn away before it reached them.
They would *not* be helpless.
They were *far* from helpless,
because there *was time*,
to walk in a whisper,
to make hidden footsteps,
mole deep into dirt,
live further in shadow,
far under rock,
in secret caves,
live in spirit,
clustered in stars,
dormant seeds,
hard shells,
waiting for time
to burst out
to share secrets,
waiting to remember it all
and live on.

They would be ready for the Crow
by disappearing.
And they would Save themselves.

And what more, she prayed for,
was that if *she* were not present,
if instead of being there, she rode away,
if instead of being witness, she was nowhere near it,
if she was not there to see it,
perhaps it would happen different.

This is what she hoped her Vision had revealed.
She had done all she could to lead them
away from their predicted plight,
short of telling them *Who* would die.
Because her every act, hope and wish
was that she could change this.

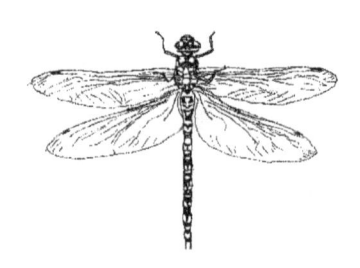

PACKING
WAÍK'IGTHISHT'AI

Spring 1852

The Ponca prepared to move on. They began a swift harvest of all that they could carry. They worked with quiet fervor, every hand busy, every arm full. They packed food stores, gathered plants and fresh roots that grew close round their village. They took some of every seed, last year's seeds and this, some of every kind. Sacred bundles were safely cloaked and transported by their Keepers.

A band of warriors and strong women made false and twisting trails away. They let travois poles drag and dig in deep, in false directions. False tracks churned into the earth with fast ponies, made it appear that here, there had already been fighting on horseback and hand to hand struggles. They shot off arrows – both their own and some Sioux trophies, taken in previous battles. They left blood stains on the ground. They left clues that a battle with a Sioux raiding band, had already chased them off... in the wrong direction.

They buried morning fires and drenched all smoke, but left some old lodges standing, as another false front, cook fires lit within them as decoys. The women, children, and elders moved well ahead, on the *hidden* trail out.

But earlier on, when breaking camp, Nóⁿzhiⁿ Móⁿthiⁿ
called to her clan women. With their help, her lodge came
down, and it was then, and only to them, that she stated
her intention. And that was to wait here for her Grand
Daughter, whom she sensed would have a sudden change
of heart and be soon returning.

Nóⁿzhiⁿ Móⁿthiⁿ simply had no strength of body or breath
of spirit to bear these upheavals. She would not be
displaced again, run out, chased. Not again. She wanted
to remain here, with the new growing corn. Held here
in the long arm of the Niobrara, its sweet and shining
water. No. She would not be moved this time.
Nóⁿzhiⁿ Móⁿthiⁿ's desire was to remain for her Grand
Daughter.

Their only protest was a dark and dead silence.
No one could agree with her. No one could let her go.

Then, they came to their senses and begged her
to leave signs for Big Horse Woman to follow
and she would find them all, together,
taking good care of Grandmother!

But Nóⁿzhiⁿ Móⁿthiⁿ argued that the Crow could read signs
just as well and could come trailing on their heels.
She was unmovable.

After her lodge was rolled, and bundles safely wrapped,
they loaded her travois, dragged it to the river's edge.
Hid it where she told them.

Nónzhiⁿ Mónthiⁿ remained
where the lodge's circle marked the earth.
She stained the circle muddy yellow
and there painted a single clue.
Then walked on to the corn field.

STORM CLOUDS
MÓⁿXPI PÍAZHI

Fires were extinguished, but Nóⁿzhiⁿ Móⁿthiⁿ pretended to be deaf, when she was told to put her fire out. The signal came, the camp was moving. Nóⁿzhiⁿ Móⁿthiⁿ did not abide it.

The chief's bonnet was staked high on its tall, bent staff, above a thick sage bed. Shúde Gáxe now bent and placed the eagle feathers on his head. In full dress, he mounted his spotted roan, and led Nóⁿzhiⁿ Móⁿthin's Red Pony behind. When he reached her place, on the corn watcher's stage, he spoke to her directly.

> "Nóⁿzhiⁿ Móⁿthin, you will ride beside me.
> Come. We must leave this place.
> You will let me know, Nóⁿzhiⁿ Móⁿthin,
> when you sense her return.
> We all know she will find us.
> And we can no longer wait for her.
> Big Horse tracks, past the river crossing,
> end in a slippery stream.
> She rides like a ghost away from us.
> Why couldn't she stay among us,
> in our present danger?"

It was not until he raised this question, that Nóⁿzhiⁿ Móⁿthiⁿ raised her head. She looked up and away, into the wide sky, where they saw storm clouds gathering force, moving towards them.

> "My Granddaughter is being chased
> by more than what appears to be
> today's enemy.
> She is being pursued by those
> who cannot fully possess her
> but who remain selfish in their efforts
> to overpower her.
> She is being haunted by a future
> we cannot imagine,
> by Crowds beyond number.
> Her visions gather above her,
> in dark clouds,
> and she will not return,
> until tempests subside
> amongst her own people.
> She can no longer bear the pain
> of seeing us cut in pieces,
> when only fierce unity
> will survive the coming storms."

Shúde Gáxe hung his head, feeling that they had failed her.
Sorrow welled up in his heart.
He raised his brow at the dark looming clouds.

"This storm will keep the Crow away,
cloud cover any moon light.
We will be blanketed in darkness.
If we run before it turns to mud,
our traces will wash out behind us.
We will be long gone,
when they are slowed by mud.
Nóⁿzhiⁿ Móⁿthin, climb down.
Ride beside me. Red Pony waits ready."

He led her Red Pony closer to the ladder and held its rope out to her. Nóⁿzhiⁿ Móⁿthiⁿ did not move towards him, or the horse.

"I have clouds to watch," she answered.
Then she started singing of her own road.
No one could disrespect her, could interrupt her death song.

So Shúde Gáxe stayed his horse,
and sang low, his own prayer song
as others gathered.
He sang a song of thanks and praise
to Nóⁿzhiⁿ Móⁿthin.

In Grandmother's corn field, they witnessed this.
They wept their tears and moaned.
Some even cut their flesh, right then and there.
But no person dared to interrupt her, medicine woman,
Grandmother to so much that protected them.

Some praised her in song.
Some watered her corn with tears.
None would deny her wishes.

Grandmother's platform was soon covered with gifts of
food and offerings, sweet grass braids, bundled sage, twists
of tobacco. Her nearby shade tree filled with flowing
ribbons and cloth prayers tied on, blowing with the winds.

Grandmother sang.
"Say your prayers.
for your selves.
Say your prayers
for our children."

Grandmother sang up to the sky,
down to the earth, in all directions,
Slowly, the people all drifted off,
heads down and weeping.
Left her with her hobbled horse.

~

Nóⁿzhiⁿ Móⁿthiⁿ worked alone, busy in the corn field as if
it were any other day. She moved slow, and when she grew
tired, she sat in the shade on her watcher's stage.
As her old body rested, she set her hands to beading
moccasins for Big Horse Woman, for the long journey that
lay before her. She had started beading above the ankle long
ago, and now finally worked down and round to beading

their very soles.

Her eyes struggled.

Nóⁿzhiⁿ Móⁿthiⁿ focused thought on her granddaughter.

She knew this was her chance

to say all she needed.

She wished she had ways to pass more on.

Through cloudy eyes, Nóⁿzhiⁿ Móⁿthiⁿ knew

these were the last soles she would bead

as she sewed her prayers into every stitch.

Prayers for her granddaughter's strength.

Prayers for her People.

Prayers for the earth they walked on.

Prayers for their path.

Prayers for their every step.

Prayers to guide them.

Along with her prayers,

she wove in secrets.

As the day wore on and light faded,

Nóⁿzhiⁿ Móⁿthiⁿ went to her kitchen booth

to prepare warm food.

As if it were any other day,

she started a soup.

She thought of events just past.
Thought how this present threat
was the direct result of *her!*
Horses stolen for *her*...
Payment intended for *her*....
To stir such a war!
Over horses... stolen for *her!*
For *her* granddaughter!
Hai! Buh!
Nóⁿzhiⁿ Móⁿthiⁿ thought it only fitting
that *she* confront this revenge directly.
That *she* take responsibility.
For the impending vengeance.
For the unfolding future.
For the ghost she felt beside her.
Kíka Toⁿgà's comrade, struck down by a Crow arrow-
the young Ponca horse-raider-
who now hung about the corn stage, lurking near.
This hungry, vengeful ghost, who now accompanied her,
drawn in by the warm soup...

She left a bowl of corn soup, to nourish him.
Yes, she would feed the ghosts.
Let them have their revenge.

Those storm clouds blew in.
Thunder rolled.

COUP

Three warriors stayed behind to wait with Grandmother;
Thédewathatha, Ónpon Zhínga and Kíka Tongà, who denied
the wishes of his father and, should he not survive, denied
himself his place in line as Chief.

They weathered howling rain that slashed across the night.
Next daybreak, it was mud and slate skies.
Wrapped against the rain, Nónzhin Mónthin sang
her death closer, made it welcome.
Her song brought the men out of hiding,
them suspecting that she knew
something they did not.

"Grandmother, those are not corn growing songs you sing."

No, she agreed, and proceeded to warn them.
She told them Crows flew on the wind,
coming to snatch those ponies meant for her.
They came because of her.
And so she was here to give her self up.
It was a fair trade.
There was no point in *them all* dying, she told them.
They came for her.

They would be of better use distracting the war party
with fresh tracks and false dividing trails,
than by giving their lives away, here and now,
defending someone who intended to die.
They should spy the northern hills,
if they did not believe her.

The men looked north- and saw the swarm of Crow
warriors descending fast upon them.

They all kicked heels into their horses and galloped,
twisting and turning, leading the Crow into wooded
thickets, away from Grandmother.
They churned up the earth around the camp.
They flew, adding false trails, zig-zagging, leading nowhere.
They would come back for her, once the Crow were run out.
They could not leave Grandmother.
They would wait in ambush.

Thédewathatha rushed to the challenge, teasing the Crow away from the abandoned village, away from Grandmother's corn stand. Like a pack of dogs, the Crow split in two, and surrounded him.

He dared them,

> "Throw my bones to your dogs!
> Hang my hair from your shields!
> Kill me, but I will never die!
> I live to haunt the winds
> around you I will ride."

He gave these last words up to the winds
as Crow arrows sang back ------> deep into him.

                    --------->

                                        --------------->

-------------------->

Óⁿpoⁿ Zhíⁿga and Kíka Toⁿgà continued to make wide loops, away from, then back to the river.

Then Kíka Toⁿgà led the Crow straight to their stolen horses, where he had them, picketed together by the water. He rode back and forth behind the line, kicking up sand, aiming his swift arrows at any Crow who caught up to him. They hesitated to shoot arrows back, to aim into their own herd, and so could not take a clear shot at him.

Just how Big Horse Woman had pictured it.

He could have got away without a scratch, slipped away
as they chose the horses, over counting one coup.
But he kicked sand up, and spun around,
and asked for it.

Nóⁿzhiⁿ Móⁿthiⁿ heard
Kíka Toⁿgà's war cries high above the others.
She wished he had less pride.
His pride went with his death.

~

Alone, Óⁿpoⁿ Zhíⁿga lashed his tired horse,
lunging hard across the river.
They ran for their lives, chased and outnumbered.

~

When the Crow war party turned and swarmed back into
the village, they found it abandoned, but for the deaf old
Grandmother with cloudy eyes, squinting, stringing beads,
and chanting. Her death came quick.
Her song fulfilled.

~

The Crow divided between one false Ponca trail after
another, always losing tracks in streams or boulder passes,
just long enough to slow them, irritate them, make them
argue amongst themselves.

The Ponca were long gone. So the Crow retreated, satisfied enough with their glittering string of Palouse ponies, two fine Ponca war horses, one old red mare, two warrior scalplocks, a warm pot of corn soup, and their bold claim to these abandoned hunting grounds.

At the center of the camp,
they aimed their Crow arrows –
shot into the ground
with bloody scraps
to mark it.

MOURNING SONG
GÍ-K'ÓⁿWAOⁿ

The day after Big Horse Woman pulled the blanket up and headed away from camp, she considered how much further she would go. She knew the Ponca had changed direction, but she did not know to where, or if they all traveled together.

But now as she offered her tobacco to the rising sun, and heard the warning calls of crows, her stomach churned. Their raucous caws filled the sky over the wide Niobrara.

Ká'xe-ma, K'á'xeNík'ashigà p'ahóⁿga uwítha
Crows warned of Crows.

She mounted Big Horse and headed back fast.
By mid-day, she made her way into the camp. Big Horse Woman saw no one as she rode the trail bordering some newly planted fields. Crows rose from the corn rows. She watched them, boldly descending upon the abandoned corn seedlings, pecking at the fields, feasting on the trampled corn shoots and swollen seed.

Ears Up showed no concern, smelled nothing to fear here. Neither did Big Horse sense an ambush, or the need to flee. But as they got closer, Ears Up cried in a low, mournful whimper as soft winds swept past.

Something was dead.
She could see now, the gathering
of vultures that roosted in the dead
cottonwood, their wings spread,
outstretched to dry in the morning sun.
Now stretching their necks to see who
was approaching.

She followed along the cottonwood
cover of the river bank, into brush and shadows. She
followed the hills of corn and saw that sprouts had been
systematically pulled, as far as hurried hands could get.

As she passed around the outskirts of the fields and watched
for clues, her heart jumped to her throat. She saw that all
fires had long gone out, but for the wisp of smoke that rose
from Grandmother's field kitchen…

Ears Up trotted ahead. Found Grandmother.
He licked the blood and nudged the hands that had always
thrown him scraps and bones. He whimpered to her cold hands.
Hung his tail between his legs, and howled.

Big Horse Woman saw Grandmother. Slid off Big Horse.
The red blood had already browned
against her skin.

There was nothing great in this.
There was nothing brave in this.

And why....
WHY had she no premonition of this?

If she had known...
could she have stopped THIS?

The only voice that answered was her own,
high wailing scream of her soul.

SCAFFOLD

Big Horse Woman took Grandmother's rake, hoe and cooking tools, gathered up her many gifts and prayers into blanket bundles, and tied them firm to Big Horse.

She lifted Grandmother's body and laid her on the black bear robe. She covered Grandmother with sage and wrapped her in the bear. Straining, she lifted her dead weight up and across Big Horse's wide back. She rode, balancing Grandmother across her lap. They carried her to the river.

Big Horse Woman wept. She bathed Grandmother and washed away the dried blood. She closed her grey eyes, stroked her coarse hair, kissed her soft forehead.

She listened carefully, an ear to Grandmother's lips, for any whispers. When nothing, not one secret more, passed from Grandmother to her, she sat up, warbled high and mournful to the endless sky.

She painted Grandmother's face, painted her with grace. She placed her antler rake and elk-shoulder hoe beside her. She filled water gourds and lit sweet grass.

She trimmed the scaffold with sage and prayer bundles.
She uncurled her small-fisted hands, and crossed her arms
over her belly. She crossed Grandmother's braids over her
heart, and as she smoothed them down over her breasts,
she felt a strange lump under Grandmother's dress.
She reached under the collar and saw shining beads
peeking out. Pulled at them to discover the most beautiful
moccasins she would ever see. She smoothed them out and
turned them over.

Onto the soles a careful design had been beaded.
Big Horse Woman uncurled them and saw secrets woven in.
This gift from Grandmother held instructions,
so carefully beaded, pictures telling.

> *"My name, I give you*
> *My lodge, I give you*
> *My bundle, I give you*
> *My heart, lives in you."*

> To the sky she cried in answer
> "A'on, ā-o^{n}thano^n'o^n -a!   Yes! Hear me.
> Āwíno^n'o^n I hear you.
> A'on, dó^{n}b-a!   Yes! See me.
> Thi-bthí^n!   I am you!
> Shó^n! Gáx-ai!"   It is done! So be it!

"Shóⁿ!" she whispered.

Big Horse Woman wept hard for Grandmother.
She took her name, her lodge, her bundle,
kept her in her heart.
She took her body, wrapped and bound within
the black bear robe, to the plateau burial scaffold,
which the people had built for her leaving.

Aⁿhíⁿga feathers, of the rarely sighted, sacred water bird,
were tied to the scaffold's four corners.
Aⁿhíⁿga feathers. Another clue. Left by the women.

She wrapped Grandmother with ashes, with sage and cedar
smudge, with tobacco and cornmeal prayers.
She took her knife and cut off half her own hair.
Cut the flesh on her forearms and shoulders,
offered up her own blood.
She placed a handful of Niobrara earth,
over Grandmother's heart.
Offered tobacco prayers,
which the winds swept up,
high into the air.
Put tobacco down on the ground.
Big Horse Woman cried out her name.
    "Nóⁿzhiⁿ Móⁿthiⁿ!"

Wailed high, as the sun set on them.
Cried with all urgency, to the winds,
> "Nóⁿzhiⁿ Móⁿthiⁿ!
> Nóⁿzhiⁿ Móⁿthiⁿ!
> *Nóⁿzhiⁿ Móⁿthiⁿ thíⁿge!*
> Now I carry us both!"

MOURNING VISION
GÍK'Oᴺ THÍᴺKE ÍTHATHASHTI DÓᴺBAI THÍᴺKE
'While she was mourning, she saw something.'

Big Horse was free to forage, old corn stalks, new sprouts,
new grass. He grazed, swished his tail, filled himself.
Drifted from one familiar field to another, ears forward,
always listening for the Ponca horses.

He left her high up on the limestone plateau,
overlooking the river.
Grandmother high up on the scaffold,
Big Horse Woman on the ground beneath her.

Her tears mingled with blood on her arms,
where she cut them.
For three days she stayed with her eyes open,
spoke Nóⁿzhiⁿ Móⁿthin's name out loud,
before she could no longer, on day four.
She offered pieces of her own flesh to Grandmother.
Put her name to rest.
Big Horse Woman stayed with Grandmother,
Rocking back and forth beneath the scaffold,
waiting for answers.
Abandoned by Spirit.
Before
Always there
Always whispering
Always telling

What to do. When.

But now-

When she questioned...

Nothing.

She was orphaned. Pitiful.

Alone.

Not a breath

not a touch

no sign

to tell

that she wasn't.

Alone.

Not a word.

Nothing-

came to her

but the angry

thirst to scream

need to scratch

claw her way out

of this deep hole

Grief.

Spirit?

No.

Just

a wide

empty

horizon

not a bird

mole or mouse

not a wind.

No sun.

Just a

flat

grey

sky

a heavy heart

utter and void

of Spirit.

No answers.

No voices.

Grandmother's tracks

left the ground.

Nóⁿzhiⁿ Móⁿthiⁿ

crossed over

to settle back to stars

not

long

away

just

over

the other side…

On the fourth day
she ran dry of tears
closed her heavy eyes
to another vision.

Saw the crowds, light flooding the plateau.
Saw the faceless crowds pushing
since childhood through her nights.
They walked, between her
and the morning star
directly towards her coming trampling
every living thing between them.
They came, grasshopper thick
flattened prairie grass
to dust rising up
Dark tornadoes
twisting
and Something Else
coming
no words to name it
Máxoⁿ! [7]
She saw it and
felt a line cut sharp
straight through her belly
dividing the earth in two
twin metal lines cutting
a trail of steam burning
a line of black smoke spilling
a sharp whistle piercing
stinging spikes slicing

at her feet
metal sparks.
She could not name it
and then something
opened her eyes

Opened her eyes to see Ears Up
licking her toes, cold and exposed.
In trying to move her,
he'd tugged off her grass boots.
To bring her back, licked her feet, to circulate heat.
Ears Up licked her ears warm. Nuzzled her neck.
His whimper and whining brought her back to the living.

HIDDEN MEDICINE
MAᴺKÁᴺ THE ÚK'INOᴺTHE

All she ever really knew was her next step.
She knew no other way to walk.
And so she stood up.
Shóⁿge Toⁿgà Wa'u departed her post at the burial scaffold.
Left the plateau. Passed slow through the cold camp circle.
Big Horse Woman saw the Crow arrows shot into the
ground. Saw their claim to it.

She rode to where their lodge had been, where the grass
was flattened by the weight of the tipi cover, as it was
folded, rolled and packed. She saw the grooved impression
where the lodge poles had been stacked. The meat-drying
racks left behind, standing empty. Their fire pit filled with
smooth river sand, in the center circle of the packed dirt
floor. She saw the shallowed path where the doorway east
had been. And in the hardened earth, she saw another clue
had been stained and marked.

A full bowl of the yellow pigment had been used to paint
a circle of sun. Below this, a waving blue line was streaked.
Under this, a full red moon.

With this, Big Horse Woman knew where to find their
hidden lodge.

She returned to the fields and filled her blanket with all she could carry of corn husks and stalks, for Big Horse. She tied up the bundle of fodder, loaded up Big Horse. They walked to the shady banks of cottonwoods and willows twisting up the river.
Found the trail which Grandmother's heavy lodge poles traced, just past the camp. Followed the grooves to the place where her first Moon lodge had been, where she had bled red into the earth under the moon, where she had seen and heard the Sun, where she had dreamed the River. Where Grandmother chose to keep their medicine, safe by the Niobrara.

Aⁿhíⁿga feathers of the sacred water bird, hung in the willow brush, to mark it, another clue and gift from Grand mother. The hidden lodge, well tucked behind a web of willow roots, waited for her. If Big Horse Woman never found it, Grandmother intended for the lodge to be returned to Wakóⁿdagi when high waters came. The same seasonal floods that once bared these roots, could wash the lodge away. This was a good way. Because, as everyone knew, the medicine it kept was so powerful, it would have brought harm and misfortune to anyone else that might find it. Better to have drowned it.

Big Horse Woman removed the wilting branches and brush that covered it, then lifted the travois from its pallet of willow branches. She propped the lodge poles up, against tall rocks.

She led Big Horse into place, then settled the poles along
either side, the slings crossed and tied at his withers. At the
crook of his withers, she lashed a parflêche, settling it flat
against his broad shoulders. The weight kept him standing
still, as she fastened another parflêche, sacks and bundles
across his rump.

She climbed up on his back, sitting between the parflêches,
legs propped up, feet resting on the slant of lodge poles.
She tapped his belly and prodded him up river.

Ears Up sniffed around the camp, found meat scraps
and bones, and the freshest churning tracks and tried to
decipher them. Criss-crossing trails made it easy to see that
it was purposefully deceptive. So she chose to follow older
tracks that were laid by habit, and did not abruptly circle
back. She followed well used routes to and from camp, to
see where they led, and which ones held most promise. Ears
Up took up a fading scent. As they rode away from there,
she did not know when or where she would again find her
People, and she called for the Voices to return to her.

Soft rains came. She turned up her face. Let the drops soak
and soothe her parched skin. She opened her mouth
to drink.

When the rain stopped, warm southern winds followed
in surging waves. She rode straight into them.

RUBY DAWN   1852 – *Today, Day One*
ÓⁿBA KÓⁿGE ZHÍDE
Day,   almost there, red

Shóⁿgè Toⁿgà Wa'u slept wrapped in her warm blanket.
At her side, the big dog kept his Ears Up all night.

Cottonwood down dusted the sky and settled on her blanket,
tickled her awake. Big Horse snorted hello, swished at flies,
gnawed on the budding trees nearby.

Big Horse Woman started her day with a whisper of thanks
that passed her lips even before she opened her eyes. She
listened to her thoughts, to the tale-end of dreams, the
sounds of insect and bird, what the smells told. She smelled
sweet grass, heavy with dew, and something new.

She opened her eyes to the morning haze, to the ever
changing sky, then rolled onto her belly and surveyed all
around her. The chill of the earth beneath her triggered the
need to rise, and so she did.

~

Standing, she made offerings to four directions,
to the Sky and to the Earth.
She prayed and circled her arms sun-wise
round her head to bring on the day.
The north wind blew its greeting
 and she pulled her blanket closer
around her shoulders.
She stood
dizzy.

It had been four days mourning.
Four days since she took anything in.
Today, she would open her mouth.

MULLEIN

SÍNI HÍ

Footsore Plant

Dew covered mullein hugged the sloping hillside.
Its large rosette made the perfect cup of drink.
The padded leaves blanketed each other as they unfolded.
She could see this plant was still dreaming, visibly soft with
sleep. She approached it, focused on the inner leaves, lush
with pillows of memories.
She thought of the countless times mullein leaves lined
her moccasins, aiding her footsore and weary treks. She
loved mullein, remembering when she'd fallen off her pony.

When Grandmother held cool, wet hide scraps against her
bruises, alternating them with steaming mullein leaves.
She saw the mullein taproot, white and hard as bone
and she saw her strong spine, like a knuckled root.
The mullein flower that opened her ears when they ached.
The tightly bundled inner leaves that held morning water,
held the clinging breath of each new day.
Drinking it in now, she listened to the Mullein Song

> *"With my root, stand tall,*
> *With my leaf, make smoke*
> *With my flower, clear your ear,*
> *With my seed, heal down deep."*

It was this she remembered, this song she heard and knew
as she knelt, gratefully drank the morning's mullein dew.

Tears came, with thoughts of Grandmother.
There were still tears yet, and no telling when they would
dry up. She turned away from them.
The tears welled up none the less.
She pushed her tears away and thought forward.
For the first time in four days.
She had to eat. She needed strength.

She took her first meal with her horse, following his whiskered nose as he nudged up tender green. Soon her pouch was filled with pepper grass seed, cattail shoots, pine and sorrel buds.

She shook dirt off and stirred them, breathing life in. The food was still alive as she chewed it and felt it fill her empty belly.

She took what was left of her green meal and laid the remaining plants flat in her parflêche, some of every kind, to share and to remember.

VOICES
HÚ T^HE

As Big Horse Woman journeyed through Tender Grass now covering the prairies, the strength of the returning sun and near full moon pulled tree buds to blooming, brought shoots unfurling. And so it was that she was searching and foraging with an appetite born of grief.

Big Horse Woman gave thought to when she would return. Now, without Grandmother, she was not eager to hurry back, to the feuding, the old scars and fresh wounds. The Crow war party sought revenge for horses stolen, in her name. Horses she refused. Horses that none the less came. Horses that left a trail of blood shed.
Despite her Vision, she could not stop them.
But it was not the Crow, she most feared. In the dark of the previous night, she'd lost the trail of the Ponca. Even Ears Up could not pick it up beyond this sandy stream. This trail they'd followed east was now lost. She came to think that her people had likely switched back west, or turned south. Intentionally deceiving their trackers, they had certainly deceived *her*. The people were somewhere, far ahead. Her mourning had kept her back.
And, something more, bothering her.
In her fasting dreams, there was something she only vaguely recollected. *Something* she was being pushed *towards*.

DEER

TÁXTI

Meat, real

They headed towards the warming sun.
A crow cawed on the hilltop.
Big Horse raised his head.
Ears Up stopped scratching.
They all listened.

Their eyes watched the hill.
A twig snapped.
Ears Up slunk forward towards the sound.
Big Horse returned to grazing, one ear listening.
Big Horse Woman pulled his head up. They followed Ears Up.
Walked down slope, angling east toward the snapped twig.
Big Horse Woman reached over shoulder for an arrow,
knowing that shortly, paths would cross.
A tuft of fur moved through branches and she saw a doe lift
her head. Ears Up tensed, waiting.

The Woman froze, arrow between fingertips,
and Big Horse stood quiet under her.

The doe stopped chewing, nose up.
Stared and flashed her tail.
>"*My young follows me... there...*"

The fawn came into view then, small tail flicking in the shadowy underbrush.

Big Horse Woman did not move, but turned her eyes away.

The deer moved on.

Ears Up set his ears down flat.
Whimpered, disappointed, when the arrow relaxed.

WATER
NÍ T^HE

Big Horse took his time climbing the next ridge, until the smell of wet pine and running water suddenly cascaded over them. He picked up speed and the travois seemed to get lighter behind him. Reaching the ridge, they caught sight of the ribbon of water glittering below. They cautiously followed the narrow deer trail down. Jays screeched at their arrival. A rabbit ran under brush. Ears Up set off to chase it.

Big Horse's careful steps brought them to the edge of a swollen stream. The Woman slid off and removed the travois, propping it against a large rock. She slipped the rope from his mouth as he lowered his neck and slowly sucked in the cool water.
The Woman sang her Water song.

> "Ní t^he, for your clarity,
> Ní t^he, for your mystery,
> Ní t^he, for your life, Níta
> that flows in all things.
> I drink you, to become my blood."

So thirsty, she drank long from her cupped hands. Then she scoured the banks to gather shiny watercress and wild onions. Put the glossy leaves and silty bulbs into a woven bag. Tied the bag and lowered it into the rushing stream to cleanse her food.

RABBIT
MO^NSH-CHÍ^NGE AK^HA

As Big Horse Woman cleared ground for a cook-fire, Ears Up returned, the rabbit in his tight jaws. Big Horse Woman scratched his back and praised his catch.

"Ú'doⁿ! Friend! We will have a good meal."

Ears Up dropped the rabbit by her feet and went to quench his thirst, tail wagging.

She gathered white bark, brown needles and dry grasses, twigs, and branches. She most carefully built her fire in that order, and then removed her burning stick from its pouch. She set it between the palms of her hands and began the quick spinning of it in its fire starter bark.

As it spun, small wafts of smoke rose, first like strands of hair, then feathered plumes. The birch bark and pine needles were set off in small sparks, which she blew into a steady flame. Gently she blew and fed it brittle grass.

She then turned her attention to the rabbit. Her hands worked more easily now, by the warmth of flames. She lifted the soft animal and stroked its open eyes shut.

She held it next to her belly, bent to whisper into its long, limp ears

> "Run home now.
> Ears Up and I thank you for giving away this body,
> to give us strength this day."

She held the rabbit, waited till she felt all life pass.
Reached for her skinning knife.
Ears Up waited, whining nearby, as the sharp blade started.
She tossed the head and limbs to Ears Up. He ripped, chewed and swallowed. She rolled and tucked the guts into a large wet burdock leaf, then pushed the roll into the hot coals. There it smoldered, tantalizing.

Ears Up paced the circle of fire, watching as she firmly set two forked sticks in the ground, on either side of the flames.
She speared the rabbit and set it across the forks. The hiss of dripping blood caused Ears Up to twitch. He watched the rabbit closely, but it did not drip again, as she turned it with a skilled hand until it was perfectly roasted in its own juices. The rabbit was a good size, already fattened by tender grass.

Big Horse Woman brought the dripping watercress and onions to the fire. She macerated these and rolled them into another burdock leaf. She removed the roasted rabbit, cut a strip of meat.

She tossed the first chunk back into the flames and watched her offering go up in smoke. Tossed the next tender bite to Ears Up. She unrolled the burdock roll of greens, and wrapped the rabbit in the steaming plant juices and let them stew longer in the coals, until the smell was strong enough to taste. When she ate her first meat, the tender rabbit and sharp bite of onion enveloped her tongue.

~

Big Horse Woman squatted, sinking her weight on her heels as she slowly chewed the last bite. She ate all she could, leaving sinewy scraps and bones for the dog. She stuffed the green roll of roasted guts into a well-smoked elk-skin pouch.

After covering the fire with dirt and wet sod, Big Horse Woman pressed a firm hand to Ears Up's nose, signaling him to stay and stand guard. She hobbled Big Horse near him, and whispered to them,

"I won't be long. I won't be far."

MORNING FORAGE
HÓᴺÉGÓᴺCHE WABÁHI
Early Morning, To graze

Big Horse Woman was a person of knowledge.
This made her free.
She did not depend entirely on any one to make life possible.
Life flowed from all directions.
Big Horse Woman was welcomed to sit at any fire.
She always brought a story, always left something behind.

The reputation of her horse preceded her to gatherings of neighboring tribes. Everyone had heard of the Big Horse, and she did not arrive to them a stranger. This granted her a warm reception, and she was always welcome.

Today she walked with her hard ash root-digger in hand, scanning the forest and clearings around her as the sun rose in the sky. The earth warmed beneath her. Dew dried from the grasses but clung to the shade plants. She walked beneath cool trees, until she came to a fallen tree, its long decaying log covered with clusters of puffballs, and cried out
>"Fallen stars!"

Big Horse Woman sprinkled the log with tobacco, in offering for the food and medicine. She removed a hand full of the mushroom clusters, carefully slicing the spongy stems clear of soft bark.

She packed the treasured mushrooms into a woven
cloth pouch. Further on, she sat on a hill, sloped under
the morning sun, gathering those plants she knew. She
murmured soft prayers during her gathering, looked
carefully before removing leaf or stem, knowing that if she
did not choose wisely, harm to the cycle of plants, birds,
animals, and people, would soon be measured.

She looked long at a new plant before touching it.
Offered corn meal or tobacco. Only then, would she
scratch, smell, lick it, sometimes chew. She knew plants by
the print of their veins, a map, of identity. A flower's petal,
thinner than the skin of a newborn mouse, had the same
force of life pulsing through it.

Smells were the voice. The smell of one thing was never like
another. Each so uniquely given. As true of taste. A taste
told everything. Each new leaf and flower, every smell and
taste, told something.

Tightly spiraled ferns collected in a coil basket.
First-year burdock and plantain leaves lay flat in a parflêche.
Bunches of field mint, bee balm, golden rod, horse tails,
yarrow feathers, all hung dying on a nearby branch.
Big Horse Woman saw more plants on that hill which she'd
never seen before. In recent years past, she found many
medicines and foods that her People had never used. Her
discoveries were sometimes shared, clan to clan, tribe to tribe.

Others were kept, her secrets, these plants from another world. Today, as she dug a hand full of familiar wind flower roots and shook the dirt, a new smell came to her, rich and deep from within the freshly dug earth. She closed her eyes. Inhaled and tried to identify the earthy scent, but did not recognize it.

When she opened her eyes, they focused on a thick patch of curly-edged leaves nearby, new to her.

She remembered her Grandmother's words.
> *"When a plant grows so abundant, áhigi,*
> *or a new one comes in crowds, on the wind,*
> *from the waters, in the path of travel...*
> *It is often a gift to the People,*
> *that they don't yet know they need.*
> *It has happened before,*
> *and many plants tell us now.*
> *Something new comes our way. You will see.*
> *Watch and learn. You will know.*
> *Wéshpahon tániⁿk^he"*

DOCK ROOT
ZHO^NKÓ^N ZÍ

Root,   Yellow

Big Horse Woman heard it whispering
>*"Dig a little deeper.*
>*My roots follow the dark."*

Her fingers, chilled in the deep earth, followed the root, exploring its length. She wriggled her wrist, scraped her fingernails deep into the dirt. As fingers worked through the darkness below, she crouched closer to the earth and pressed her cheek against it. The smell of baking clay wafted from the hole to her nostrils.

She removed enough of the surrounding dirt so that she had all fingers of both hands wrapped firmly around the root, and slowly extracted it like a strong and stubborn tooth. Pushing clumps of caked earth back, she re-filled the gaping hole. She kept the plant in the shadow of her tunic as she carried it whole to the stream. Only then did she expose it to the light and look long at it.

>*"You moved me.."*

The root spoke.

>"You called me,"

Big Horse Woman answered.

She lowered the root into the cold water, to quench its thirst.
Then, its whispering continued,

> *"We've arrived ... crossing the muddy water.*
> *On skirts, hems and fur.*
> *We've covered hills and filled ditches.*
> *This is a Wave,*
> *as happens, be it air, land or water...*
> *the breaking wave, of trampling wheels,*
> *feet and horses.*
> *Heavy with seed, clinging, carried away*
> *on new trails.*
> *Under the fullest moon, sinking deep*
> *from blue skirts*
> *here*
> *to*
> *root."*

Big Horse Woman curled her toes into the dirt
and thanked the earth.

DREAM
HÓᴺBTHE

Wrapping the root to dry, she started downstream, back
to where Big Horse and Ears Up waited. Her strength
wavered, weary. Her head was light. The soles of her feet
ached, stiff and heavy with over-use. In the cold water,
they became a sudden knot of hardness, cramping,
stabbing, until she could no longer feel the sand beneath
them. She sat to rub them, brought them back to life.

She walked slowly back to where she'd hung the gathered
plants and bundled them. She padded her grass boots thick
with mullein leaves, to comfort her sore feet.

Muscles spasmed, this, her first food, after four days
of fasting. Before she could walk further,
drowsiness overcame her.
She thought it good to briefly rest.
She rolled into her blanket on a bed of pine needles
under cover of low pine boughs.
In this small cocoon, she quickly drifted,
the yellow root in her hands,
    "Why did you call me to dig you?"

The root smell sifted into her nostrils,
filtered into her dreams...

ZHÓNMÓNTHIN
WOOD WALKING
Walking Wood; Wagon

Muffled voices hushed each other.
A massive wagon hull on rolling wheels
floating over prairie grass
Strange faces, devoid of blood or color
faces shrouded, skin stretched tight over
bone cheeks, dust covered lips, clenched
the voices stopped.
A young girl
blue eyes catching the sky
Watching up
a shadow grow, against the blue.
Listening up,
to screech-high piercing
iiieeeeeeeeeeeeeeeeeeeeeeeeeee
of a hunting hawk
Watching the hawk
dive down swift
brought
Big Horse Woman
hurtling fast
back
to earth.

MOON STREAM
NÍOᴺBA WACHÍSHKA

Moon Stream   Night One

Big Horse Woman sat up, startled. The sun had set.
A cool, wet fog crept downstream towards the sleeping
pines. She shook off a deep chill. The grass held blue
shadows. She carried her harvest in the dark, followed the
stream by moon light, carefully avoiding slick rocks at the
water's edge.

The dream haunted her.
The unforgettable face of the young girl.
The strangest eyes - blue- that she had never seen.
Looking up to the rising moon, she asked,
> "Is this girl a child of the sky?
> Of the water?
> Such eyes cannot be a daughter of the earth.
> Perhaps her blood runs blue, instead of red.
> No color on those faces-
> but for eyes - that catch the sky."

Big Horse Woman whispered up
> "Who sends me this strange dream?
> Moon?
> Stars?"

There was no answer from the sky,
but at her belly the root stirred, in answer,
> *"No - not a Dream.*
> *A Memory."*

She felt her skin crawl at the thought.
These ghostly people were real?
And had been *Here?*
Passed through? Here?

She felt the urge to run. Far.
She rushed to get back to Big Horse.

~

Ears Up met her on the deer trail, licking the tips of her chilled fingers. Big Horse stood sleeping, his ears dancing forward. Big Horse shifted his weight and snorted.
The Woman approached him, warmed her hands and face in his thick mane. She removed the hide hobble and stroked his strong back.
> "Wake up Big Horse. Stretch those wooden
> bones. It is time to come alive, dear friend."

She patted his rump and set him to grazing, and they all went to the water and took a long cool drink.

Big Horse Woman took the root once more and moistened
it in the stream. This time she rubbed off the dirt residue
and admired the strong root, its coppery skin, before
wrapping it tight in its crown of leaves. She tied the root
bundle close to her belly.

Big Horse Woman packed Big Horse with the travois,
bundles and parflêche, and prepared to ride. They set off
at a steady pace over unfamiliar terrain, watching again
for signs of her People.

~

For the first time, Big Horse Woman was not sure she
wanted to hear all the voices that swirled inside her. For the
first time, she wondered if she shouldn't have left this root
where she found it. She did not like this most recent dream.
Her most vivid glimpse.
Those faces.
Those *eyes*.
Worse even than the gaping holes.
This was not the first time she dreamed the crowds.
And the last time, the last time a dream of this sort woke
her, it brought the wave of wagons. More men.
More women. More children.
Then, the winter in hiding, alone with Grandmother.
Big Horse Woman's eyes filled with tears that came,
unexpected, remembering Grandmother,
and those winter moons, when they'd left camp and stayed safe,
alone together.

But now… now the dreams of crowds came stronger, more often, and the haunting faces were not washed away by warm squash soup upon awakening. Grandmother's hand was not there to soothe her brow. No ears to listen.

These recent dreams remained haunting
wide wheels churning over the land
pale skin and grey eyes
and this time the blue.
Those clear blue eyes that she had never seen.

She did not move carefully as the urge to run crept up again.
The moon rose full and bright. So she allowed Big Horse
to cut across the shining foothills, dragging the travois over
bramble, following the widening, bright stream.
As they hurried along in the dark shadows of a downward slope,
Big Horse tripped, lost footing, stumbled to his knees.

Big Horse Woman lurched over his shoulder
and landed hard.

Ears Up circled back.

POULTICE

UBÉTÓ[N]

To Wrap

The Woman tumbled and curled in a ball. She caught her breath and pulled herself up, and back to Big Horse. She reassured him with her voice as she carefully felt his legs over. When he pulled his front hoof away from her grasp, the warm stickiness of blood filled the palm of her hand. Lifting again with care, she looked at it more closely, saw the deep gash at his heel.

She coaxed him to the water. Submerged his hoof in its iciness, and held him there, with her thumb pressed tightly over the wound, until the water no longer flowed dark with fresh blood. She pulled out the puffballs, plantain, and wind flower roots from bags she had filled that very morning. These would stop the bleeding, start the healing. She pounded them between water smoothed stones, into a fibrous, pulpy poultice, which she applied directly to the wound. She scooped muddy sand and with a scrap of bark, plastered this over the fresh plants. Over this, she lashed a soft hide scrap, to keep the poultice in place, stop the bleeding. Big Horse Woman threw her blanket over his steaming back. As her fingers stroked Big Horse, she spoke softly into his ear,

"I am careless, friend, to forget who you are
and ride you like a slave to my own fear.
Now let me see you walk and we will see
how you go."

She coaxed Big Horse to take a step. Watched him shift his weight off his injured foot. They hobbled a ways, Ears Up leading, ears back, making sure they followed. They had to get away from the open, find somewhere safe for the night.

But Big Horse stood, tail swishing, head hanging,
foot curled under, and could not be moved.
She whispered now,

"No, there is no need to push on.
We must rest your foot and my weary spirit,
before we go further in any direction.
We will be still as stone, my friend,
until you are able.
Perhaps if you feel better, we will move
before first light."

Big Horse turned to her, breathing warm air over her face.
She looked into his dark eyes and felt herself relax.
She could not worry. She let the lodge lie, leading the horse
out from under its weight. Then, by scratching his ears,
she coaxed his neck to relax, his head to lower,
and soon he bent his knees to the deep grass
and lowered his haunches to the earth.

She stroked his neck until his breathing grew rhythmic and slow, and she knew he was deep sleeping. She nestled against his shoulder, and watched her mind spin.

Big Horse Woman again questioned when she would return to the tribe. This root had stirred things up. But this much was clear- she could not answer the many questions she knew they would ask upon her return.

She could not share a story so full of holes. A spotty vision. She could not warn of something she could not even name. How could she tell them, without them seeing her crazy.

She relaxed against Big Horse's breathing.
Here, she did not feel the pull for home.
She did not want to go back, to all that was gone.
She felt like a sack of fish-eggs clinging to a slippery rock,
against a current pulling toward a predestined place.
Something was the root of it.
At the center.
She felt the urge to define
what was pushing and pulling them.
Something soon to happen.
Some bursting seed planted.
Something loosely woven
but tugging tight at her.

The sight of those blue eyes

catching the sky

had sent her rushing through the darkness

of this vaguely familiar valley.

Something haunting

that had completely pulled her in.

Something *was* the root of it

at the spinning center

strong feelings

pulling

her

deep

under

....

...

..

..

.

.

.

.

.

.

THE ROOT OF IT ALL
ZHO^NKÓ^N UTHÍZO^N BTHŪGÁXTI

Root,   Center,   All, the whole

Big Horse Woman dreamed vivid, images flooding in
> *Strong, white-dusted hands,*
> *kneading thick, brown bread.*
> *The unwrapped root on her lap,*
> *held against her belly.*
> *Her wrists blue. Her hands stained red...*

She heard the root's raspy whisper once again,
> *"Yes... Rest....*
> *Do not rush like the wind*
> *to spread fear to the People.*
> *There is much more to this dream we share."*

The root stirred its story deeper into her belly.
She felt it pulse through her blood.
> *"This - a season of great changes.*
> *You will be split - down the middle,*
> *in the distant light.*
> *There inside, you will see,*
> *a core of strength*
> *of earth, rain, and stars*
> *the sun and moon, the power of life*
> *The treasure that you carry,*
> *the root, that needs be tapped,*
> *the nurturing earth,*
> *the thundering sky,*

> *the root strength*
> *in you..*
> *the power*
> *Split in two."*

Big Horse Woman opened her eyes, surrounded by silence.
Black night enveloped them. The moon hid behind a mass
of clouds. Big Horse did not stir from his heavy sleep.
Ears Up, curled up at her feet, seemed deep in dream.
The air, still with a sudden chill.
Big Horse Woman waited.
Listened.

> *Find shelter....*

was all she heard.

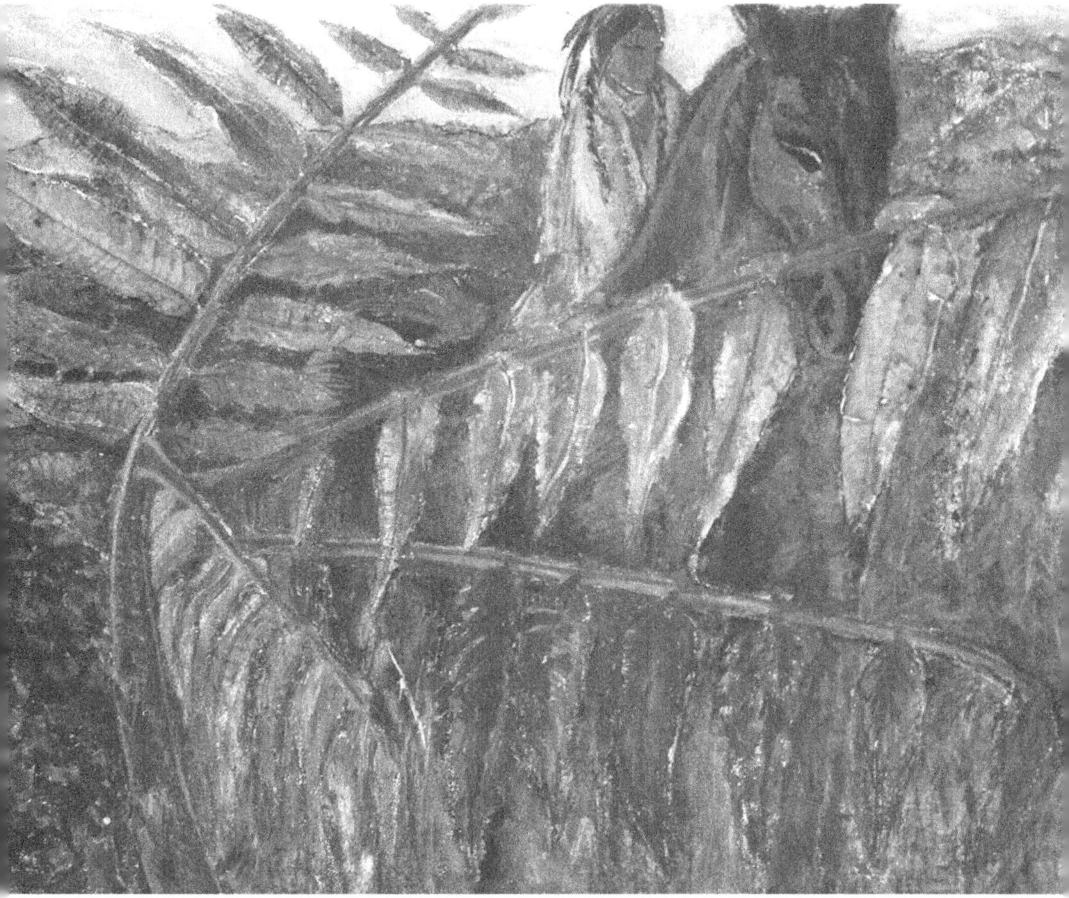

SUMAC AND CEDAR
MÍ'BIDEHI KÍ MÁZI

In the black sky, there was not a single star. They reached the base of the limestone bluffs and cold night air descended. She walked ahead of Big Horse, to reduce the weight of his burden. As she carefully led, she considered the nearest safe place.

She could stay in this valley, and follow the narrow creek south around the foot hills, till they eventually met Ni^{n}shude t^{h}e. They could then follow the river west and north, along its sandy banks. This would add time to her journey, depending on many things - like Big Horse, his footing, and approaching weather. Tonight, as cold north winds pushed them, it was good to be going south.

She led Big Horse in the dark, followed the bristling tail
of Ears Up, who seemed to know this way.
Moonlight broke through, revealing a clearing.
Ears Up sniffed the ground, catching a scent.
Big Horse Woman smelled the crisp air.

There was a spill of boulders at the foot of the bluffs ahead. These could provide the safe place to hide, if it was not already occupied. The travois scraped behind them over the gravel littered ground.

If anything else waited in that clearing, it was either asleep, or as still as a stalking spider. Big Horse Woman hissed softly, tossed pebbles around her, waiting for any response. Finding a large dead branch, she beat the brush around them. The startled flight of a nearby quail flushed out of the brush. The dog let out a yip. Quick, disappeared after it.

Big Horse blew air at the night, tugged to be free to graze. The woman led him behind large boulders and a sheltering clump of cedar. Unlashed the travois from his back, removed blankets, sacks and par fleches. Concealed the lodge with rusty sumac and cedar branches.

Big Horse lowered himself to the dirt and rolled. Watching him rub up his back against the earth always pleased her. A cloud of dust rose as he shook himself out. She did not need to hobble Big Horse. On his wounded foot, he would not go far.

Tired, stretched her toes inside her boots. She watched clouds closing in. She whistled short, and brought Ears Up back, rushing up the creek, lapping water into his empty mouth. No catch this time.

The Woman explored the rock walls to her left, and chose a nearby slant of darkness, well hidden behind a thick stand of sumac. Ears Up led the way under velvety branches, following his nose. A shadowed cave was barely visible as they approached it. Ears Up circled its floor, tail wagging.

The Woman entered, slowly feeling her way, expecting bats and spider-webs. She felt the walls, knelt and gingerly touched the floor, grateful to find a soft, windswept layering of years of fallen leaves. No spot felt warmer than any other, and so she knew she had not discovered someone else's bed. She arranged the leaves under her comfortably, spread out her robe and blankets. With the knot on her waist finally loosened, she shifted the pouches, bags and parcels off her hips and shoulders, laid them close, beside her.

Big Horse Woman tied three sticks into a tripod and hung her pipe bag and medicine from it. Finally, she wrapped herself up in a sound sleep.

Ears Up sniffed the cave's perimeters, then paced the shadowed entrance. He lifted his leg, left his mark and howled, daring any one to cross his line. The moon slipped in and out. Ears Up ended his song and sauntered in. With a sharp-toothed yawn, he curled up beside the Woman, his eyes slit on the clearing. Followed her into dreaming.

BLACK EYES WOMAN

ÍⁿSHTA SÁBE WÍⁿ

*Iⁿshta Sábe Wíⁿ was a very large
Woman. She bore a baby
every year and in months
between, kept her wide belly.
She always had arms full
of babies. Then high fevers
came, and their hot breath
against her breasts,
red mouths and swollen throats,
soft skin erupting, blisters oozing,
finally crusting, over cold skin.
She was not able to accept losing.
She was not able to let go of them.
When their bodies stiffened blue, the people tried
to take her babies but she would not let go her grip.
Iⁿshta Sábe Wíⁿ clung to them until her heavy eyes
fell shut. Her heavy arms, relaxed. While she slept,
the People traded brim-full corn seed sacks, wrapped tight
in blankets, replacements for the stone-cold babies.
The fevers had invaded so quickly, conquered so completely,
that those remaining thought only of escaping.
Those remaining, delirious with grief and shock,
had no strength for proper burials.
Walked in fogs.*

*They set heaping funeral fires, burned bodies to ashes, wailing
as they strayed, hopelessly away, orphans, forever feeling lost.
Upon awakening, late, Iⁿshta Sábe Wíⁿ saw her camp was moving,
saw the funeral fires blazing and she panicked.
She could not move so fast. She and her remaining children,
so over-packed, so weighted down, so many mouths
to feed! She hoarded, more than most, and for the baby
stirring in her stretched belly, expecting soon to come out,
she would be prepared, determined, against all fears.
She would feed her baby well, make it strong, against fevers
and hunger. So overburdened, with her dead-weighted arms
and the child with-in her, she felt worn out.
Her older children carried more than small backs should.
They took turns resting, balanced atop their careless, unsteady
travois. Iⁿshta Sábe Wíⁿ's husband was far ahead,
bow across his lap, full quiver at his back, war club at his waist.
It was not his place to carry anything else, keeping hands free
for weapons, free to protect his scattered tribe and children.
They followed Planting Creek, straggling West, North.
Soon entered a boulder canyon in the foothills.
It was thick with sumac and cedar, and sheltering stones.
They stopped to rest. People, dogs and horses watered at the
creek. It was then that Iⁿshta Sábe Wíⁿ finally uncovered her
tightly bundled babies. Gently laid them down, heavy on the
ground. Perhaps it was shock that made her decide,
to hide them. Perhaps it was just too much to carry.
Iⁿshta Sábe Wíⁿ called her eldest daughters, and filled each
of their folded arms with a wrapped bundle. Told them to*

hide them well and high in the nearby caves, and to mark
the place, so they could come back for them, one day.
The girls chose a slanted cave behind the sumac and boulders,
as the hiding place to be. Stories of spirits, snakes,
wolves and bears, roared in their heads.
Bats and spiders. They were scared!
They stood terrified of their own shallow breathing,
their eyes adjusting, as dark walls became visible,
and no other eyes stared back at them.
One climbed the other's shoulders, stuffed the seed sacks
high up on a rock shelf. They shoved their bundles away,
from reach of bird, mouse, man or bear.
They marked the wall with limestone chalk,
drew two ears of corn, pointing up.
Then they ran from there, and were glad to help their mother,
stand and rise back to the trail.

    Some dreams were not hers.
    As certain things occurred or crossed her path,
      they felt expected, meant-to-be, already known, memories,
    but not her own.
    The reminders certain dreams provided,
      meant for someone else,
      came to benefit herself.
    In this dark cave,
      came this one revealing dream,
      and its hidden treasures.

TRAIL OF MEMORIES   Day Two
UGÁSHO[N] SÍTHEWATHÈ

Big Horse snorted and stomped the cold ground,
shook the Woman awake.
She felt his breath stream through her hair as he came closer
and pawed the dirt.
    "*Stand. Woman. Move.*"

Ears Up stretched. Shook out his snow-dusted coat.
A glitter of flakes filled the air, some landing on the Woman's
warm skin, the melting chill quickening her movements.
    "Yes, yes, I'm AWAKE, and without
    memory of a single dream.
    My body so heavy from deep sleep.
    Slow *Down,* Big Horse!"

She'd have to catch him up and get him back to load him,
she thought. He whinnied back,
    "*I will not cannot carry the skins!*
    It will slow us down
    and we are almost there!"

What did he mean by *that?*
Almost *where* were they?
And why was Ears Up, who dashed out of the cave,
obliging his urgency? Was there something near to hunt?

She thought of the lodge, still hidden in the cedar, and the struggle it would be to get Big Horse back to pull it. She would have to keep the lodge, safely camouflaged here, until she caught up with Big Horse and determined their course. This was strange on his part. Something was pulling him, too. Even so, she did not hope to go far from the lodge, before returning for it.

Big Horse merely snorted louder, stomped harder, then headed off without her, following Ears Up, who was sniffing a warm trail. *What was he after?!*

She moved faster, rolled up her bed, tied belts and bundles to her waist and shoulders. Big Horse Woman peered out from the cave. Thin snow clung to everything like a rabbit skin moccasin on a tender foot. Trees trembled in their new coats, shivered a muffled morning song. The Woman felt the scrunch beneath her booted feet. She stood still, circled her arms sun-wise round her head, offering tobacco.

Big Horse Woman adjusted pouches and checked the root, still tied against her belly.
> "Well friend, our journey continues.
> What will we dream or remember today?"

Big Horse Woman paused. Closed her eyes. Heard no root words. No answer. During the night, the voice frozen.

The Woman covered the lodge with more sumac and cedar
branches, swept out their tracks with a pine branch.
Called ahead to Big Horse.

    "*Slow Down*, Big Horse!"

Ears Up caught up to him and nipped his heels till Big
Horse whirled back on him. He slowed to a circling stop,
threw his head back, filled the air with impatient breath.

When she approached, he gave a belligerent snort. She
snorted back and scratched his neck, snatched his mane and
circled a rope around his nose. Feeling down his front leg,
she lifted the hoof, and untied the poultice. The wound,
sealed clean, looked much better. She rubbed away crusted
blood with fresh snow. Letting the hoof down, she packed
it over with soft sumac leaves, a handful of fresh cedar, and
some cold snow, then firmly wrapped it tight again.
She patted the great animal.

    "That healing looks fine, friend.
    I imagine you speeded it up
    because you have somewhere to go?
    Well, *let's go then.*"

She slung the parflêches over his rump and shoulders,
bridled him and mounted, appreciating the warmth of his
wide back on this chilly daybreak. Feeling his body sprung

tight, she tried to hold him back and relax him.
But he kept a slow prancing trot, leading the way.

They had not seen this obvious trail in the black of night.
It was a clear path through these thick scrubby woods.
Though she did not recognize it in the coat of snow,
somehow the way felt familiar.

Thin snow quickly thawed, evaporating into plumes of
cool mist. Along the way Big Horse consumed pine and
cottonwood buds, chewed twigs of crooked witch hazel
and willow.

Big Horse Woman did not deter him from his voracious
browsing. He knew just what he needed for healing.

She listened to the horse and to the dog.
They were still heading south, *aiming.*
Big Horse's movements below her were purposeful, directed.
They were taking her somewhere, and so she settled in for
the ride.

CORN SEEDS AND TEETH
WATÓNZI WAMÍDE KÍ HÍ
Corn   Seeds   and Teeth

A rose sky unfurled, pink light washing gold over the
rock walls. She heard Ears Up just ahead, digging, nails
scratching against rock. Big Horse caught up to him.

She slid down to ground and found another slanted cave,
its entrance grown over with cedar and sumac.

Ears Up stood on hind legs, scratching up the shadows of a far
wall with his paws, straining towards what he'd discovered,
high up. His quivering nose pointed to an inaccessible shelf of
rock above him. He whined.

In the dim light she saw a chalky white image scratched
onto the wall. As her eyes adjusted she traced her fingers
over a simple drawing of two ears of corn. Big Horse
Woman looked up into the shadowy crevice, to where they
pointed, Ears Up already aimed there.

A slant of early light filled the hollow. The reach was much
too high for her. She gathered up Big Horse, coaxed and
prodded him to enter the cave. Ears Up helped to shepherd
his hooves, as she held him standing under the ledge, long
enough to see the tightly sewn corner of a seed sack and

blanket with beaded trim that she immediately recognized
as Ponca. As Big Horse shifted under her, she quickly
reached up and took the sack into the crook of her arm,
and was surprised to find another one, behind it.
She took this too and left her hand print
and a prayer feather, in thanks.

On the ground, she touched the dusty corner of the sack,
pressing with her fingertips. Felt the grains of corn give
way. She pushed at the bulging bag and heard the kernels
scrape each other awake. A pulse went through her fingers,
to her wrists, up her elbows.

> *She remembered now – that she saw all this*
> *– somewhere – before –*

She slid her hands under the sack and, feeling the weight
of it, knew they had uncovered someone's heavy secret.
This feeling was immediately intensified by the weight of
the other sack beside the first. She knelt to untie them,
and reaching in, brought two hands out full.

A *mix* of native seed, most deep blue, some speckled,
golden, some grey, creamy white, and a few, precious red,
mixed in, as was tradition. But the tradition of mixing
them *all* like this, she had never heard done.
Who would ever *mix* so many seeds?
Why would the sacks be so brim filled, in such a hurry?

Ears Up's tail whipped against her leg. He nudged his nose against the hard tip of something else, buried deep in the seeds. She brushed him aside and saw the cover of a small, green clay pot, jutting out. She scooped corn seed aside. The pot, hastily lashed shut with sinew, had not been properly glued. Big Horse Woman knew no one who would pack so carelessly... unless they were in danger!
Were they running? From what?

Ears Up nosed the loose sinew and the lid fell off the pot, exposing a strange collection of children's teeth, straight locks of hair, a black braid, a fingertip, all cut off, in mourning. Blood stained it all and Ears Up could smell it.

She dropped and smashed the clay pot. She took her rattle from her hip and shook the gourd at it. She shook the gourd rattle, again and again. Drove the trapped spirits out. Chills passed through her as a strange wind carried them, free from the cave.

Her tribe and others often spoke of those seeds lost in all these wandering years. Driven from one village and camp to the next, there'd been so much lost.

>So many Seeds
>lost
>So many People
>gone

So many Words
forgotten
So many Traditions
broken
So many Seeds
lost.

If she could not save her People
If she could not speak the right Words
If she broke Tradition
Nothing mattered so much as the Promise
she made at birth.
To know and keep the Seeds.
To be a Seed keeper was her duty.
In her travels, she traded for seed,
saving quantities of all varieties.
She had always done this.
But never, ever, had she been so led, to such a treasure.
She had been guided, and felt Grandmother's hand in this,
the corn at her feet, whispering...

"Watónzi ukéthin![8]
We return to those
that lost the seed.
To plant, again,
follow Planting Creek."

GHOSTS
WANÓⁿXE AMA

As she loaded the first sack into her parflêche, Big Horse
fidgeted. She held him close and spoke firm. He curled
his injured foot under him - yet he was anxious to move
on. She pushed the second sack in, secured and tied the
bags shut. She grasped his mane and with a running jump,
pulled herself up his shoulder. As her leg swung up over
his back, he started off. She felt like a child, scrambling
to regain balance and scolded him for his adolescent start.
Once fully in her seat, they again moved in unison, heading
steady, due east.

It was *then* that she fully realized she had not been this far
east *since*...she *was* a child... and that...
Planting Creek had once been her home.
She *knew* Planting Creek.
And knew *why* she did not remember leaving.
And she was not sure she *wanted* to return.
Some time ago, the Ponca stayed west of the Mississippi.
Then, the Ponca kept west of the Missouri.
Word spread of the changing world, and proof soon followed
on the Muddy River's shores. Posts and Forts raised up,
infested by the strange new people, black smoke,
offal smells, bad spirits. Since *then*, they had *always*
stayed west of these Niobrara hills.

Her people respected the warnings, always traveling within-the-between places, never making themselves visible by common tracks or trails, or bold silhouette, on new horizons. Even so, they could not always escape the change they were avoiding. Big Horse tugged ahead.
What *was* pulling him?
She tucked her toes under his wide belly to warm them, and he quickened, slapping a wet pine branch against her, momentarily blinding her. Shaking her wet hair, she pulled him in.

    "Tell me Big Horse, what *is* it you're after?"

His lips quivered as if to attempt speech itself,
> "*A MARE, A MARE…There is a MARE.*
> *She walked this way, with a Woman,*
> *like You.*"

Big Horse Woman gave *this* her full attention.

"Shóⁿge míga wíⁿ?	A mare?
Wa'u wiáxti?	A woman?
Thegóⁿ i a?	This way?
Wí éte égoⁿ?"	Like me?

And so he filled her head with images. So she could see…
> *A cloaked woman, on a huge grey dapple mare*
> *Red wet nostrils blowing hot breath*
> *Trotting far ahead, through thin air.*

A Ghost they all clearly saw.

PINE GROVES
UXTHÁBE MÁSI

They followed clear water bending south. Big Horse Woman could feel this valley's climate, carved differently than the snowy bluffs and foothills from which they had descended. They walked all day at a steady pace. The day grew warmer and the grass taller as they went.

The sun reverberated from one side of the wide valley to the other. Along the way they foraged lush shores. When they finally stopped at day's end, she chewed on t'agát'ubè, tossing some to the dog. The sun began its descent and the sky filled with birds, swarming to catch the late feast of flying insects.

The woman dismounted and examined the trail for signs of recent use. Big Horse grazed, still curling and favoring his foot. But he did not like stopping for long, and swung his head from side to side, to tell her so. They rode on, keeping their eyes on Ears Up, his nose to the ground, tail flailing, wild with excitement. Every inch of this trail held fresh scents. He was losing his head. She whistled short and quick, and he came back in bounding circles through the thick grass. Big Horse Woman spoke.

> "Listen up! You both follow your nose
> without thought. Something new,
> something sweet makes you reel,
> like headless birds!

A'ón! We will follow this trail,
but we will stop now and consider,
where it is that we are going,
and a *silent* approach."

While clearly coming upon something tantalizing, yet unknown, she had to pull them back – until she could *see* what they already *smelled.* Although she knew, by their loud behavior, that nothing ahead was an immediate threat, she needed them quiet. She chirped to Ears Up and gestured him back to her side. The dog trotted up and stayed there, prancing along beside them like a young buck.

It was then that the sweet smells finally traveled on the crisp wind to her, and she slowed them all to a standstill. Someone was cooking up a storm. It was time to head for cover. She steered Big Horse into the pine woods, staying in thick shadows. Big Horse picked his way over slippery pine needle slopes and brought them to the thick shade of old trees.

She tied Big Horse under a low branching pine that he could scratch and forage on. Draped the bags and heavy seed parflêches over thick pine limbs, out of his reach. He settled down and stretched his neck tall, to keep watch. Ears Up spun circles, making a spot in the soft needles, then lowered himself to it with a resigned groan.

Big Horse Woman leaned against the wide trunk and asked,
> "Where are we, big trees, and who lives
> among you, making such sweet smells fill
> the air, without care?"

The Pines above her whispered.
Big Horse Woman listened.

They did not answer her question directly,
but began with formal introductions...
> *"Long have we been rooted here,*
> *watching comings and goings*
> *We remember you child...*
> *the way you came...from stars...*
> *yet born of earth. Strong,*
> *you played in our streams*
> *like a fish in water.*
> *Like a tree with roots,*
> *you stood and heard us.*
> *Thixu wi^n*
> *they called you"*

Big Horse Woman remembered her girl name-
Thixu wi^n.
Water Willow, she was called.
And, now, Big Horse Woman remembered it all.
Living in these hills as a child, always dreaming.
Of distant places. Hearing Voices

from other lands, oceans, mountains, passing clouds,
far away stars. Listening, as a child,
to ghosts, spirits roaming, many lost,
who cried across the plains, who wept for moons.
She heard warnings, and laughter, too.
Children, wanting to be born.
She learned new tongues, different songs,
distant cries, distinct calls. *Here*
in her childhood
where dreams and vision came
strong with fever
the fever
that decimated them.
Here.
Where her family was lost.

\\./

Big Horse Woman returned from her memories and realized
these were not burial grounds, but should have been.

Big Horse Woman shuddered.
It was the greatest Death her people remembered.
Two hands full of winters had passed since.
They still lived in fear of the Spotted Fever. *Di'xe.*[9]
They wanted nothing to bring it back.

So her people never spoke of it.
They did not look back.
They lived a good way, kept a clean camp, heeded warnings,
carried medicine, lived in beauty, lived for joy,
journeyed well. This was their way.
But today, the tears came.
She wiped away their flood,
listened to the trees.
> *"You have walked a strong road.*
> *Tears are good medicine.*
> *Do not scold yourself for the bursting dam*
> *that waters the earth at your feet.*
> *Let them flow; you are safe*
> *held in our branches.*
> *Soon you will pass from under our cover*
> *And arrive at the place*
> *that was home. "*

Because in her fevered state, she did not, could not, remember the Trail Away, she had no idea where she left her childhood home. It had remained, buried in memory, until now. The trees whispered,
> *"When you passed childhood*
> *Grandmother buried it all*
> *so it would not carry the fever.*

She buried your Life cord,
your Cradle charm,
your dream catcher,
here, in our roots,
offered in thanks for your life.
She thought the dream catcher failed you
because it failed to keep the nightmares
from you.
But it did catch your dreams
Here, deep in earth.
Our roots still hold them.
You are not alone
holding your memories
and Visions. We share
Your dreams
of Great Crowds..."

Big Horse Woman stopped breathing,
her wind knocked out with these words, and the memories
instantly conjured... *Great Crowds...*
Yes - Here was when the dreams started...
Yes - She had been *dreaming crowds* ever since *the fever...*
She remembered these dreams woke her to fear as a girl.
Nightmares that came, where death loomed,
but did not take her.

Visions that came with the spotted fever,
sweeping through camp,
wiping some out,
passing through her.
......DÍ'XE.....
....Smallpox....
Ears Up bolted up sudden.
The hair rose on his spine, to form a perfect fin,
through hair raising waters. His nose to the stars,
he let loose from his deep chest and sang up
his long throat. His plaintiff howl, piercing, an arrow
through the silence. He remembered this place.
Big Horse Woman rose to stand beside him.
Though perhaps she should have, she did not silence him.
With memories of funeral fires burning,
the sun set blazed the sky.

She sat down dizzy. Her head hot.
She pinched some new growth of tender needles from the
white pine branches above her. She chewed on the tart
pine needles, to ground herself, bring herself back to earth.
Stretched out her legs and... *Manónzhinha-hi!*
A hot stinging burned her ankles, made her flinch.
She poked away fallen branches to uncover the green-blue,
creeping shoots of early *stinging nettle!*
Its pungent smell triggered delirious memories,
more sudden flooding, a vortex, she was spinning,
near to drowning, floating back and forth...

NETTLES 1843
MANÓ^NZHI^NHA-HI

Water Willow's head, so heavy.
It hurt to open her eyes. Pain throbbed.
She dragged her tangled, smothered limbs,
out of the twisted robe covers.
Crawled, stumbled by the flames.
She was so hot, fire did not scare her.
Her tongue, so dry
swollen in her throat, choked for breath.
Gasping, rasping... *"Ní... Ní...Ní..."*
Begging for... *Water...water...water...*
Her steaming face, like broth
she stood, her legs like soup
scuffing bare feet out the door
crackling fire behind her...
hissing... *Water...water...water...*
Outside cold air tickling
and she heard *giggling*
Heard the stream bubbling ...
Water... water... water...
its bright surface, sparkling
against black depths...
She ran with every drop of strength
cool air gave her.

The giggling surrounding...
but she saw no one.
Did not see more stalks bent towards her,
or the shoots covering shore,
or the potent roots,
breaking through eroded earth,
across the sandy surface, a fiery brush...
She ran through and
all at once her ankles *burned.*
She was on fire with needles,
stinging...stinging...
she rolled downhill
toward cool *water...*
into the smooth *water...*
rolling under *water...*
the burning stopped,
in the black cold.

SQUEEZE
THÍSHKI

Big Horse Woman pulled a flask from her waist and trickled cool water onto her nettle-stung ankle. She rubbed in wet pine needles and cool dirt. She had no more plantain or wind flower paste on hand. The stinging was like fire and Big Horse Woman stood to search for another immediate remedy. The rolled root fell from her waist bundle and thumped to the ground. When the Woman picked it up, she heard its dry voice,
 "*Squeeze.*"

So, *this* root was an answer to the *stinging?*
She picked up the pouch and loosened its ties.
The root was neatly encased in its thick clump of curly edged leaves. She unfurled and pinched a stem from the thick crown. It came away with an oozing, slimy substance, which she carefully transported to her ankles. She spread the acrid juice over the red welts, rubbed it into her skin.
And now she clearly heard the root *sing!*
 "*Nettle out, dock in.*
 Dock remove the nettle sting."
The singing stopped.
The stinging stopped.
Big Horse Woman asked…
 "Dock? … Your name is Dock?"
But it did not answer again.

Cautiously she pinched some tender tops off the young nettle shoots at her feet, crushed them between two rocks, then scraped the nettle leaves into her water flask. She lay this on the slope to steep and soak up sun. Whether Moon or Sun-brewed, nettle tea would sooth and nourish her.

She unrolled the burdock wrap of roasted rabbit guts and gave them to Ears Up. He wolfed them down, then curled up between wide pine roots and began to groom. He took to preening as if something whispered in his ear that his appearance mattered.

She cut nearby grass and sprouting branches and put piles under Big Horse's nose, where he remained tied off, in the shadows of the tall pines. She stroked his tall neck and leaned against his shoulder.

> "With the sunrise, we will see
> and perhaps I will discover
> what you both already seem to know."

~

Big Horse Woman could not sleep. She had been dreaming wide awake all day and now she could not close her eyes.
The trees whispered in the darkness.
The wind swirled up through the branches.
The rustling pines, a soothing sound.

She tried to imagine what and who she would see
when she opened her eyes to morning.

Would there be scaffolds crumbling?
Lodges collapsed?
Would there be tracks...
from so far back?

She thought about the seed corn she found this morning.
The old Ponca trail that led them back to the Planting
Creek, that was once home.

Would she see the village as she remembered it?
Who would be the occupants?

The sweet smell was inviting.
It was not the smell of death or the unforgettable stench of
burning hair and flesh, the smell of funeral pyres that she
remembered. As a child on the edge of life and death,
and even now, its memory lingered in her nostrils.

No, this was not a burial ground, but it should have been.
These plateaus should have been marked with scaffolds.
But they were not.

So how would a newcomer *know?*
How would they know that the People had died here?
The core of them - forever gone here.
How would they know?

If they were Umónhon, they would know.
If they were any of the many bands of Sioux,
they would know.
The Pawnee would have heard of this village,
and stayed away.
The Crow would never sweep this far east.
And none of these would ever dwell here.
None of these would as much as dare pass through,
or step upon, this sacred Ponca ground.
Umónhon, Sioux, Pawnee, Crow, would all pass wide around.
No...whoever it was
was *unfamiliar.*

Even the smell...
Sweeter than she had ever ...
Unpredictable...
but someone skillful ...

Big Horse Woman's thoughts were broken by the comforting
nicker of Big Horse, who found her still awake.
He could smell what she was thinking.
He snickered

> *"Wake up!*
> *Wake up and look ahead*
> *There are no fires…*
> *No pyres or scaffolds…*
> *But there is corn…*
> *and more more more."*

Big Horse Woman looked at him.
> "Corn?"

He answered.
> *Not ready yet…but there…just planted*

They looked to the line of light on the horizon.
As the sun woke, she whispered her morning prayers
and circled her head with hands, wide open,
released corn powder.
Floating from sky to earth, the wind took her offerings.
> *"Big Horse Woman asks permission*
> *to look again upon what was home.*
> *She seeks protection, so as to know…*
> *Who masks the distant haunting*
> *smell of burning flesh?*
> *Who fills the air with brazen, sweet scents?*
> *Who walks among our ghosts?"*

The trees grew quiet. Gave no answer.
Today she would see over the hill for herself.

BLUE DAWN   Day Three
ÓⁿBA KÓⁿGE T'Ú
Day Lies Pale, Blue

Light came up. Standing at the edge of woods, Big Horse Woman watched over the horizon. Her eyes and heart slowly drank in the beautiful bowl of the hidden valley below her. Big Horse Woman spoke softly,

> "I will never forget this beauty!
> Like the stars above and the creek below,
> there are patterns in everything!
> I sit here, not dreaming,
> yet thinking I must be..."

Blue and green meadows measured across the horizon in wide, curving stripes. Patches of brambling bush were already covered with walls of berry blossoms, waking up the pollinators.

Birds plucked their fill of insects and worms. Accustomed to the abundance in these fields, they thrived and crooned, songbirds, crows and jays, birds of color she seldom saw. The air filled with their music and morning calls.

A loud bird crowed above it all, as the sun cracked brightly over the east horizon.

> *Ark ark ark aa aaauuuuuuuuu!*

Ears Up growled.

Big Horse Woman held Ears Up close, wishing she could
walk among the flowing patterns in the fields below,
that she could smell and touch and taste these gardens.
But she knew she would first explore from a distance,
with keen eyes, slow, careful, wary.

She watched the rising vapors of melting dew, frail to the
soft southern wind. She smelled flowers opening, scents
carried to the hills. She hadn't expected such perfumes for
another moon!

There were spiral gardens, planted in a wheel pattern.
In the east, yellow buds spilled down to the creek.
A bright white blossom fringed the spiral south.
Deep blue trumpeted as it spiraled west.
Red marched boldly, a carpet spiraling north.

She did not recognize many plants and this was the strangest
surprise.
She wondered if somehow she had lost days, in her fasting,
sleeping, mourning, dreaming?
> *She wondered if she were dreaming now...*
> *Could another moon have passed without her?*
> *Is this where the painters of the seasons*
> *made their first strokes?*

Big Horse Woman held her breath, sank deeper into the
earth. Became still as a stump, but for her roaming eyes.

Surrounding the spirals were patterns and shapes all carefully planted. Continuous plots of green and brilliant flowers, in curves, crescents, snakes and serpents. In the center of it all was a perfect circle, filled with yellow blossoms, radiating like a high desert sun.

Every plant thrived, as if somehow coddled there by the seed spirits.

> *Was this a Wiharu?*
> *A garden of the southern tribes?*
> *There were stories of such,*
> *but she had never seen one.*
> *What amazing people had painted so*
> *with flowers and grasses???*

She was surprised to hear the answer...

> *"Welcome to the center of a shifting world."*

{{{{{{{{{{{{{{{{{{{O}}}}}}}}}}}}}}}}}}}

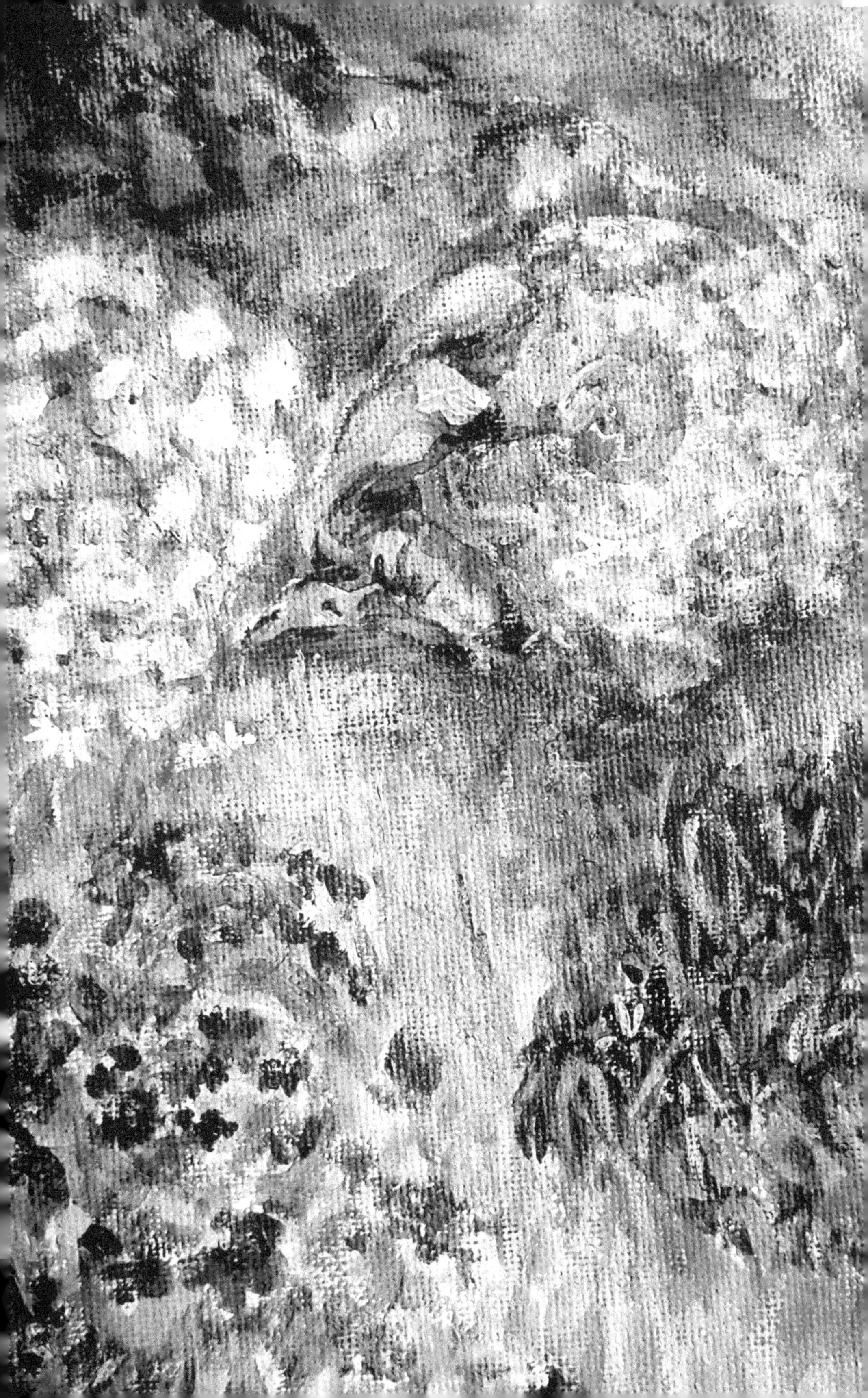

BLUE SKIRT
WÁTE T'Ú
Skirt, blue

Shóⁿge Toⁿgà snorted from his lonesome place. She crept back towards him, snatching wet grass, filling her arms as she approached.
He pawed at the ground and snorted impatiently.
For this, she grabbed the bridge of his nose with one firm hand and pinched his nostrils shut. Big Horse's eyes were wide as she warned him. He pushed his forehead against her chest, but he did not snort again. She left the grass in a heap in front of him and he started in. She buried his fresh dung in dirt and pine needles, to keep the smell from carrying.

Ears Up sat up, eyes sharp. He circled them, tail up and whipping, excited.

A wisp of smoke scented with yesterday's flavor rose again, the sweet smell of bread baking. Big Horse Woman could see a smoke hole, on an earth lodge well hidden, shadowed against a hill, camouflaged by years of thick grass grown over it, fenced by a huge fallen sycamore in front.
A bright, shining creek flowed behind.

She immediately recognized the wide white tree on the ground. After the people, it too had fallen.

Ears Up let out a sudden whimper, laid his ears back.

Big Horse Woman glared and raised a silencing hand to him,
then turned to watch the hill. Ears Up kept his eyes on
the smoke hole, lowered his head, raised his nose.
The hair down his neck stood up.
He growled low.

There was a person in shadow, walking toward the gardens,
who turned to face to the sunrise and squatted in the grass.
The large bird crowed. Momentarily, the figure stood.
Walked on, throwing grain from apron to dirt. Several
more large birds came scurrying out from their well-hidden
hut and pecked at the seed in the dust.

Big Horse Woman had never seen such big birds gather
around a person before. They were bigger than prairie hens.
Louder than crows. Fancier than water birds.
Clumsier than storks. Some wore feathered slippers.
She remembered stories of a Grandmother to the south
that could keep wild turkeys this way. But these were not
wild turkeys. And so loud! Looking at the bird that crowed,
she assumed he was the male, strutting around that way.

Her thoughts screeched to a halt when the stranger turned
towards the hill and walked into light and view, her face
now visible.

It was the girl she dreamed,
this blue skirt woman with *blue sky eyes!*

Big Horse Woman watched her.
Big Horse Woman was flooded with questions.
>*Who was this? Did she alone create these patterns?
Or was she simply their Keeper?*

She watched the Woman tend the gardens, watched her odd movements, observed her use of tools, and what she tended, picked, tasted, harvested. The Blue Skirt spoke to the plants as she visited them. Big Horse Woman could not hear a word, but was enchanted by the gentle tone that flowed to the flowers, which grew abundantly in answer.

She saw that the woman did not move smoothly. There was a limp in her hip and a drag to her feet. And when she bent to the plants, she was crooked. She moved with slow and steady purpose, not wasting steps that took such effort. When she tired of standing, she sat leaning to one side, and pulled weeds or planted seeds as far as she could reach in a circle, arm's length around her. She would then slide to the next spot, and start again, working a new circle around her.

Big Horse Woman saw that this created the patterns, circles and spirals. Not some grand design, but a function of necessity. The woman was hindered and her movements reflected this. Her gardens mirrored her arm's reach.
Big Horse Woman's fear that she was a trespasser, softened with these observations. Somehow, this woman had been injured, settling here, hidden, safe from predators.

She was a survivor, her own care taker,
and had created a place of beauty with her sole efforts.

Still, suspicions and questions jumped ahead.
> *Was she alone?*
>> *Were there others? Near or far?*
>>> *Where did she come from?*
>>>> *Why did she come* here?

Questions spun into knots until pine winds soothed her.
> *"Open your eyes, ears and heart*
> *there is a voice in every thing*
> *there is a voice you can see*
> *in every shape a meaning*
> *in every pattern a song*
> *that you can hear*
> *by looking long."*

ROSE
WÁXTA ZHÍDE

Big Horse Woman left her overlook and crept closer.
Ears Up stayed low at her heels. They followed the berry
bushes, whose flowering would cover their scent.

She came to a thick hedge of wild rose and was distracted
by their overpowering fragrance. She pinched a tight bud,
placed a petal on her tongue. She inhaled, mesmerized by
the delicate flavor. As the rose melted on her tongue,
it sang

> *"From the heart of the Mother we come,*
> *The kind Mother of Life and of All;*
> *And if ever you think she is voiceless,*[10]
> *You should know that flowers are her songs.*
>
> *And all creatures that live are her songs,*
> *And all creatures that die are her songs,*
> *And the winds blowing by are her songs,*
> *And she wants you to sing all her songs."* [11]

Big Horse Woman opened her eyes.
When she looked again to the spiraling gardens
the Blue Skirt Woman was gone.

GONE
THIᴺGÉ

Big Horse Woman slipped back to the pine slopes, quietly clucking her tongue to announce her return to Big Horse. There was a strange quiet. She looked over the knoll into the pines. Big Horse did not stand where she had tied him! All that remained was frayed rope and deep stomping in the soft earth, where his hind legs dug in to pull back.

She scolded herself for not thinking!
There might have been more to his dream.
Perhaps it *was* the scent of *the Mare* that had pulled him.
He *was* a stallion, strong willed and stubborn.
She wanted to run out, call him out, search high and low, but...
She needed to calm down...
Big Horse had *never* left before.
Silence surrounded her.
She felt so small.

> "Shóⁿge Toⁿgà!
> Were you scared up by the angry ghosts?
> I should not have left you!
> How will I walk without you?"

Big Horse Woman scanned the churned earth, the peeled bark and gnawed pine roots. She saw his impatience, watched where his tracks led.

Ears Up went ahead, over the hill, tail wagging.
He did not seem at all concerned at the loss of his horse.
He came back at Big Horse Woman and nudged her onward,
past the pines, his tail high.
Ears Up slipped off, over the hill.
She started after him onto a trail he discovered through pine
and poplar. She kept sight of the dog running ahead
and heard the distant nicker of Big Horse.

She moved forward and whispered *thank you*
to winds in motion that would listen.

   "Táde ama...
   Wíbthaho[n]."

FOUND
ÍTHE THÍ^NK^HE

Ears Up led Big Horse Woman through the underbrush,
an easy trail of recently broken branches.
She approached the clearing where Big Horse grazed,
gorging on thick grass and tight clover.
He did not seem bothered by Ears Up, who nipped his heels.
He kept on eating, did not even look up at the taunting
dog.

Over the hill further, Big Horse Woman heard the rhythm of
a smooth and easy trot. It sounded so familiar that it shook
her. Big Horse stood, alert, ears forward, now arching his
back, lifting his tail, standing on his toes, making himself
taller, aiming which way to go...

Big Horse Woman wished she had his eyes. Looking into
the forest, she could not see movement where he clearly
perceived it. She peered into the trees, expecting someone.
Remembering the blue cloaked woman and the dapple
grey mare... loping... *Passing through...*
But there was no one... though they'd *all* heard it...

Big Horse Woman slipped the rope over his nose and secured
his attention before she mounted. She rode with the rope held
short, pulled his head up, and aimed back into the woods.
It bothered her that she did not see where the Blue Skirt
had gone. It bothered her that Big Horse had run off.

She kept Ears Up close. Watched his nose point and his ears pin and twitch. He seemed splintered by too many smells. He snaked through the tall grass on his belly, until they were well off the ridge.

Big Horse jerked his head forward and pulled at the rope. She tugged his nose back.

> "Now, I know that there is something,
> just beyond that cliff.
> I feel the pull. I know you do.
> We can *all* smell it.
> But you must stay *with* me,
> until the time is right."

The wind picked up, muffling distant hoof-beats and sounds. Ears Up circled Big Horse until the horse relaxed and settled. They moved on, quiet. Big Horse Woman whispering,

> "She is not there...
> and there is no grey mare...
> Eyes open, what will we see then?"

It bothered her that they could see something that she could not. They were not helping to make it clear to her.

SUN DOWN   Night Three
MÍ'ÍTHE

Sun has gone

The day came to a crashing halt.
She had come full circle, the trail of memories streaming by, and visions fresh, all seeming to make sense.
Water Willow's childhood home, carrying her back, pulling them in this direction, leading here, but still such a mystery.

> *Why was she led here?*
> *Why was she led back?*
> *To this Woman?*

As they moved further back into the dark woods, she imagined how she would approach this woman.
She did not feel threatened. She did not sense danger.
There was no hair raising on the back of her neck.
She needed to overcome the fear that came with the dreams of crowds that came with her.

A brassy glow caught her eye, as a sliver of light shone on the silver bark of slippery elm. She rode Big Horse to this hollow, where an elm grove stretched exposed roots over a green knoll. She tied him there *and* hobbled him. Grass to graze, elm bark, ferns and tufts of moss, would keep his muzzle busy. Big Horse stretched his neck to the ground. Ears Up grazed dog grass beside him.
Guard him, she signed, and he answered, tail wagging.
> "I won't be far," she assured them.

Big Horse Woman scanned the valley's shadowed hills as the sun set. Darkness quickly blanketed the valley. She crept over the slope, staying well protected behind the old pine trunks, and made a thick nest in the pine needle floor. She spread her buffalo robe and smoothed out her blanket. She rolled up in it, her eyes on the sky, her thoughts on her People.

The deadly spirits had swept through here, killing one in two. They'd heeded its warning by leaving and never returning.

>*Was the power lingering yet?*
>*Could its wrath be rekindled?*
>*Had it crept away from this valley,*
>*or settled into the very dirt?*

Her bones told her to remain invisible and pray for direction.

SMOKE
SHÚDE

Shóⁿge Toⁿgà Wa'u quietly uncurled the quilled doeskin that held her pipe and smoke pouch. She opened the pouch and felt into it, scraping flakes of river tobacco, dust, the last of it. She pinched it together and carefully placed it in the pipe's bowl.

Tomorrow, she would gather willow bark and mullein to shred and dry. Refill her smoke pouch.

Since childhood, she had watched her heart's desires carried to the clouds. She waited for their answers, to know which way to go, what to do, when. The wind always answered.

She looked at the small pinch of sacred tobacco.
Her words softly hung in the dark.
> "Shóⁿge Toⁿgà Wa'u calls to you
> with a whisper of fear, a call for help.
> My body is racked with keeping still,
> my muscles knotted with not knowing.
> Not knowing who we wait for?
> Why we are called back?
> Headless birds, we are, skittering in circles.
> Hiding, in the dark, keeping our distance,
> while someone walks in our place.

>Strangers, smoke and unfamiliar smells.
>Let me dream tonight and know
>that nothing but good may pass between us.
>Nothing but truth may cross our lips.
>To you Grandmother-Grandfather,
>Shónge Tongà Wa'u now raises
>and lowers her pipe."

Stem to the sky and bowl to the earth, she lit the tobacco with her flint. She took short puffs and watched the smoke curl as she blew towards each direction, then cupped the smoke over herself, in prayer,

>"Shónge Tongà Wa'u walks with you
>All she knows, she gives away
>to be empty again, to hear
>each new voice, to listen
>each new way, of living.

>We will see by morning...

>I will walk again on earth
>made of my People.
>I will see the hair and skin of my mother
>in the flowers that bloom here.
>I will see the arms and eyes of my father
>in the corn and sapling trees.
>I will see the People and their horses
>growing in the grasses,

> from the blackened soil, born of their fire,
> from the ash and dust of their bones,
> hooves and blood.
> And if our morning prayer
> cannot rise in smoke,
> if there is no tobacco or corn meal to offer,
> Please hear it in Big Horse Woman's
> beating heart...
> At daybreak, we will blow to the sky
> with only our breath.
> Drum with our heartbeat.
> Circle, with pitiful, empty hands.
> So to All, we now call
> so that tomorrow, you may still be listening."

She blew her prayer into the silent night.
Warm wind came up all around in answer.
She tucked the pipe bowl carefully into its moleskin pouch,
the stem back in its doeskin wrap, and placed these carefully
away in her quilled pipe bag.

She knew the moon would be rising nearly full, and the
night would be well lit. She curled up in her spying place,
wrapped her blanket closer and watched the valley.
Heard Big Horse and Ears Up breathing behind her.
A low hanging mist rolled in from the nearby creek.
A single, thin line of sweet smelling smoke hovered.
The dusted wings of moths began their silent rhythm
in the growing dark.

CAMPFIRE IN THE VALLEY
USPÉ MÓNTE UNÉTHE
Valley (Dented), Fireplace, hearth

Big Horse Woman peered down through the pine trees.
She saw a bright campfire grow in the center of the dark bowl
of the valley, in the middle of the spiral garden.

The Blue Skirt was there, wrapped in a worn blanket,
staring up into the bowl of stars and singing soft.
She sat quiet, patient, did not fidget, but was still as stone,
waiting, unmoving. She watched the sky, watched the
trees in the breeze. The woman talked to herself, and to
whoever might be listening. Big Horse Woman crept
down closer to hear her.

As Big Horse Woman watched her, she observed a gentle
nature that seemed harmless. She felt her own fear and
apprehension evaporate, replaced with the feeling that
this woman was *familiar.*
Big Horse Woman watched and waited until the fire died away.

* *   *

*

The Blue Skirt had spread a cloth on the ground, and laid
out food in bowls, a water gourd and cups, used shiny tools
to eat with. Eventually, she spread the cloth over the feast

of uneaten food. Reluctantly, she walked away from it, back to her earth lodge, bone weary. Before entering the lodge, her eyes swept the valley, settling on the western hills, looking long and hard, peering into the thick pines as if she could see through them.

Big Horse Woman held her breath and froze, until the Blue Skirt Woman slowly turned away, into the shadow of her door.

~

The moon was high, and the fire coals were black, before Big Horse Woman dared to slip downhill into the garden. She slipped out again, with the bowl, the bread and the water gourd.

Big Horse Woman returned to the elm grove and surveyed her gift. She looked long at the painted gourd and admired the wooden burl bowl. Such a feast it held! Greens and flowers and a strange pronged spoon, which resembled Grandmother's antler rake, in shiny miniature. This speared and held the food well enough, and so she ate with it.

She ate every leaf and bud which blended newly on her curious tongue. There were many tastes that pleased her, many that she did not know. This surprised her, because she knew well most all the tastes that needed knowing.
She reveled in the sharp sweetness of young leaves.
Crisp green life and flower petals lingered on her tongue.

The bread was good, hard-crusted and dark brown outside and in. It tasted like the sweet morning scent that drew them in. She chewed, soaking pieces in the water gourd, for Ears Up and Big Horse. They all shared in this generous gift. Ears Up licked his lips and Big Horse stretched his neck in search of more.

~

She watched Big Horse drifting, his eyes half open, lower lip flapping, sleeping standing, breathing low. She watched Ears Up's ears follow every rustling. Even sleeping, his ears moved, like a moth's feelers. Once, he opened his eyes to see a pinecone drop.

She wrapped herself in her warm blanket and looked long at the stars. She lay still, staring into space, listening through crescendos of crickets and beetles. She turned over and watched the forest floor, the shadowed slopes, the thick tree trunks, the moonlight. She watched the night until her eyes grew heavy and fell shut.

With the sky full of stars, a chill in the air, and bellies full, they were all soon asleep.

*
*

*

She dreamed the voice
coaxing her to waking....

> *You will proceed*
> *Until you meet kindness.*
> *Once there, she will take your hand*
> *and guide you forward.*
> *Join your hearts.*
> *Join your voices.*
> *Together you will*
> *Speak for the Voiceless.*

*

*

*

*

*

FISH CATCHING HUGÁSI

Day Four

It was still dark when the trio crossed the mossy clearing and continued downhill to the bright stream. Without permitting Ears Up and Big Horse to muddy the waters, she let them take a long drink, then tied them.

The stream was wide here, and there was a shallow pool at the bend that was the perfect place for fish catching. She crept to the edge on her knees and peeked over. She held her head very still while her eyes roamed the surface waters and depths of the pool. She saw the first silvery flash in the shadows of ledge rock.

She slipped her fingertips into the water, mimicking the pattern of wavering fins. She fluttered her fingers as she lowered them. When her hands were fully submerged, she kept them still.

The fish were curious now, and approached her fingers with their groping mouths. She wiggled them. The fish swam away, and then just as quickly, swam back. And thus enticed, one swam alongside, nibbling. She rubbed his under belly till he stilled, then she clutched him up with the speed of a stork. She played this game again and again, until she had tickled up enough fish for a good meal.

Ears Up did not wait for his fish to be cooked. She split and filleted it, tossed it to him and he devoured it. She split and wrapped the others in water-soaked corn husks, then speared them with green sticks. Big Horse Woman built a small fire of dry wood and brush. It was a quick, hot fire, and she roasted the fish quick.

Ears Up drooled and paced, keeping watch on both the roasting fish and the valley below. It seemed almost too much to follow all at once. He was bursting restless and Big Horse Woman knew it. Once the fish were cooked, she doused the smoking fire, buried the steaming ashes, and threw the fish heads to Ears Up. He snapped them up. She lined the clean burl bowl with wide burdock leaves and packed the grilled fish neatly into it. She wiped her oily fingers over her braids, giving them a black shine. There was one more task to tend to before they could move on.

Big Horse Woman reached into a corn seed sack and brought out a handful of seed. She placed this on a smooth river stone, and with another stone, began grinding. Once reduced to a fine powder, she scraped it up into the small pouch around her neck. Always close to her heart, when it hung empty, she felt it.

So she filled it with the corn powder, comforted to know she could now make proper offerings this day, as would be needed.

SKY FAWN
MÓⁿXÈ TÁXTI ZHIⁿGÁ
   sky,   deer, little (fawn)

Big Horse swept his tail furiously, snorting and stomping
with impatience and frustration, demanding,
> *"Noⁿshtóⁿ'-ga! Stop! Shénoⁿ! Enough!*
> *It is time to go."*

Ears Up followed grinning,
tail wagging over the bowl of fish.

Big Horse pawed the earth,
tired of the wall of trees between them and the valley.

Ears Up jumped at him, firmly taking hold of his tail with
his teeth. There the dog dangled, while Big Horse wheeled
around to get after him. Big Horse Woman whistled short,
and Ears Up released his grip.
> "Oⁿthábahai móⁿka.
> We will be known.
> Settle down. It is time!"

She dipped her fingers into bear fat. Into a palm full of
this, she sprinkled the precious vermilion pigment, mixing
them together into warm paint. She placed her red palms
against her forehead, painting a band from hairline to temples,
then stroked her red fingertips, in lines down her cheeks,
from under her eyes, straight to her jaw.

Finally, she painted red in the part of her hair.
She then painted a thin line of cobalt blue, circling her wrists, to make her hand-talk fluid.

She gathered her blanket neatly around her, pulled up her downy, cattail collar, let her charms loose, to hang freely. She balanced the burl bowl on her hip and gathered the lead line in hand. She led Big Horse to a boulder mount, and swung herself up onto his wide back.

She held him standing. On the hilltop she voiced their names, loud and clear, to all that could hear her-
> "Shónge Tonga Wa'u.
> Shónge Tonga.
> Níta Ánonzhin."

Big Horse stomped the ground, making certain that their arrival had been properly announced. With a pinch of corn powder, she circled her arm, sun-wise round her head, gave her thanks. Breathed her morning prayer...

> *"Shónge Tonga Wa'u walks with you.*
> *All she knows, she gives away*
> *to be empty again, to hear*
> *to each new voice, to listen*
> *to each new way, of living.*

Let me see and know
that nothing but good may pass between us.
Nothing but truth may cross our lips.
Wíhe, to you, little sister,
Shǿⁿge Toⁿgà Wa'u
now raises her voice."

Wind carried the corn prayer. Powder floated, sprinkling over Big Horse, on to grass. A soft southern breeze nudged at her like a hungry fawn. She rolled her hips, gently squeezed her thighs and walked Big Horse on.

THE PONCA LANGUAGE:

Ponca is a Siouan language spoken by the Omaha (Umónhon) people of Nebraska and the Ponca (Panka) people of Oklahoma and Nebraska. The two dialects differ minimally but are considered distinct languages by their speakers. Ponca Tribe of Nebraska https://poncatribe-ne.tv/category/language/

Omaha-Ponca, a Dhegiha (LAY-gee-ha or THEY-gee-ha)* language, spoken by the Omaha and Ponca peoples. Omaha-Ponca is a Siouan language belonging to the Dhegiha group in the Mississippi Valley branch. The number of speakers is not known, but it is probably a majority of those Omahas born before WW II (several dozen?), and about a dozen among the Southern Ponca. The Omaha (UmaNhaN) center is the Omaha Reservation in Nebraska, especially around the town of Macy, near the Missouri River. The Ponca (PpaNkka) are represented by a group in Nebraska (the Northern Ponca) and a group in Oklahoma (the Southern Ponca). Differences between Omaha and Ponca are barely perceptible to outsiders.
Access to material on Omaha-Ponca is made more difficult by the fact that almost every reference has its own orthography.
John E. Koontz http://spot.colorado.edu/~koontz

'All of my orthographic suggestions are based on the current Omaha writing system. If you are wanting to use the Ponca system, you will have to locate someone from the Ponca tribe who knows their current system and ask them to re-spell everything.'
Dr. Mark Awakuni-Swetland, UNL Omaha Language Instructor, Anthropology, Ethnic/Native American Studies.

AUTHOR'S NOTE:
In many orthographies, the **D** (đ with slash through it, or 'led' sound) is often rewritten or typed *without* the slash, therefore losing the correct **th** sound, with the reader assuming it is a **d** sound.
(**th** is used in most Omaha (Umónhon) orthographies.)
The letters **l** (and sometimes **r**) have also been used in some orthographies, example; **Wiblaha**
(but **l** and **r** are *not* used in the Ponca alphabet.)
I use **th**, to make it easier for new readers.
 In this book series: **th** = d —

Similarly, the **ą** (a-cedilla) which represents the **nasalized** *a* sound, (*aⁿ*, *ahⁿ* or *awⁿ*) is almost always written here as **oⁿ**, (used in most Omaha (Umóⁿhoⁿ) and some Ponca (Póⁿka) orthographies.) Otherwise, the **ą** often gets read or rewritten as just a plain **a** and loses the nasalization in translation.

In this Book Series: **oⁿ, óⁿ** = ą, ą̀, aⁿ
(*Exceptions:* **Máⁿchu** - Grizzly Bear (Móⁿchu)
Máⁿkaⁿ - medicine (Móⁿkoⁿ)
...because these are common spellings for these words, as used by the Ponca Tribe of Nebraska.)

Also note, some readers don't understand the '**raised ⁿ**' nasalization, (example - **Wíbthahoⁿ**) and it is often left off when reading, writing or speaking. Common interpretation includes saying **Wíbthaho**, especially when said by men, although this is not a traditional or 'correct' way of saying or spelling this word. Likewise, **Uda** has become a very common slang for **Udaⁿ** or **Udoⁿ**.

In this Book Series, we use **raised** ⁿ : **oⁿ, óⁿ, aⁿ, áⁿ, iⁿ, íⁿ**

<u>Long **O** words</u> ō - *o* as in 'boat' or 'note'
Rarely used in Poⁿca, only a handful of words,
  and by male speakers only, or male signifiers, as in:
ho - now, at this time
aho (M) - hello; term of agreement (*never said by females)
tho ho - an exclamation... a call to Wakoⁿda; to arrest attention; to announce that something is in progress...
yo come; a form of call
negi'ho (M) negiha (F) - direct uncle or mother's brother or mother's brother's son, grandson, great grandson mother's clan
niçi'ho (M) - direct son
tushpa'ho (M) tu'shpaha (F)-direct grandson/granddaughter
osku – man's middle braid
Cook, Thurman. *UmoNhoN iye te ede'noN'ya*
[*How do you say in Omaha?*]
Otherwise, **o** is always **oⁿ**, the nasal sound.

Therefore, in this book series*: to avoid common misunderstandings, mispronunciations, mistakes, or misuses by the reader or language learner, I chose to consistently use:*
th = ð
oⁿ, óⁿ = ą, ą̀, aⁿ
raised ⁿ : **oⁿ, óⁿ, aⁿ, áⁿ, iⁿ, íⁿ**
(**In Footnotes and all quoted material:*
all spelling and diacritics are those used in the *original* materials.)

PONCA PRONUNCIATION GUIDE
Letter / Closest English Sound / Examples of Ponca Words

Vowels

a	a in **father**	s**ká** white	w**á**haba corn
e	a in **hay**	k**é** turtle	t**é** buffalo
i	ee in **see**	s**í** foot; seed	z**í** yellow
o	o in **boat**	**aho (M)** hello	**ho** now, at this time
u	oo in **toot** or **boot**	n**ú** man	t'**ú** blue
a^n	nasal a in **want**	Má^{n}ka^n medicine	Má^{n}chu grizzly bear
i^n	nasal ee in **seen**	sí^{n}ga squirrel	thábthi^n three
o^n	nasal o in **donkey**	shó^{n}ge horse	sho^{n}tó^{n}ga wolf

Consonants

b	b in **boy**	sábe black	búta round, circular
ch	ch in **chip**	ichó^{n}ge mouse	má^{n}chu grizzly
d	d in **dog**	dúba four	xúde gray
g	g in **go**	gáxe make; do	zhí^{n}ga small, little
g^h	g in **ghost**	g^{h}i brown	maág^{h}ig^{h}ibe mud
k	c in **cut** or k in **keep**	ké turtle	ishtí^{m}ike monkey
m	m in **mom**	má' snow	míxa duck
n	n in **need**	ní water	ná^{n}ba two
p	p in **pot**	pa head, nose	pétha^{n}ba seven
s	s in **sing**	sí foot	siká^n fox
sh	sh in **show**	shó^{n}ge horse	sho^{n}tó^{n}ga wolf
t	t in **top** or **bent**	té buffalo	tú blue
th	th in **that** or **them**	thábthi^n three	xítha eagle
w	w in **walk**	wí one	wasábe black bear
x	x (German **Bach**) not in English	xítha eagle	xúbe sacred
z	z in **zoo**	zí yellow	zizíka turkey
zh	z in **azure** or g in **beige**	zhábe beaver	zhíde red

F, L, Q, R, Y, are *not* used in the Po^{n}ca Language.

THE NAMES

The main character, whose girl name is ***Water Willow***,
is later given the name ***Big Horse Woman***.

English
Po"ca

Girl name
Water Willow
Thíxu wí"
Willow, (water) the, one, *or* girl

Woman name
Big Horse Woman
Shó"ge To"gà Wa'u
Horse, Big, Woman

Her horse
Big Horse
Shó"ge To"gà
Horse, Big

Her dog
Ears Up
Níta Áno"zhi"
Ears, Standing

Her Grandmother
Rain Walking
Nó"zhi" Mó"thi"
Rain, Walking

My grandmother
Wikó"
(How granddaughter refers to her grandmother)

My granddaughter
Witúshpa
(How Grandmother refers to her granddaughter)

Her Grandfather
Bear Medicine
Má^{n}chu Má^{n}ka^n
Bear,   Medicine

Her mother
Plum tree Woman
Kó^{n}dehiWi^n

Her father
Facing the wind
Kímo^{n}ho^n

A Principal Chief
Smoke Maker
Shúde Gáxe
smoke, he makes

Chief's son
Curlew
Kíka To^{n}gà

Her Uncle
Wolf Looking Back
Thédewathatha
(Refers to the frequent cautious looking backward of the wolf as he trots along)

Her cousin
Young Elk
Ó^{n}po^n Zhí^{n}ga
Elk,   little, young

Black Eyes
Íⁿshtá Sábe Wíⁿ
Eyes, black, woman

Big Little Sister
Wihétoⁿga
Little sister, Big

Rabbit
Moⁿsh-chíⁿge

Moccasin Flower Medicine
Máⁿkaⁿ Híⁿbe-zha
medicine, moccasin, flower

Magghie
Blue Skirt Woman
Wáte T'ú Wa'u
Skirt, Blue, Woman

The Five Đhégiha Tribes

The Omaha Legend of origin says, "In the beginning the people were in water...They dwelt near a large body of water, in a wooded country..."

A Ponca story of origin says "In the real beginning... Wakónda made the people...and told them to 'Go!'... so they started west to the setting sun and came to a great water..."

An Osage origin story begins "Way beyond... a part of the people lived in the sky. The sun told them they were his children. The moon (told them) that she gave birth to them. She told them they must...go down to the earth, which was covered in water... In their wandering, they came upon other peoples and were taken in as one of their seven bands."

All the traditions of the five cognate tribes, speak of movement from the east to the west over a long period of time. Specific stories or knowledge of place origin are vague in the public record, but all legends indicate that there was a large body of water, 'which may have been the Atlantic Ocean,' Their movement west has no definitive tracings, or clear accounts of the many separations, though some stories are shared as common among them: The name Umónhon "against the current" or "upstream" was recorded as early as 1541 by De Soto, who met the Quapaw– translated as "with the current" or "downstream" - these names referring to when they were split 'while crossing the *Uha'I ke* River.' The Omaha then went north up the Mississippi and onward to the Pipestone quarry region of Minnesota. The Omaha spent a long period of time in the northern regions (Iowa, Minnesota, North and South Dakota) and between the Mississippi and Missouri Rivers, lands which they gave up in the Prairie du Chien Treaty of 1830, as well as in another treaty 6 years later.

An estimated 300 years passed between the time that the Omaha and Quapaw parted at the River and the cession of Omaha land to those treaties. At about this time the Omaha and Ponca also made contact with the Arikara and learned from them the building of earth lodges. They also renewed their knowledge and use of corn, as was shared with them by the Arikara.

Eventually the Ponca and Omaha separated, with the Ponca going far west 'toward the Rocky Mountains', as far west as the Black Hills. They encountered the Padouca (Comanche) and horses, which they then adapted, calling them *kawa*. The Ponca returned to the Missouri, and then upriver to the Niobrara, where they settled.

The Ponca tribe was divided by forced government removal in 1877 to Oklahoma territory. Some returned to Nebraska; those remaining in Oklahoma being called the southern or 'hot-country' Ponca and those that returned to Nebraska being called the 'cold country' or Usní Ponca; the Ponca Tribe of Nebraska. The Usní Ponca were never given a reservation in Nebraska, and so are more scattered, but their tribal headquarters remain in Niobrara. The Southern Ponca, the Ponca Tribe of Indians of Oklahoma, is in White Eagle, OK. The Osage are now headquartered in Pawhuska, OK. The Quapaw settled into four villages at the mouth of the Arkansas River, until their removal to Indian Territory, where they now remain, in Ottawa County, Oklahoma. Kansa, or Kaw, tribal headquarters are in Kaw City, OK. The Omaha Reservation is in northeastern Nebraska and western Iowa, with headquarters in Macy, and approximately 5000 enrolled members.

Despite geographical and physical separations, the five cognate tribes – the Omaha, Ponca, Osage, Kaw and Quapaw – remain linked together, not only in language but in tribal organization, community, and ceremony, and show trace of relations by maintaining gens or kinship groups that share common names. Further commonality is evident in personal names being present from tribe to tribe, which were once derived from gens of other tribes.

Also see:
www.poncatribe-ne.org/culture/history/
www.ponca.com/ponca-history
www.ponca-nsn.gov/
Đhégiha Preservation Society -
https://www.govserv.org/US/Pawhuska/1565094350411631/Dhegiha-Preservation-Society

TIMELINE OF RECORDED VISITORS
- NIOBRARA AND MISSOURI RIVERS -

THIS TIMELINE of recorded Visitors tells what has been documented by Visitors of the Ponca, Omaha, and other Missouri River Tribes.

Their origins are shrouded in the mists of time... We can be certain they were in the Ohio Valley around **1500 A.D.** There is a strong school of thought that suggests that they originated in the Carolina and Virginia Piedmont region and moved from there to the Ohio area. Another theory is that their earliest origins were in the Ohio Valley where they eventually divided, some going to the southeast and others to the west and the northwest.
Cash, Joseph H., *The Ponca People*, Indian Tribal Series, 1975, p. 2

The Ponca, together with the others of the Ðhégiha group, probably migrated from the southeast by way of the Ohio River valley. Around **1540**, they arrived at the Mississippi, with the Quapaw going south and the rest going upstream. The Osage and Kansa left the group at the mouth of the Osage River, while the Ponca and Omaha continued on to Minnesota, where they settled on the Big Sioux River. Driven from this area by the Dakota, they traveled to the Lake Andes area of present day South Dakota, where the Ponca and Omaha separated. The Ponca continued west as far as the Black Hills, and eventually turned east again. They rejoined the Omaha and went down the Missouri to Nebraska, finally, by **1673**, settling near the Niobrara River. There the Omaha left them, finally settling on Bow Creek.
Indian Tribes of North America, *Ponca* p. 374-375

The Ponca lived for a short time in the Iowa area and apparently ranged as far north as the pipestone quarry at Pipestone, Minnesota. There is some evidence that they had

a village there. They left the Minnesota when the Yankton Dakota moved into the region, and apparently the Ponca separated from the Omaha in the vicinity of the James River in South Dakota and migrated west of the Missouri River. There is also evidence that about **1650** they ranged as far west as the Black Hills. It is certain that they were on the Niobrara in **1673**, and it is also certain that during this period they somehow managed to arrange peaceful relations with the Lakota of the west and the Yanktons of the east. This arrangement, while occasionally ruptured, remained basically unchanged until the middle of the 19th century.
The Ponca People, p. 3

1673 - Approximate time of removal from Illinois to Nebraska as a result of the domino effect of the Beaver Wars, mentioned as *Mahas*, a wandering nation on a Pere Marquette map which placed them just east of the Missouri in central Iowa
http://fourdir.com/ponca.htm

1673- earliest historical mention of the tribe- on Marquette's autograph map ('Pana')
B.A.E. Bulletin 30. p. 278-279

Marquette placed the Panas or Poncas near the Omahas on the Missouri River at the mouth of the Niobrara River.
White Eagle, p. 48

The Platte River valley is an adopted home for the Omaha tribe. Oral history tells of the greater Ðhégiha people's origins in the Ohio River Valley. They migrated to an area around what is now St. Louis in the 17th century, pushed by the warring Iroquois. From there, the tribe split. Factions now known as the Osage, Omaha, Ponca, Quapaw and Kaw each headed in different directions, spawning their own offshoots of the Ðhégiha language.
Those that traveled north, up the Missouri River, became known as the Umónhon, which means "upstream people" or "against the current." That would eventually morph into "Omaha," a name given to them by white settlers. The Umónhon settled near

the Platte and Missouri Rivers and, after a split with the Ponca tribe, lived around modern-day Bellevue in a place they named Ní Btháska, "land of flat waters."

Peters, Chris, *Omaha Tribe trying to revitalize endangered language*, Omaha World-Herald, 23 February 2015

Lake Andes, South Dakota; There, according to Omaha and Ponca tradition, the sacred pipes were given and the present gentes constituted. From this place they ascended the Missouri River to the mouth of White River, South Dakota. There the Iowa and Omaha remained, but the Ponca crossed the Missouri and went on to the Little Missouri River and the region of the Black Hills. They subsequently rejoined their allies, and all descended the Missouri on its right bank to the mouth of the Niobrara River, where the final separation took place. The Ponca remained there and the Omaha settled on Bow Creek, Nebraska, the Iowa further down the Missouri (to Dixon County NE.)

Bureau American Ethnology, Bulletin 30., p. 278-279

As game decreased they had to move their camp from year to year. The introduction of the horse helped some. Eventually the Poncas reached the Big Sioux River to live and here they built a fortified village but even thus equipped they were unable to resist their foes the Sioux and again they had to move, going to Lake Andes, South Dakota.

This home was only temporary and they moved again this time to the mouth of the White River ... the Iowas and Omahas who had joined forces with Poncas remained. But the Poncas crossed the Missouri and went on to the Little Missouri and continued on to the Black Hills. After a short time there, they again returned to join the Omahas on White River as a means of protection, descended to the mouth of the Niobrara River on the Missouri, chosen as their permanent campsite.

Zimmerman, Charles Leroy, *White Eagle, Chief of the Poncas*, Printed by the Telegraph Press; First Edition (1941), p. 48, 57

"After finally abandoning the Big Sioux (River) village locale, the confederated tribes traveled west and northwest to the mouth of the White River, where the Omaha and Ioway remained for a time. The Ponca, however, set off on their own to the Black Hills. The three tribes eventually reunited and traveled back down the Missouri River. Driving the Arikara out of northeastern Nebraska cleared the way for the eventual settlement of the region by the Ponca, Omaha, and Ioway ..."
The Omaha and Ponca migration, www.american-languages.org/198

The Poncas were originally a part of the Omaha Tribe which separated and lived along a branch of the Red River near Lake Winnipeg and later relocated to the west bank of the Missouri River.
The Ponca Tribe of Nebraska - www.poncatribe-ne.org

The Ponca established themselves in the area drained by the Niobrara River, which enters the Missouri... They built their major village at the mouth of the Niobrara, but they established other settlements as well.
The Ponca People, p. 3

There is folklore tradition that the Eastern Sioux were the source of the Ðhégiha, moving down the Ohio River and westward... *White Eagle,* p. 58

In the nineteenth century any one of the larger tribes, such as the Comanches, Sioux or Blackfeet, had more horses than all the herds from New Mexico in 1680, but at that early period the Plains tribes were fewer in number and smaller in size, with a total population south of Nebraska of about twenty thousand people. Since those tribes at first considered a horse or two for each hunter real wealth, five thousand horses would have sufficed to equip them all, yet a century later any one of the tribes would have felt poor indeed with fewer than five to ten horses for each hunter. As each tribe desired more and more horses with the passing years, its wants were supplied in part by the natural increase of its herds and in part by new stock from the settlements. Haines, Francis, *Horses In America*, 1971, p. 53

The Ponca were the first to fission off from the larger group, signaling a new political and economic arrangement for the allies. When the confederated group reached the mouth of the Niobrara River, the Ponca permanently separated from the Omaha and Ioway. The Omaha eventually settled near the mouth of Bow Creek in northeastern Nebraska, and the Ioway continued eastward to establish a village near Ponca, Nebraska. (Ritter 2002: 276) Around this time the generally more mobile Ponca received their first horses from the Padouca (or Plains Apache). There is no oral history of how and when the Omaha received horses.
The Omaha and Ponca migration www.american-languages.org/198

1700 - The Poncas adopted **the horse** about the year 1700. *White Eagle*, 1941

1735 – First Omaha village west of the Missouri established on Bow Creek in present Cedar County, Nebraska
http://fourdir.com/ponca.htm

1738 - La Verendrye
The French-Canadian explorer the Sier de la Verendrye noted in 1738 that the Mandan Indians had not only "corn, meat, fat, dressed buffalo robes, and bearskins" but also European goods. The village dwelling Mandan traded with the Cheyenne and other mounted nomads, bartering guns, beads, and corn for horses and buffalo meat and robes. By the early 1800s guns and horses had given Indians new strength and mobility, but the fur trade had snared them in a net of dependence on European commodities that was desolating their traditional culture.
The Making of America NORTHERN PLAINS, Cartographic Division, National Geographic Society, Washington, D.C. © 1986

1750 - The first Ponca villages near the confluence of the Niobrara and Missouri Rivers. [O'Shea and Ludwickson]
Đegiha tribes migration, (North American Languages: A fragmentary survey with focus on Siouan languages)
www.american-languages.org/145

1755 – Village established near present location of tribe (Knox County, Nebraska)
http://fourdir.com/ponca.htm

1758 - Omaha population dropped by 800 vs. their number in the year 1700, which could be the roughly the number of Ponca who may have departed. [O'Shea and Ludwickson]
Đegiha tribes migration, www.american-languages.org/145

1761 – The Poncas were also visited by an agent for the Missouri Fur Co., Manuel Lisa in 1761, he was accompanied by an English trader named H.M. Breckenridge...who made notes of his trip and specifically mentions the Poncas whom he states he met at their village after passing the Platte River....At that time they were located on the east side of the Missouri River beyond Iowa and near the Big Sioux River.
White Eagle, p. 59

1780 - a century later,(when) any one of the tribes would have felt poor indeed with fewer than five to ten horses for each hunter
Haines, Francis, *Horses In America*, Ty Crowell Co, 1971, p. 53

1786 - French map identified the Ponca on the Missouri River, near Ponca Creek and the Niobrara River.
[James Henri Howard] www.american-languages.org/145

1789 –The Upper Missouri and all of Louisiana was at that time in the hands of Spain.... During the period of Spanish control, the fur trade remained in the hands of Frenchmen. The first to ascend the Missouri as far as the Poncas was Jean Monier. When Monier reached the Poncas fortified village at the mouth of the Niobrara, he traded some, talked a lot, and returned. p. 26

In **1789** Jean Baptiste Monier of St. Louis is said to have discovered the Ponca tribe and in consideration of this fact was granted the exclusive trade with that nation.[38] During the nineties Francis Benoit, J. D'Eglize, R. Jusseaume, and Joseph Garau were regular traders up the Missouri river.[39]
South Dakota Historical Collections, vol. IV, p. 329;
Billon's Annals of St. Louis.
http://www.usgennet.org/usa/ne/topic/resources/OLLibrary/nea b/pages/ neab0019.htm

1789/1793 Jean Baptiste Monier - Traded and lived with the Ponca. He was the first European who actually was in a Ponca settlement.
Đegiha tribes migration, www.american-languages.org/145

1793- Indians Intercourse Act provided "That the purchase or grant of land, or any title or claim thereto from any Indian Nation or Tribe of Indians within the bounds of the United States, shall be of any validity in law or equity unless the same be made by a treaty or covenant entered into pursuant to the constitution."
The Indian is a ward of the government.
White Eagle, p. 168

1794 Jacques Clamorgan - Located the Ponca "on the bank of the Missouri about thirty leagues above the village of the Maha [Omaha] nation."
Đegiha tribes migration, www.american-languages.org/145

1794-1795 Jean Baptiste Trudeau - Opened a trading post that came to be known as the "Ponca House" on Ponca Creek
    Đegiha tribes migration, www.american-languages.org/145

1795-1797- James Mackay traveled up the Missouri and wintered with the Omahas slightly above the mouth of the Platte and made contact with the Poncas in that manner.

1800 – Loisel's post founded many miles above the Poncas. Trade by that time was fairly constant, and the Poncas were not in the best fur trading area, but they did do some trapping and sold a considerable number of hides. In addition they were able to trade their garden produce, or at least their small surplus, to the fur traders. The white men came to admire the Poncas as an honorable, peaceful, handsome, and moral people. *The Ponca People,* p. 30

    It was the French who came here first, to trade their beads and kettles and blankets for the furs of the Poncas. Spain claimed the land, but it was the French who came among the Poncas and left their names with the people. In **1800** France took the Louisiana territory from Spain and in **1803** Napoleon sold it to the United States.
    For the next half century fur traders traveled up and down the Missouri, and there was always a white man with a French name living among the Ponca
    Mulhair, Charles, *Ponca Agency,* p. 2

    The Ponca tribal rolls contained some French names from marriages of French traders and trappers with Indian girls, some of them being notable French families as Delodge, Leroy, and Primeaux.
    White Eagle, p. 46

    Wherever a Frenchman traded, he intermingled and frequently married. Famous French names such as Primeaux, LaPointe, La Flesche, and LeClaire began to appear among the Ponca people. At the same time Poncas intermingled considerably with the Omahas and the Yankton Sioux, who ranged across the river.

Ponca historical information; encyclopedia

1800 - less than **30** non-natives in S. Dakota /Nebraska
Fradin, Dennis B., Fradin, Judith Bloom, *South Dakota*, Childrens Press, Chicago,1995

The Poncas were a small tribe numbering approximately 700 during the **1800's.** Lewis and Clark reported that the tribe, once a part of the Omaha Tribe, separated and lived along a branch of the Red River near Lake Winnipeg. However, the Sioux forced the Poncas, as well as many of the smaller plains cultures, to relocate to the west bank of the Missouri River in the early **1700**'s.

Nebraska Indian Commission, Lincoln, NE

1803- Louisiana Purchase: a vast territory from Napoleon; the French Republic...one of the greatest diplomatic coups in American history... *the treaty added some 830,000 square miles to the United States for $15,000,000,* **nearly doubling the Nation's size.**

The ill-defined boundaries of the purchase extended roughly from the east bank of the Mississippi to the Rocky Mountains, and from northern Texas to just beyond the Canadian border.

Grosvenor, Melville Bell, Ed. In Chief, *In the Footsteps of Lewis and Clark*, National Geographic Society © 1970. p. 20

President Thomas Jefferson assigns Lewis & Clark to explore the region and People, to... "let them know of the Change of Government, the wishes of our government to Cultivate friendship with them, the objects of our journey and to present to them with Some Small presents."

Grosvenor, *In the Footsteps of Lewis and Clark*, p. 44

Lewis and Clark in their trip on **July 15th, 1804** reached the mouth of Little Nemah River and on July 20th were at Weeping Water in Cass County. Here, near the village of Rulo in Richardson, they met Indians. The next day they camped at the mouth of the Platte River. Later they reached Omaha's site and Fort Calhoun and here on August 3rd was held the first council with the Nebraska Indians. Fourteen Otoe and Missouri chiefs attended [including] Little Thief, **Big Horse** and White Horse, and the site was called Council Bluffs. They reached Calumet Bluff and held a council with the Sioux Indians, with Chief Shake Hand, and White Crane and on Sept. 4th they reached the Niobrara River. **Here they met the Poncas** who had long made their home in Nebraska... *White Eagle*, p. 65

On **August 18, 1804** the leading Missouri Chief, **Big Horse**, and main Oto chief, Little Thief, met with the Corps. Lewis gave his speech, but Big Horse responded with pointed requests for goods and whiskey. The Corps gave them tobacco, paint and beads, but the Missouri warriors were not satisfied and went away unhappy.
www.pbs.org/lewisandclark/native/mis.html 7/12/98

[Clark] 5th **September 1804** Wednesday
Sent Shields & Gibson to the Ponca Towns, which are Situated on the Ponca River on the lower side about two miles from its mouth in an open beautiful plain. At this time this nation is out hunting the buffalo.
http://www.nps.gov/jeff/LewisClark2/TheJourney/NativeAmericans/Ponca.htm

The Poncas were a Siouan-speaking tribe, whose language was nearly identical to the Omaha. They were horticulturists living in earth-lodge villages but made seasonal tribal hunting trips far out onto the plains; because of their absence on such a trip they did not meet Lewis and Clark. The village was on Ponca Creek, in Knox County, probably not far from the present village of Verdel.

It is now known as Ponca Fort and was occupied in the late eighteenth century and abandoned about 1800.

Atlas map 19; Hodge, 2:278–79; Wood (TL); Wood (NPF). https://lewisandclarkjournals.unl.edu/item/lc.jrn.1804-08- 31#lc.jrn.1804- 08-31.01

Also See: *The Lewis and Clark Journals* (Abridged Edition) *An American Epic of Discovery, Meriwether Lewis, William Clark, and Members of the Corps of Discovery,* Edited by Gary E. Moulton, Bison Books, Lincoln, NE., 2004.

There was no Ponca village on the explorers' (Lewis and Clark) map, although their journals refer to one on the south of Ponca Creek and to another on the north side of the Niobrara.

Jablow, Joseph. *Ponca Indians* Ethno-History of the Ponca with their Claim to Certain Lands (1950's) U.S. Government Report, NY/London, Garland Publishing,1974

1804- Lewis & Clark

Meriwether Lewis and William Clark: The explorers camped a little above the mouth of the Niobrara River at the place that came to be known as Lewis and Clark Point on **September 4, 1804**. They saw the Poncas, met them,* and found them living in the same location where they had been for years before. (They found them) greatly decimated. The Poncas, who had numbered an estimated 800 in **1780**, had been reduced to approximately 200 people. They had been ravaged by a smallpox epidemic, which had also decimated their cousins the Omahas during the winter of **1800-1801**. Two hundred people on the northern plains is not many. Yet they held on, planted their crops, and survived to eventually rebuild their numbers and their strength.

The "Poncars" as Lewis and Clark called them, took the explorers for some side trips and showed them the land. The expedition leaders were most reluctant to leave the camps of the friendly Poncas. Thus, they stayed for some time. At the time, their **chief was named Smoke**, and his sub-chief was called Pure Chief. *The Ponca People,* p. 31-32

*All accounts, by Lewis and Clark, report that they did *not* meet the Ponca *on Sept 4th,* as the Ponca were on a buffalo hunt.

During this time they succeeded in consolidating their hold over what is now Knox and Boyd counties in Nebraska and portions of Gregory County in South Dakota. They possessed fine agricultural land, good grazing areas, and an abundance of water. This was an ideal homeland.
The Ponca People, p. 32

Epidemics had reduced the Ponca population by over 90 percent by the time they encountered the Lewis and Clark expedition in **1804**.
Ponca historical information; encyclopedia

1806- Alexander Henry & Charles McKenzie*

1807 – Manuel Lisa ...established a trading post in 1807 along the Missouri River and made a permanent settlement.
White Eagle, p. 65

1809: the St. Louis Missouri Fur Company is chartered by The Chouteau family in 1809
TIMELINE: Peabody Museum, Boston, Massachusetts

1810-1811*Bradbury and Brackenridge
See; Bradbury, *Travels in 1809-1811, Early Western Travels 1748-1846,* Ed. By R.G. Thwaites, Cleveland, No. 8, Vol 5 & 6 (main 592. T54)

1815 - The first treaty between the United States and Omaha was signed in 1815.
Omaha and Ponca Tribes, Educational Leaflet #2, Nebraska State Historical Society

1817 - U.S. Treaty with the Ponca Tribe-
A treaty of "peace and friendship" between the two nations.
    Nebraska Indian Commission, Lincoln, NE
    The interpreter for the treaty negotiations was Joseph LaFlesche, whose descendants would play an important role in later Ponca history.
    The Ponca People, p.33

1825-26 - Expeditions funded by William Henry Ashley explore the Missouri, Platte and Green rivers. The American Fur Trade is developed further.
    Peabody Museum, Boston, MA.

1824-34 the decline begins
    Fletcher, Alice C. and LaFlesche, Francis,
    The Omaha Tribe, See Chapter 9.

1825 – In the Treaty of 1825 the Poncas acknowledged that they lived within the "territorial limits of the United States" thereby recognizing the supremacy of the government.
    Nebraska Indian Commission, Lincoln, NE

1829- Ponca population **about 600**
    B.A.E. Bulletin 30., p. 278-279

...in the **1830**'s, Indians in the Upper Missouri country were supplying Americans with as many as 25,000 muskrat pelts and 50,000 buffalo robes a year. But furs were becoming scarce and tribes were under attack from smallpox and white settlement.
    *See Map: *The Making of America NORTHERN PLAINS,* Cartographic Division, National Geographic Society, Washington, D.C. © 1986

1832* Written descriptions of Indian life and art since LaVerendryne's time, are scanty and often lacking in detail, and it is not until the 1830's that we have pictorial records of life in the Upper Missouri River villages and surrounding Plains tribes.

George Catlin was the first artist of record in **1832** and **Karl Bodmer**, who traveled with Prince Maximilian in **1833**, was the second and more important of the two.

Crow Indian Art Papers, Presented at the Crow Indian Art Symposium Sponsored by the Chandler Institute, Chandler Institute, June 1984.

1833-34 - The explorer scientist Prince Maximillan zu Wied and Karl Bodmer visit Indians along the Missouri River.

Peabody Museum, Boston, Ma.

1832-34- Karl Bodmer
See portraits and paintings of the Ponca tribe

It is of interest to note that the Duke writes of this man as "the" chief, whereas previously he had met "a" chief. Although the individual was undoubtedly the principal and responsible leader from the government viewpoint, and the Ponca, for this and other reasons, must have recognized him as the most important tribal leader, he was not the chief from the traditional point of view. The institution of Chieftainship underwent considerable change as a result of white contact. Chiefs arose where there were none before; traditional chiefs were replaced by new chiefs who possessed qualities demanded by the conditions resulting from intercourse with whites; where there had been several chiefs on more or less the same level, as was undoubtedly the case among the Ponca, there was a transmutation to one of greatest importance.

Jablow, Joseph. *Ponca Indians*, p. 160

1832- August 16, 1832, the Duke arrived at the Niobrara River not far from its mouth. This was an extremely favorable region of tall grass, timber, wild fruits, and a variety of animal life including deer, wolves, hare, ducks, geese. Here he met the next day "the chief of the Poncas **Chu-ge-ga-chae, the Great Smoke'** who arrived with his son and others after an all night ride.

After conversing with "the chief of the Poncas", the Duke resumed his journey and shortly met the main body of the tribe. The procession "advanced in the same order as had the Omahas, only they maintained strong and well-armed rear guard as protection against probable attack on the part of the Dakotah or Sioux"....

The Duke journeyed up the entire length of the Ponca River whose valley was fertile and contained bison trails. The Plains around the valley were covered with vast herds of bison, while at the same time there were antelope grazing on the prairie. Jablow, Joseph. *Ponca Indians*, p. 160-161

Catlin was in Nebraska twice; once in **1831** and again in **1832**. http://monet.unk.edu

1832-1834 - George Catlin- see portraits and paintings of the Ponca tribe

1830-33 - George Catlin travels among Plains Indians and paints village scenes as well as portraits.
Peabody Museum, Boston, Ma.

George Catlin – North American Indian portfolio; eight years travel, 48 tribes, London: Egyptian Hall, 1844

November 1833 - *Shooting Star Showers -*
Big Horse Woman born during Shooting Star shower.

"To understand the use of the word shower in connection with shooting stars we must go back to the early morning hours of Nov. 13, 1833, when the inhabitants of this continent [of North America] were in fact treated to one of the most spectacular natural displays that the night sky has produced... For nearly four hours the sky was literally ablaze ... More than a billion shooting stars appeared over the United States and Canada alone."
Peter M. Millman, "The Falling of the Stars," *The Telescope*, 7 (May-June, 1940), p. 57.

1837 – Alfred Jacob Miller selected by Capt. William Drummond Stewart as artist to record a journey to the Rocky Mountains. The expedition journeyed by wagon along what was to become the Oregon Trail.
http://Monet.unk.edu/mona2/artexplr/miller/miller.html

1838 - The first Indian treaty for a reservation was made with the Cherokee when they were removed to Indian Territory. 'Trail of Tears' *White Eagle,* p.169

1840 – Census reveals booming population: The U.S. census records 17,069,453 inhabitants, an **increase of one third since 1830.** The number of immigrants is estimated at 620,000, the majority of whom are Irish or German. Numerous people migrate to the western frontier in Missouri.
http://www.catlinclassroom.si.edu
Smithsonian Institute, Washington, D.C.

1842 - Ponca population **'some 800'**
B.A.E. Bulletin 30. p. 278-279

1842 - the trade at the (Union) Agency amounted to half a million dollars, among the items being 25,000 buffalo tongues. As a result of this prosperity there was a partial suspension of hostilities against the white man.
White Eagle, p.174

Also see: *Women of The Earth Lodges, Tribal Life on the Plains*, by Virginia Bergman Peters, regarding the first Missouri River explorers, visitors.

1847 Magghie- *Magghie travels from Pennsylvania, across the Missouri, along the Niobrara, settles at Planting Creek.*

1848 - Gold discovered at Sutter's Mill, CA.
1849 – Gold Rush – heavy traffic crossing through.

1852 - *Meeting of* **Big Horse Woman** *and* **Magghie, Together To Gather** - *Niobrara, Nebraska*

"The Indians became cats-paws for the contending forces that coveted their dominion and sought their undoing."
Dunbar, Seymour, *A History of Travel In America*, Volume 1, The Bobbs-Merrill Company, 1915

Forced by the US Government to march to central Oklahoma in the spring of **1877. The Ponca Trail of Tears**: nearly 1/3 died of disease, starvation and exposure.
-Ponca Tribe of Nebraska www.poncatribe-ne.org

The Ponca, as a component of the Omaha, were a hunter/farmer tribe which were plains buffalo hunters in the summer. Little changed after they fissioned from the Omaha in 1755. At first White contact, they were located on the Missouri at the mouth of the Niobrara.

The forced removal of the tribe to Indian Territory resulted in the death of about 200. There are two tribes today, located in Nebraska and Oklahoma.
Ponca Tribe of Nebraska, Niobrara, Nebraska.
Ponca Tribe of Indians of Oklahoma, White Eagle, OK.

Ethnie: **PONCA**
Language: Omaha-Ponca
Family: Ðhégiha
Stock: Siouan Proper
Phylum: Siouan
Macro-Culture: great Plains
Ponca Speakers: **1986**: 60
Ponca Speakers: **2020**: estimated, less than 20 speakers
http://fourdir.com/ponca.htm

Also see: **www.poncatribe-ne.org**
www.ponca.com
www.ponca-nsn.gov/

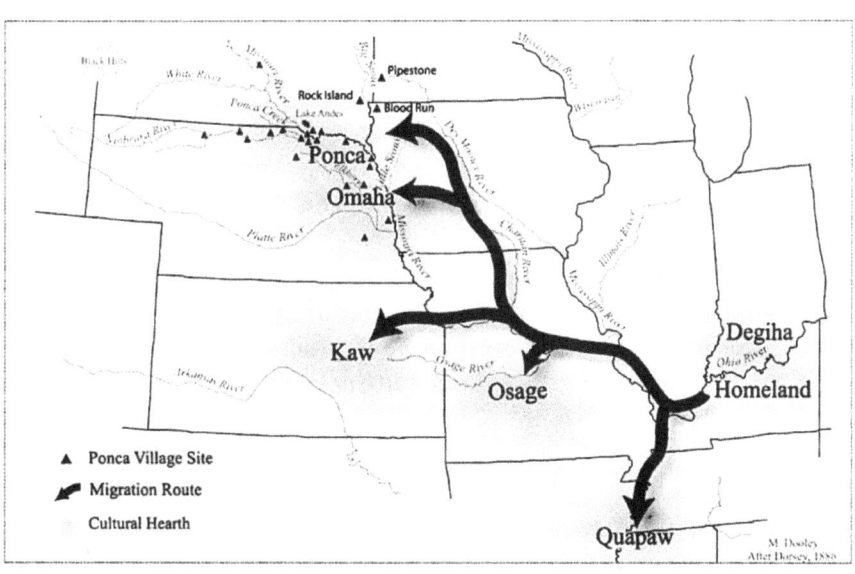

FIG. 3. *Map of Degiha migration routes and Ponca village or occupation sites.* [Adapted from James Owen Dorsey (note 6), Plate X, and James H. Howard (note 42), p. 111.]

Ðegiha migration routes and Ponca village or occupation sites.
p.328- Map by Matt Dooley, after J.O. Dorsey 1866,
Beth R. Ritter, Great Plains Quarterly, Fall 2002

MORMON TIMELINE - Associations with Ponca -

Niobrara River and cliffs, Niobrara, Nebraska

Sept 1846 to Feb 1847 - Group of 500 Mormons winter with the Ponca on the Niobrara
Mormons on the Missouri, *Ponca Tribe*

1846 – T.P. Moore of the Upper Missouri Agency reported that a Sioux war party had attacked a party of Ponca, killing one and wounding another. Apparently the Ponca were in fear of the Sioux again, for Moore stated that the Ponca welcomed the group of Mormons, who were building winter quarters near the mouth of the Niobrara, "as protection against the Sioux" (ibid., p. 295.) The St. Joseph's Journal on September 21, 1846, reported that "the Sioux attacked the Ponca at their village on the L'Eau Qui Court a few days before the Clermont arrived, killing several" (Notes, 1922, p.167) The same source also stated that 'the most western post of the Mormons was found at the Ponka village,' under Elder Miller...they made arrangements with the Ponkas to settle for the winter on their land" (ibid, loc. cit) Moore had also said that he found at the mouth of the Niobrara an encampment of 200 Mormons, and perhaps a similar number of Poncas.

Niobrara in 1846 - One of the Mormon pioneers has said that he was sixteen years old at the time the encampment was established at the mouth of the Niobrara. According to this source, a group of Ponca who had been visiting the Pawnee led the Mormons to the place of settlement, "a country of verdure-

plenty of food and timber and game". He said also that the young men of the Mormons went with the Ponca on their winter hunts along the Niobrara where "the timber stretches were abundant with wild turkeys and the prairies alive with buffalo". At the same time, he stated, there were Indian camps from the mouth of the **Niobrara** to **Five Mile (Bazile) Creek** (Fry, 1922, p.5 dft ex a-19)

We therefore have the Ponca at this time (a) in friendly relations with at least some of the Pawnee;(b) making winter hunts on the Niobrara; (c) **inhabiting the area along the Missouri between the Niobrara and Bazile Creek.** The Ponca have apparently reoccupied their village on the Niobrara site since **it was no longer safe to risk meeting the Sioux on the plains**.

In his communication, Agent Moore referred to **the Niobrara as "the dividing line between the Sioux and the Poncas"** (Ann rep 1846,p.295; dft ex c-230.) This is a statement difficult to accept at its face value, for it would seem to place the Ponca below the Niobrara. It may simply mean that because of the Sioux hostilities being directed against virtually all tribes in the area, including the Ponca, the latter found the territory below the Niobrara safer ground and, as a result, may have spent more time there during this period of intensive Sioux action.

Jablow, Joseph. *Ponca Indians*, p. 250-251

"Cross the Platte, stay on its north side and go north to the Loup. Follow the North branch to its end and stay due WEST. You will find the southern tributary of the Niobrara River where the Ponca people (stay). They call this valley their own but they will welcome you there."

Inman, Henry, *The Great Salt Lake Trail*, Crane,1899
Mormons with Ponca on Niobrara - 1846 Road to Niobrara Winter Camp, near (Soldier) Road
Wall map: Middle Missouri Valley Settlements 1846-1852
Film: *From Nauvoo to Wilderness 1846* Mormon Trail Museum, NE

*FOOTNOTES:

NOTE TO READER: Detailed Footnotes, and accompanying Ponca Language notes and lessons, as in this sample, are available for the entire manuscript, and will be published separately upon completion.

*1) page 16 - Omaha Prayer – *Birth of a Child (excerpt)*
    Alice C. Fletcher & Francis LaFlesche, *The Omaha Tribe, Volume 1,* University of Nebraska Press, Lincoln and London,1992. ("Rites Pertaining to the Individual; Introduction of the Omaha Child to the Cosmos.") p. 115

*2) page 20 - She made a generous bundle of t'agát'ubè-
    t'agát'ubè- Ponca word for pemmican, or jerky; dried strips of meat, salted, and pounded with fat, berries, cherries.

*3) page 30 - "If you are willing to remain ignorant and not learn how to do things a woman should know, you will ask other women to cut your moccasins and fit them for you. You will go from bad to worse: You will leave your people, go into a strange tribe, fall into trouble, and die there- friendless."[2]
    Omaha elder (quoted from *The Omaha Tribe*, Fletcher & LaFlesche), *Through Indian Eyes, The Untold Story of North American Peoples*, p. 206

*4) page 32- Míkasi-máⁿkaⁿ, -
    Mikasi - Makan (Omaha - Ponca); Jack in the pulpit 'Coyote medicine'
    Gilmore, Melvin R. *Uses of Plants by the Indians of the Missouri River Region.* p. 65

*5) page 52 - Zhon-zi-zhu -
    TOXYLON POMIFERUM [*Maclura pomifera*]
    Raf. Osage Orange, Bois d'Arc.
    Zhon-zi-zhu (Omaha-Ponca),
    "yellow-flesh wood"
    (*zhon*, wood; *zi*, yellow; *zhu*, flesh).

This tree was not native to Nebraska, but its wood was used for making bows whenever it could be obtained. It was gotten whenever southern trips were made into its range, which is in the southern part of Oklahoma; or it was obtained by gift or barter from the tribes of that region.
Gilmore, *Uses of Plants by the Indians of the Missouri River Region*, p. 35-36

>   Zhóⁿzi   Osage Orange Tree.
>   Wazházhe   Osage Indian
>   Stabler, Elizabeth, compiled by Swetland, Mark J., *Umonhon iye of Elizabeth Stabler*, Nebraska Indian Press, Winnebago, Ne., 1977, p. 130

*6) page 78 - Grandmother chewed on **juniper berries,** breathing its juices onto Water Willow's face. The juniper berries were a barrier to the fever's spell.
JUNIPERUS VIRGINIANA L. Cedar.
Maazi (Omaha-Ponca).
  The Omaha-Ponca name for the cedar is *maazi*. Cedar twigs were used on the hot stones in the vapor bath, especially in purificatory rites.
  As a remedy for nervousness and bad dreams the Pawnee used the smoke treatment, burning cedar twigs for the purpose.
Gilmore, *Uses of Plants by the Indians of the Missouri River Region*, p.18

*7) page 207- ***Máxo*ⁿ** - *to cut; to cut with a knife*
   Umonhon iye of Elizabeth Stabler, p. 53

*8) page 254- ***Watónzi ukéthi*ⁿ*!***
   Watóⁿzi-ukéthiⁿ - Indian corn
   Sherman Bold Warrior -1994- Ponca Language, Disc 1
   Watóⁿzi-ukéthiⁿ - Indian corn -Sylvester Bold Warrior, Ponca
   Watóⁿzi - corn (native) - Eagle Rhodd 10202021
   Wáhaba or Watóⁿzi - Corn
   Wáhaba ukethin - Indian corn
   Umonhon iye of Elizabeth Stabler, p. 47, 102

*9) page 260, 263- ***Di'xe*** – smallpox – p. 68 LH - DOPP
    Dixe - Epidemic, prevalent disease, such as smallpox.
    Uki abtha – Epidemic (spreading sickness).
    Umonhon iye of Elizabeth Stabler

*10) page 279 - 'Song of the Wild Rose'

    *And if ever you think she is dumb**
    *dumb: mute; unable to speak
    Author's note *dumb, as in mute, changed to 'voiceless'
    And if ever you think she is voiceless, [10]

*11) page 279 - 'Song of the Wild Rose'

    "From the heart of the Mother we come,

    The kind Mother of Life and of All;

    And if ever you think she is dumb,

    You should know that flowers are her songs.

    And all creatures that live are her songs,

    And all creatures that die are her songs,

    And the winds blowing by are her songs,

    And she wants you to sing all her songs."

'The people of the Dakota Nation, and other tribes, think of the various plant and animal species as having each their own songs.'
    Gilmore, *Uses of Plants by the Indians of the Missouri River Region*, p.34

MOONS - NÍᴺBA-AMA - page 35

She was born at The Beginning of cold weather.
Mí' Osní ahóⁿge   The beginning of cold (weather)
November, the 11th month of the year.

The next full moon brought Snow, and frozen water.
Mí' Máthe oskóⁿska   Middle of the time when it snows
December, the 12th month of the year.

Deer pawed the snow, in search of food- a hungry hardship moon.
Mí' núxe dá-tethè   moon when ice begins to form
The elders also used these names for January:
Mí' Táxti má anáⁿge   when deer paw the snow, in search for food.
Má'spàⁿ   snow melts
Lakota: **Te' hi wi**   hardship moon
   Wiote' 'hika wi   moon of hard winter
January, the first month of the year.

When Geese came back, trees snapped free of ice.
Mí' uthúnoⁿzhiⁿwatházhi   Undependable moon.
The elders also used:
Míxa agtháike   When the ducks go back [north]
Lakota: **Cannapopa Wi**   Moon of popping trees
February, the second month.

The Sore-eyes moon signaled the end of glaring snow.
Mí' Míxa agtháikedi   when the waterfowl returns home.
The elders also used:
Mí' Iⁿshtá-ukíaⁿdà   sore eyes [caused by snow glare]
Lakota: **Istawicayazan wi**   sore eyes moon
   Ista' wi'ca niyan wi   snow blindness
March, the third month.

With Rains came tender grass.
Mí' Noⁿzhíⁿshtoⁿ   Constant or recurring rain
Lakota: **Peji to wi**   moon of tender grass
April, the 4th month of the year.

They planted under the Moon Spring begins,
when leaves held potent medicine.
Mí' Mé pahóⁿga Springtime begins
Lakota: **Canwapeton wi** Tree leaves potent moon
May, 5th month of the year.

Hot weather, and they dug Núgtha.
Mí' Moⁿshté p'ahóⁿga Beginning of sunny days; Hot weather
Lakota: **Timpsila wi** Wild turnip moon
June, the 6th month of the year.

As the Green Corn grew, so the Buffalo fattened.
Mí' nugé oskóⁿska Middle of summer
Omaha: **Tehu'ton ike** Moon when the buffalo bellow
July, 7th month of the year.

Prairie roses bloomed in the middle of summer and they
picked chokecherry. Corn in silk, with the Moon of ripening.
Mí' Wathá pipizhe Corn is in silk; prepare corn for drying
Lakota, July: **'Canpa' 'sa wi** moon of red cherries, black; chokecherry moon
Lakota, August: **Wa 'suton' wi** moon of ripening
August, 8th month in the year.

When all leaves had color, Elk bellowed at the moon.
Omaha, August: **Oⁿpon hutoⁿ ike** Moon when the elk bellow
Ponca, September: **Mí' Óⁿpoⁿ hútoⁿ** Moon when the elk bellow
Lakota: **'Canwape'gi wi** moon of colored leaves
September, 9th month of the year.

Then they Stored food in caches, to prepare again,
Mí' T'óⁿde moⁿshóⁿde uzhí Store food in caches
October, the 10th month in the year.

for the Beginning of cold weather.
Mí' Osní ahóⁿge The beginning of cold (weather)
November, the 11th month of the year.

Ponca Moon Names, as well as moon names from the neighboring Omaha and Lakota, inspired the descriptions below:
Each moon was named for food, or lack of it.
She was born at The Beginning of cold weather.
The next full moon brought Snow, and frozen water.
Deer pawed the snow, in search of food, under a hungry hardship moon. When Geese came back, trees snapped free of ice.
The Sore-eyes moon signaled the end of glaring snow.
With Rains came Tender grass.
They planted under the Moon Spring begins,
when leaves held potent medicine.
Hot weather, and they dug Núgtha.
As the Green Corn grew, so the Buffalo fattened.
Prairie roses bloomed in the Middle of Summer and they picked chokecherry. Corn in silk, with the Moon of ripening.
When all leaves had color, Elk bellowed at the moon.
Then they Stored food in Caches, to prepare again,
for the Beginning of Cold Weather.

MOON NAME Sources:
Howard, James H. *The Ponca Tribe*. U. Nebraska Press, 1995, p. 73

Fletcher, Alice C. and La Flesche, Francis. *The Omaha Tribe, Volume I*, University of Nebraska Press, 1932. p. 111

Headman, Louis V., O'Neill, Sean. *Dictionary of the Ponca People,* Lincoln, NE: University of Nebraska Press, 2019.

Headman, Louis V., *Walks on the Ground, A Tribal History of the Ponca Nation*, Lincoln, NE: University of Nebraska Press, 2020.

Eagle Rhodd, Ponca Language speaker, teacher, Ponca Tribe of Oklahoma, Classes, 2020-2022.

Awakuni-Swetland, Mark. *The Omaha Language, The Omaha Way, An Introduction to Omaha Language and Culture,* Lincoln, NE: University of Nebraska Press, 2019.

Cook, Thurman., et al., *Umonhon iye te ede'non'ya? [How do you say in Omaha?] ENGLISH TO UMOnHOn DICTIONARY*, Berkeley, CA.

https://aktalakota.stjo.org/lakota-seasons-moon-phases/

Historical Images - Source

viii - *Outline Map of Indian Localities in 1833*, George Catlin. (public domain.)

p. 4- *Punca Indians encamped on the banks of the Missouri* – Karl Bodmer, pub. 1839, London (public domain.)

p. 6- *Uses of Plants by the Indians of the Missouri River Region, 33rd Annual Report, BAE, 1911- 1912*, Washington Government Printing Office, 1919, Melvin Randolph Gilmore - *field stand* (public domain.)

p. 7- *Uses of Plants by the Indians of the Missouri River Region*, Melvin Randolph Gilmore - *antler rake* (public domain.)

p. 11- *1833 Meteor Showers*, newspaper illustration print (public domain.) Illustration based on this print.

p. 15- *Dakota Star Showers* – (Native artist unknown) Dakotas, 1833.

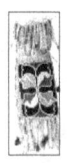

p.24 - *Wagónze's pipe bag* – Wagónze Ūthixide thingé, Professor Mark Awakuni-Swetland, Phd., University of Nebraska–Lincoln, Umónhon -Pónka Languages. Illustration made from image used with his permission.

p. 60- *Trotting wolf* – stock photo, altered

p. 90- *Small pox, Native American*, historical photo. (public domain.) Illustration based on this photo.

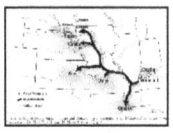

p.328- Map by Matt Dooley, after J.O. Dorsey 1866, *Ðegiha migration routes and Ponca village or occupation sites.* Beth R. Ritter, Great Plains Quarterly, Fall 2002

BIBLIOGRAPHY - Suggested further reading
TRADITIONAL PLANT USE AND NATIVE GARDENING

Buchanan, Carol. *Brother Crow, Sister Corn- Traditional American Indian Gardening.* Berkeley, CA: Ten Speed Press. 1997.

Caduto, Michael J. and Joseph Bruchac. *Native American Gardening: Stories, Projects and Recipes for Families.* Golden, CO: Fulcrum Publishing. 1996

Davis, Natalie. *Ho-Chunk Plants ~Indigenous Plants of Winnebago Reservation, Nebraska,* Little Priest Tribal College, Winnebago, NE, 2010. https://littlepriest.edu/images/Ethnobotany/HoChunk%20Plant%20Catalog%20FINAL.pdf

Densmore, Frances. *How Indians Use Wild Plants for Food, Medicine and Crafts.* New York: Dover Publications, Inc. 1974.

Gilmore, Melvin R. *Uses of Plants by the Indians of the Missouri River Region.* Lincoln, NE: University of Nebraska Press, 1997. http://www.swsbm.com/Ethnobotany/MissouriValley-Gilmore-1.pdf

Gutzmer M.P., Jensen D., Shank C., Jenson D.L. *A Field Guide to the Flora of the Winnebago Indian Reservation, Nebraska (Flora species remaining on the reservation early in the 21st Century)* Columbus, Ne: UPS Store Publishing Department. 2014. URL: http://newcenturyenvironmental.com/WinnFloraGuide_Intro.pdf

Hutchens, Alma R. *Indian Herbalogy of North America.* Windsor, Ontario: Merco, 1974. Reprint: Boston- London: Shambhala, 1991.

Kavasch, E. Barrie, *American Indian earth sense: Herbaria of ethnobotany and ethnomycology,* Washington, CT: Birdstone Press, the Institute for American Indian Studies, 1996.

Moerman, Daniel E. *Native American Ethnobotany.* Portland OR: Timer Press Portland. 1998.

Peschel, Keewaydinoquay. *Puhpohwee for the people: a narrative account of some uses of fungi among the Ahnishinaabeg.* DeKalb, IL: LEPS Press, 1998.

Vogel, Virgil J. *American Indian Medicine*. The Civilization of the American Indian Series. Norman, OK: University of Oklahoma Press, 1990.

Will, George F. and Hyde, George R. *Corn Among the Indians of the Upper Missouri,* 1917; reprint: Lincoln, NE: University of Nebraska Press, 1964.

Wilson, Gilbert L. *Buffalo Bird Woman's Garden: Agriculture of the Hidatsa Indians.* St. Paul, MN: Minnesota Historical Society Press, 1987.

NEBRASKA TRIBES

Bergman Peters, Virginia. *Women of the Earth Lodges: Tribal Life on the Plains.* North Haven, CT: Archon. 1995.

Cash, Joseph H. and Wolff, Gerald W. *The Ponca People,* Indian Tribal Series, Phoenix, AZ. 1975.

Catlin, George, *The Boy's Catlin,* My life among the Indians, New York, NY: Scribner's sons, 1909. URL: https://babel.hathitrust.org/cgi/pt?id=uc1.$b305034&view=1up&seq=10

Dunbar, Seymour, *A History of Travel In America, (Volume 4)* The Bobbs-Merrill Company, 1915.

Fletcher, Alice C. and La Flesche, Francis. *The Omaha Tribe - Volumes I* and *II.* Lincoln, NE: University of Nebraska Press, 1932.

Headman, Louis V. *Walks on the Ground, A Tribal History of the Ponca Nation,* Lincoln, NE: University of Nebraska Press, 2020.

Hofsinde, Robert, *The Indian and His Horse,* William Morrow and Company, 1967

Howard, James. *The Ponca Tribe,* Smithsonian Institution's Bureau of American Ethnology; bulletin 195. 1965, reprint: Lincoln, NE: University of Nebraska Press, 1995.

Jablow, Joseph. *Ponca Indians (Ethno-History of the Ponca with their Claim to Certain Lands (1950's))*. U.S. Government Report, NY/London: Garland Publishing, 1974.

Markstrom, Carol A., *Empowerment of North American Indian Girls, ritual expressions at puberty,* University of Nebraska Press, Lincoln and London, 2008.

Mulhair, Charles. *Ponca Agency,* Nebraska, 1992.

Ponca Tribal Encounter Kit – Teacher's Guide – URL: https://museum.unl.edu/file_download/inline/6b8eb2ef-a872-404d-a441- 2e90aa288f22

Starita, Joe. *"I Am a Man": Chief Standing Bear's Journey for Justice*. New York, NY: St. Martin's Press, 2009.

Taylor, Cliff. *The Memory of Souls,* Middletown, DE, 2020.

Thwaites, R.G., *Early Western Travels,* 1748-1846, Volume XXV, Comprising the series of original paintings by Charles Bodmer (to illustrate) Maximilian, Prince of Weids, Travels in the Interior, North America, 1832-1834, Cleveland, OH: The Arthur H. Clark Company, 1906.

Tibbles, Thomas H. *The Ponca Chiefs: An Indians Attempt to Appeal from the Tomahawk to the Courts*. Boston, MA: J.S. Lockwood, 1887. reprint: The Old Army Press, 1970.

Tibbles, Thomas Henry. *Standing Bear and the Ponca Chiefs.* reprint, edit: Lincoln, NE: University of Nebraska Press, 1995.

Wood, W. Raymond. *NA' ᴺZA, The Ponca Fort,* Archives of Archaeology, No. 3. Washington D.C. and Madison, WI: Society for American Archaeology and the University of Wisconsin Press. 1960. J&L Reprint Company, 1993.

Zimmerman, Charles Leroy, *White Eagle, Chief of the Poncas,* Harrisburg, PA: Telegraph Press, 1941.

The Editors of Time-Life Books. *The Woman's Way* (American Indians Series) Alexandria, VA: Time-Life Education, 1995.

PONCA AND OMAHA LANGUAGES

Cook, Thurman. *Umonhon iye te ede'non'ya? [How do you say in Omaha?]* Ed: Margery Coffey, PhD. Michael Wetmore, richard chilton, Gretchen E. Goodman, Dennis Hastings, OTHRP (Omaha Tribal Historical Resource Project) Berkeley, CA: Portland, OR: 2014

Dorsey, James Owen, *The Ðhegiha Language,* the speech of the Omaha and Ponka tribes of the Siouan linguistic family of North America Indians. Washington D.C.: Government Printing Office, 1890. [*Cegiha – original spelling used by Dorsey]

Headman, Louis, Project Coordinator, *Ponca Tribal Master/ Apprentice Language Project*, Ponca Tribal Language Office, White Eagle, Oklahoma, 2010.

Headman, Louis V., O'Neill, Sean. *Dictionary of the Ponca People,* (with the Ponca Council of Elders: Vincent Warrior, Hazel D. Headman, Louise Roy, and Lillian Pappan Eagle) Lincoln, NE: University of Nebraska Press, 2019.

Lieb, Curtis., Williams, Ceasar. $^{B}poh^{n}ka$ *Phraseology of Tulsa, Oklahoma*, Tulsa, OK, October 2005-2010

Omaha and Ponca Digital Dictionary, University of Nebraska Omaha Language Class, in collaboration with University of Nebraska Center for Digital Research in the Humanities. UNL, Lincoln, NE. 2008-2012. http://omahaponca.unl.edu/

Omaha Language Curriculum Development Project, UNL Omaha Language Class. http://omahalanguage.unl.edu/

Saunsoci, Alice., Eschenberg, Ardis. *500+ Verbs in UmoNhoN (Omaha),* Saunsoci & Eschenberg, 2016.

Awakuni-Swetland, Mark. *The Omaha Language, The Omaha Way,* An Introduction to Omaha Language and Culture, (Omaha Language and Culture Center, Omaha Nation Public School, Macy, Nebraska, and the Omaha Language Instruction Team, University of Nebraska–Lincoln; Mark Awakuni-Swetland, Vida Woodhull Stabler, Aubrey Streit Krug, Loren Frerichs, Rory Larson, collaborated with elder speakers, including Alberta Grant Canby, Emmaline Walker-Sanchez, Marcella Woodhull Cavou, Donna Morris Parker, to write this book.) Lincoln, NE: University of Nebraska Press, 2019.

Stabler, Elizabeth. Ed; Swetland, Mark. *Umonhon iye of Elizabeth Stabler:* A Vocabulary of the Omaha Language First Edition, Winnebago, NE: Nebraska Indian Press, 1977. Second, expanded version Macy, NE: 1979.

Umónhon Íye-wathe Let's Speak Umónhon! Level 1 Umónhon Language Textbook, (Jan Ullrich, Marcella Woodhull Cayou, Donna Morris Parker, Susan Freemont. Series Editors: Vida Woodhull Castro, Pat Phillips, Binah Gordon, Allison Horner.) The Umónhon Language and Culture Center at Umónhon Nation Public School and The Omaha Tribe of Nebraska and Iowa, 2017.

Umónhon Úshkon – title VI Umónhon Language and Culture Center, Umónhon Nation Public School, Macy, NE.
https://sites.google.com/a/unpsk-12.org/ushkon/

Audio Files:

Angie Starkel, Ponca vocabulary and phrases
https://poncatribe-ne.tv/category/language/page/2/

Curtis Lieb, Henry Lieb, Suzanne MakesCry, Ponca Basic – Phraselator, White Eagle, OK.

Henry Lieb, Ponca Stories and vocabulary words,
https://poncatribe-ne.tv/category/six-stories/

Louis Headman, Project Coordinator, *Ponca Tribal Master/ Apprentice Language Project*, Audio CD, White Eagle, OK. 2010.

Sherman Bold Warrior, Ponca language, audio recordings, Ponca Tribe of Oklahoma, 1994.

Sylvester Bold Warrior, Ponca language, audio recordings, White Eagle, Oklahoma, 2014, 2015.

Eagle Rhodd, Ponca Language, Audio recordings and Ponca Language classes, White Eagle, Oklahoma, 2020 - 2022.

BIG HORSE BOOKS

ILLUSTRATIONS

Original Illustrations are by the author

Barbara Salvatore © 2022
ALL RIGHTS RESERVED
No reproduction, sharing or duplicating in any form
without written consent from author and publisher.
Prints and reproductions:
www.bighorsewoman.com
bighorsewomanbooks@gmail.com

SERIES

BIG HORSE WOMAN
Shóⁿge Toⁿgà Wa'u
(born November 1833)
Ponca Tribe - *Niobrara, Nebraska*

MAGGHIE
(born May 1832)
German settlers
Conestoga Valley, Pennsylvania

THE TRAIL
(1847)
Magghie's journey West
Pennsylvania to Nebraska

TOGETHER TO GATHER
(1847)
Magghie settles by the Niobrara
(1852)
Big Horse Woman and Magghie
Niobrara

MAGGHIE

MAGGHIE (born 1832) First-generation born in Conestoga Valley, Pennsylvania, daughter to German settlers. Magghie's mother, an old-world herbalist and midwife, trains Magghie as such. Her aristocratic father, breeder of fine draft-horses, manages the estate, crops, and orchards, and passes on his superb equestrian skills. In 1847, when a progression of emigrants trail Cholera into their valley, Magghie is forced to abandon her home, and head West.

BIG HORSE WOMAN and MAGGHIE are Seed Savers, medicine carriers, from different cultures, with a common purpose. They've each been raised with the directive and instinct to be guardians of the plants, keepers of the seed, providers of medicine their people will need. As irrevocable tides of change sweep through the country, their lives and purpose fatefully intersect.

MAGGHIE

Maye Wilder, Hans Wilder, my Mother and my Father

There is no need to try to remember them
that went ahead.
I will always know them, and cannot forget,
so need not have to remember.
Always they are there in the air around me, in the leaves
and grass, and hair standing up on the horses' backs.

Here they are, in my words, on this page,
they still stride before my eyes,
and if only I could draw a line as swiftly as a thought,
they would be dancing - alive - in front of yours,
they would be a picture
any eye could plainly see.

My mother and my father were known to me,
known to the land they walked on,
known to the horses, known by the trees.
And known to me...

Otherwise, they kept almost entirely to themselves.
But I shan't do that. Cannot keep them to themselves.
In words and pictures, I will draw them out,
for everyone to see.

And remembered they will be.

Magghie
22 February 1850, still Winter

MAGGHIE

Magghie was the only child of an industrious German couple who arrived in Northern Pennsylvania with a small fortune to start them off. By the time Magghie was born, they had developed an orderly and prosperous farm, cleared hundreds of acres, ploughed and cultivated using their teams of strong and solid drafts. Their horse stock was well chosen, well-bred, and impeccably trained by Magghie's father, Hans.

For Magghie, they were perfect friends. Before Magghie was twelve, she could drive a team of two or four and ride any of the wide-backed geldings and mares. She covered ground on the back of a big horse.

Magghie could catch flutter-bys and dragonflies, and frogs under water, with her bare hands, and name practically every plant living around her. She filled baskets with blackberries, raspberries, mulberries, barberries, strawberries, bilberries, rose hips, stream pebbles, flower blossoms, honey mushrooms, caterpillars, salamanders and wildflowers. Magghie climbed the twisting fruit trees that her father had planted long before she was born. Gathered plums and peaches. Shook the apples, sweetly ripened, from their branches. She competed with squirrels for nuts.

Magghie mostly talked to herself. Talked, as well, to the horses, trees, bugs, and flowers. Chatted through the garden as she weeded and dug for carrots. Her world was perfectly normal, with nothing else to compare it to. She never knew to feel lonely.

Wild yams wove through patches of potatoes, rows of old world turnips, giant parsnips, cabbage, carrots, sugar beets. Hills of pumpkins and squash spread under pole beans, growing up corn. Tangled hedges separated acres of alfalfa, lucerne, legumes, and clovers. Fields of oats, barley, English rye, and German wheat grew beside sloping hills of flax and sorghum. Narrow deer trails crisscrossed the hills, cutting edges into ridges. Turkeys flocked in the woods.

Hans Wilder's was the most prosperous, well-managed farm in the region. Less fortunate immigrant families were attracted to the valley in the hopes of reaping such abundance. Magghie's father leased them sufficient land to farm in exchange for a fair portion of their hay and crops. His holdings sprawled across the hills.

The hay fields, cropped three times a season, were stacked and forked into the barn lofts for winter fodder. In the heat of summer, the horses and tenant cows grazed the cool, untamed northern hills, gradually planting grass further with their manure.

In winter, the big horses emptied the lofts, heating their own barn in the process. Magghie spent long winter days brushing them, warming her hands in their breath.

In exchange for a needed skill, or added strength, Hans sometimes rented closer quarters to transients. Their best masons came and went that way. They left when their work was done, with only the stone barn and house evidence of their former presence.

Thus, Magghie was regarded as a rich man's daughter. She was not aware of this, since she spent all of her life with her parents, there being no other surviving children in her home, and none alive on the tenant farms who had time or want enough to play with her. They'd been told that her mother was a witch, and they were not to speak to her.

Magghie sometimes watched them, busy herding geese or goats over a far hill. Once they felt her stare, they always ran from sight of her, calling out a warning

"Kleine Hexe! Kleine Hexe!"

Little witch! Little witch!

ACKNOWLEDGMENTS

On November 13th, 1995, I dreamt I was a Native woman, covered from neck to hips with pouches and seed-bags, riding a Big Horse, packed with seed-sacks, across a tall-grass prairie, trailing over pine ridges, to a flat hilltop. A valley spanned out below, flowers fanning in spiral patterns, gardens of crops, circling and snaking through abandoned earth mounds.

On the ground, a woman in a faded blue dress was bent to planting seeds, knees tucked under her. Behind her, a ribbon of shining water ran beneath steep, limestone cliffs. When the woman in the garden turned her head to look up, a dog barked, and I woke up.

I wanted to know who I was in this dream; why she saved seeds, where she was going, how she named the plants, the places, the people. Who was the woman in the blue dress, planting seeds in circles?

I followed this dream for years, and *Big Horse Woman* and *Magghie* led me down the road to their whole story and their story led me to *Níbthaska*. I am thankful for my dreams, and to those who make them real. I focus here on those teachers, guides, relatives and friends that accompanied me on this Nebraska journey. My humble apologies for excluding anyone, or for not saying enough.

Special acknowledgment goes to Dr. Mark Awakuni-Swetland, thiⁿgé, and his life's work. His dedication and care set an example for us all. His Omaha (Ponca) language class at the University of Nebraska - Lincoln, laid my foundation of understanding the language, and led to my being able to teach the language to Ponca children in Nebraska. Thank you to his family, for helping us to learn the Omaha way.

I also want to acknowledge our elder speakers in class, Emmaline Walker-Sanchez, thiⁿgé, who was always so kind and patient, and who is deeply missed. Wíbthahoⁿ, to her sister, Arlene Walker, who is such a good friend, and calls me Wíhe; *little sister*. And to Delores Black, who trusted me, and taught me through her good example.

Thank you, Rory Larson, for your dedicated years, assisting us in class. Your brilliant linguistic skills and respect of the Umóⁿhoⁿ people inspired us. John Koontz, thiⁿgé, talented linguist and friend, was one of the first to help me with resources and detailed, instructive emails, whenever I asked. We miss him.

Wíbthahoⁿ to Vida Woodhull Stabler, Pat Phillips, and Binah Gordon, Umóⁿhoⁿ language educators at the Umóⁿhoⁿ Nation Public School, and NICC, Macy, who also hosted the Umóⁿhoⁿ-Póⁿka Language Gathering, held yearly at Nebraska Indian Community College in Macy. Thank you for the countless lessons and opportunities to learn.

Wíbthahoⁿ to the Ponca Tribe of Nebraska, for allowing me to participate and learn, to the many friends and relations I have made, who welcomed me, taught me, and allowed me to find my path. Wibthahoⁿ to friends from the Ponca Tribe of Oklahoma, who hosted and welcomed me at their annual Celebration, honor dances and gatherings. I hope to always be of service in the revitalization of the Ponca Language.

I am grateful for my friendship with the Robinette Family, especially Stanford (Sandy) Taylor, thiⁿgé, Gary Robinette, thiⁿgé, and Debbie Robinette, who have been my home away from home, and showed and told me more than I can measure. Thanks to Diana Vallier and family, for your love and kindness, and for accepting me with big hearts.

Elders, speakers Curtis Lieb, thiⁿgé, Henry Lieb, thiⁿgé, and Dr. Louis Headman, Sylvester Bold Warrior, thiⁿgé, and Eagle Rhodd, of the Ponca Tribe of Oklahoma, helped me and so many others on our language journeys. Randall Bruce Ross, thiⁿgé, and Dwight Howe included me in many cultural and language lessons and gatherings, where I learned so much.

Wíbthahoⁿ to Umóⁿhoⁿ friends, to the descendants of Mary Lieb Mitchell, to Alice Saunsoci, thiⁿgé, and descendants, to speaker and storyteller, Eugene Pappan, thiⁿgé, John Pappan and family, and to all those who host language classes, who participate in Ðhégiha Language gatherings, and who are dedicated to learning and teaching.

With every loss of an elder, a speaker, there is a hurt that is impossible to put words to. As their words and knowledge go with them. We must strive even harder to awaken the words within ourselves and our children, and keep them alive.

Póⁿka bthíⁿ mázhi. *I am not Ponca.*
Umóⁿhoⁿ bthíⁿ mázhi. *I am not Omaha.*
I come from the Eastern door.
I am a dreamer, storyteller, artist. As a writer, the journey is often one of solitude, and on this long road I am grateful to many mentors and friends.

Thank you, to high-school teachers, Mr. Collins, thiⁿgé, and Mr. January, thiⁿgé, for nurturing my ability to express myself, with words and pictures. My thanks and respect to R.I.S.D. Illustration Professor, Mahler Ryder, thiⁿgé, who watched me sketch a sleeping boy on the bus, and then paved my way to art school, scholarships, and opportunities.

Our circle of writers that met regularly in Walton, NY, has been a core support through the years, no matter our geographic distance. Virginia Frances Shwartz, Denise B. Dailey, Leslie T. Sharpe, thank you. May our words continue to flow from our hearts.

I appreciate the professional commitment of Lisa Pelto and staff at Concierge Marketing and Book publishing of Omaha, Nebraska, for making my book real, allowing me to include illustrations, poetic structure, and Ponca language. Many editors and publishers told me this would not be possible, but ever since I was little, I wanted to make stories with pictures, for grown-ups. We did it!

When I moved to Lincoln, Nebraska, Rex Walton took me under wing. Rex has guided and supported so many talented writers, giving us venues to test our words with wide audiences. It was a continual source of inspiration to participate in readings with a vibrant community of local writers who feed our souls.

Rex introduced me to Clifford Taylor III, sensing that our paths were destined to cross. Cliff, Ponca poet, author, storyteller, has such a unique and authentic voice, his heart and blood streaming way back, and stepping forward for the people. I am grateful for our friendship, and for that bookshelf we are filling.

To my Lakota, Sicangu, Santee, Ogallala, Omaha, Ponca and all tribal relations who have shared sacred ceremonies, prayers, songs, ways and lessons, I am most grateful. I pray that your spirit and teachings have come through in these stories, and will carry on into future generations, an ongoing circle of remembering. Special thanks to Chief Leonard Crow-Dog, thiⁿgé, Auntie Joann and family, to Chief Luciano Perez, thiⁿgé, and family, and to all the lodge-builders, firekeepers, water-pourers, pipe-carriers, Sun Dancers, bundle-keepers, seed-keepers, singers, who carry on this sacred way of life.

I did not expect to settle in Nebraska, but the pull was strong and has not let me go. My life started east, and I especially want to thank my Family. Thank you to my sister, Dianne, Wihe thiⁿgé, who shared the love for horses since we could walk. My mother, Christine, who never caved in to our begging for a horse, but who was our anchor to home and the ocean where we grew up. She worked hard to raise us, and encouraged me, in school, with my talents, and my imagination. Thank you to my father, my dad, brother, sisters, grammas, aunties, uncles, friends, and teachers, who shaped me, and who all taught me something of life and love.

These stories sparked to life when our daughters were six and three, and I have always been writing for them. From the start, Ruby and Illa have inspired me from the inside out, and it has been a joy to watch them become themselves.

Thank you, William Klopping, for your partnership, in their creation, in this journey, and for supporting this path, all along the way. I could not have done this without you.

Thank you to everyone who showed love for this story and begged to hear more. A heart full of thanks to you, the reader!

Big thanks to our Big Horses, Fred, thiⁿgé, and Barney, thiⁿgé, for carrying me, teaching me, and for your very big hearts.

Every day under the sun and moon, I thank the Plants, for their voices, lessons, love and nourishment.

Thank you to our ancestors,
who have placed all seeds of hope in us.

Barbara Salvatore
Verdigre, Nebraska

2022

Wíbthahoⁿ – thank you, thanks, praise, I praise you; expression or acknowledgment of gratitude, giving praise
thiⁿgé gone; refers to the deceased
(In honor of the many lost since I began.)
Wíhe – (female's) little sister

TESTIMONIALS

"When I read your story, I imagine you telling it to a circle of Ponca children, here in the big room at the Agency."
Stanford Taylor, thiⁿgé, Tribal Historian, Ponca Tribe of Nebraska

"Barbara, keep up the good work. You go teach the Language. You go get that story published. Indian people need to be heard."
Gary Robinette, thiⁿgé, Santee Tribe, Tribal Cultural Director- Ponca Tribe of Nebraska.

"It is your dream. It came to you. Of course, it's true."
Rosetta Arkeketa LeClaire, Honored Elder, thiⁿgé, Otoe-Missouria, Ponca

"The story is really good. I really, really enjoyed it. Watching her grow from a willow, wispy child, to a big, strong woman."
Deborah Robinette, Elder, 12-year Tribal Council Member, Ponca Tribe of Nebraska, Oglala, Sicangu

"This is a very good story. The Ponca Tribe should be very happy with this. It is so good to see the Language in a story this way!"
Henry Lieb, thiⁿgé, Ponca Language mentor, Ponca Tribe of Oklahoma, Omaha.

"I enjoyed the book very much. The Story was very good and kept me wanting to see what was next. I got very emotional when it came to the grandmother. I really didn't expect to get that shook up. The historical facts seem true and put myself in that time while I was reading. I liked how the use of Plants were included in so many various ways and it made me think of my grandmother and how she would tell me about her mother and some of the herbal medicines she would make to help cure her ever growing family. I am letting my daughters read this book and when they are done, I will send it on to my sister, as she wanted to read it too. I know this was an effort of love on your part. Thank you."
Faythe Hurd, Elder, Ponca Tribe of Nebraska

"Barbara, this story is so good! I can't wait until it's published, and I can share this with my kids! We don't have any stories like this. It's so good." **Hehaka (John) Garza**, thiⁿgé

These stories sparked to life when our daughters were six and three, and I have always been writing for them. From the start, Ruby and Illa have inspired me from the inside out, and it has been a joy to watch them become themselves.

Thank you, William Klopping, for your partnership, in their creation, in this journey, and for supporting this path, all along the way. I could not have done this without you.

Thank you to everyone who showed love for this story and begged to hear more. A heart full of thanks to you, the reader!

Big thanks to our Big Horses, Fred, thiⁿgé, and Barney, thiⁿgé, for carrying me, teaching me, and for your very big hearts.

Every day under the sun and moon, I thank the Plants, for their voices, lessons, love and nourishment.

Thank you to our ancestors,
who have placed all seeds of hope in us.

Barbara Salvatore
Verdigre, Nebraska

2022

Wíbthahoⁿ – thank you, thanks, praise, I praise you; expression or acknowledgment of gratitude, giving praise
thiⁿgé gone; refers to the deceased
(In honor of the many lost since I began.)
Wíhe – (female's) little sister

TESTIMONIALS

"When I read your story, I imagine you telling it to a circle of Ponca children, here in the big room at the Agency."
Stanford Taylor, thiⁿgé, Tribal Historian, Ponca Tribe of Nebraska

"Barbara, keep up the good work. You go teach the Language. You go get that story published. Indian people need to be heard."
Gary Robinette, thiⁿgé, Santee Tribe, Tribal Cultural Director- Ponca Tribe of Nebraska.

"It is your dream. It came to you. Of course, it's true."
Rosetta Arkeketa LeClaire, Honored Elder, thiⁿgé, Otoe-Missouria, Ponca

"The story is really good. I really, really enjoyed it. Watching her grow from a willow, wispy child, to a big, strong woman."
Deborah Robinette, Elder, 12-year Tribal Council Member, Ponca Tribe of Nebraska, Oglala, Sicangu

"This is a very good story. The Ponca Tribe should be very happy with this. It is so good to see the Language in a story this way!"
Henry Lieb, thiⁿgé, Ponca Language mentor, Ponca Tribe of Oklahoma, Omaha.

"I enjoyed the book very much. The Story was very good and kept me wanting to see what was next. I got very emotional when it came to the grandmother. I really didn't expect to get that shook up. The historical facts seem true and put myself in that time while I was reading. I liked how the use of Plants were included in so many various ways and it made me think of my grandmother and how she would tell me about her mother and some of the herbal medicines she would make to help cure her ever growing family. I am letting my daughters read this book and when they are done, I will send it on to my sister, as she wanted to read it too. I know this was an effort of love on your part. Thank you."
Faythe Hurd, Elder, Ponca Tribe of Nebraska

"Barbara, this story is so good! I can't wait until it's published, and I can share this with my kids! We don't have any stories like this. It's so good." **Hehaka (John) Garza**, thiⁿgé

"Beautiful book! I enjoyed reading it. I'm an avid reader, and the book must captivate me, or I won't read it. Big Horse Woman did! Being an enrolled member of the Ponca Tribe of Oklahoma, I endorse the book Barbara Salvatore has written. I loved it!"
Memahashay (Darlene) Pensoneau Harjo, Ponca Tribe of OK.

"I really enjoyed it. What I tell people is, anything you write is how you see it and I'm nobody to say you're wrong or it should be changed. When a story comes to you like that, no one is anyone to criticize it or you. It's yours. It's good."
Dr. Louis V. Headman, *Dictionary of the Ponca People*, and *Walks on the Ground*, A Tribal History of the Ponca Nation, Elder Language speaker, Ponca Tribe of Oklahoma, Pastor, Church of the Nazarene, Ponca City, OK.

"We made it home [from Ponca Pow Wow] safe and sound. My daughter started reading Big Horse Woman immediately and is already halfway through! She loves it!"
Delrayne Roy, Ponca Tribe of Oklahoma

"I have known Barbara for several years through a collaborative research relation. Barbara contacted me from her home in New York (1995) with a request that I read and comment on her *Big Horse Woman* manuscript. Because it portrays a Ponca character she wanted to make sure the Ponca language and culture were being correctly represented. Over the ensuing years we exchanged ideas that have been incorporated into her work.
Barbara's passion for her research and work has brought her to Nebraska and South Dakota on many occasions. She has established collaborative working relations with members of the Ponca Tribe and Sioux Tribe. As an artist, she has explored Indigenous cultures as the source for her manuscript illustrations. She has worked diligently to refine how people and material culture are displayed in her art. In 2011, Barbara moved herself and family from New York to Nebraska in order to be closer to the people whose history and culture she is becoming deeply involved with. Barbara enrolled in my 3-semester Omaha language series as one avenue to learning more about Ponca language, history, and cultural practices."
Mark Awakuni-Swetland, thiⁿgé, Ph.D., Professor Anthropology/Ethnic Studies (Native American Studies), Collaborator, *The Omaha Language, The Omaha Way*

"My grandson was putting my bookshelf in order and found your manuscript. I had to read it again, and call to tell you how much we enjoyed it. It brought back so many memories of being a boy by the river. It is such a good story, Barbara, when are you going to publish it?"
Logan Fontenelle, Omaha Tribe of Nebraska and Iowa

"This is wonderful...wow...At first I thought in the beginning of the Dream share...that you were a Traditional Trader, or Traditional mishkiiki kwe on a journey (a traveling pharmacy woman). You are wonderful to listen to. It is so good to hear a storytelling, that is so organic and awakens the imagination within. A beautiful gift of story-telling. Please everyone, listen carefully to the hidden teachings in the story. Chi miigwetch (many thanks.)"
Kanzee Gitimido, Anishinaabe/Ojibwe, Language Teacher & Student, Traditional Storyteller

"I found the story captivating and it drew me in from the start. I initially worried that she may lose an audience that was unfamiliar with the ways and customs of Native Americans, or more specifically, the Ponca people. However, she instantly proved me wrong, as I was pulled in and got lost in a different time and place where I was completely immersed in the musings of Water Willow and her grandmother. Her provision of the pronunciation guide, historical context, and timeline makes it lucent and simple for the reader to understand.
I love how Barbara was able to weave in the educational aspects of the Ponca history and language, as well as showcasing her wisdom of plants, herbs, and horses. Salvatore shows such a humble and compassionate regard to the authenticity of the story and writes with care and respect towards the historicity of the people. Barbara Salvatore completely mastered a perfect blend of subtle nuance mixed with educational facets that show great equipoise in her writing style. I found the story well-paced and kept me yearning to know more. *Big Horse Woman* is an amazing testament to Salvatore's talent as a writer, linguist, and herbalist. I finished the book having learned so much and at the same time yearning for more! I look forward to the next novel!"
LeAndra Hallowell Nephin, Omaha Tribe of Nebraska and Iowa, University of Oxford, England

"I truly found myself becoming Big Horse Woman - In a sense, I was her, feeling each of her emotions, thoughts, actions. Marvelously written! Such sensitivity and authenticity to the native culture... and the portrayal of relationship to Mother Earth, each other, to the medicines. The flow of *Big Horse Woman* is so real; I find myself re-reading portions almost daily."
Leah Droubie, Licensed Nurse, White Earth Nation, Anishinaabe, Minnesota

"Nice! I love the story; took me to a different place in such a short time... You do good work, very much appreciated, and thank you - left me with a good feeling."
Travis Blackbird, Ista Ska, Ledger Artist, Omaha Tribe of Nebraska & Iowa

"What a stunning piece of work... It is a mammoth labor of love."
Barbara Lucas, thinge, Author, Educator, Founder & Director, Institute of Publishing & Writing; Director, Lucas-Evans Books

"Your writing, as with all great fiction, is like entering a dream, another world... It is iridescent, beautiful, very moving, very engrossing."
Leslie T. Sharpe, Author, *The Quarry Fox and Other Tales of the Wild Catskills*, Editor, Professor, Columbia University School of Arts

"A well-written, honest, faithful rendition of *Big Horse Woman* and life within the Ponca tribe in the mid-19th century. The author has definitely done her research in this area."
Michael Mirolla, Editor in Chief, Guernica Editions, Canada

"It is impossible to read this book without admiring it. It is likewise impossible not to recognize the amount of work and love that went into it. *Big Horse Woman* is as much a poem as it is a novel. Big Horse Woman is a character that you're not likely to meet in other novels of this ilk, nor forget her stunning portrayal. So too, the spirituality of this book shines through on virtually every page. The respect and understanding, indeed, the language between human, animal, and land is represented in such a way that is impossible not to believe. The Ponca Tribe would have to be proud of their representation here and the honor of their tradition and culture the author shows."
Michael Lee, Judge, Leapfrog Press, Author *Paradise Dance*

"*Big Horse Woman* is a story of people so connected to the land, its plant-life, and animals, that communication, through dreams or an inner language, seems not only possible, but natural. The voice is so authentic that the words feel not so much written, as channeled. The story is as real and visceral as a reading experience can get of the traditions, customs, and way of life of a Native American tribe before ongoing contact with the westward push across the American continent."
Evan Anderson, Author, *Downriver: A Tale of Moving Pictures Before Hollywood*

"Barbara Salvatore is one of the most powerful and inspiring writers and narrators I have ever heard. She puts John G. Neihardt in the second seat. Hold onto your reins, folks."
Phil Schupbach, Host *Platte River Sampler,* KZUM Radio, Lincoln

"Big Horse Woman was a lovely, evocative poem. The pictures were as much a part of the work as the verse. But what impressed me most about the story was the willingness to take risks in order to paint moods and scenes. I felt that there was a deep connection between the visual art and the verse in the sense that both were directed toward creating images rather than telling intricate stories; I saw the forest. I saw Big Horse Woman on Big Horse. I saw what was being described. This is very unusual and nice work."
Michael Graziano, Leapfrog Press Judge

"I have enjoyed hearing your incredible and alive fiction. In the writing, there is a rhythm, a unique rhythm that mirrors the people, their language, a unique cadence, like a drum. I have been deeply affected by the main character and think you have touched something primal or primordial. There's something deeper there, I sensed. That's why it has power. I was immersed. What I heard was a woman who struggles, who questions, who won't shut up, who at times wishes to give up but then returns to battle. That is not dark, but inspiring. It was a voice on a journey, on the edge. It was riveting. The scenes have lingered. I don't think I will ever get the image of her out of my mind. Reading it has inspired me as a woman, a seeker, a healer, and as a writer."
Virginia Schwartz, Author, *Send One Angel Down, Initiation, If I Just had Two Wings, Messenger, Among the Fallen*

"It is the Kind of Story you don't want to end."
Martha Reich, Artist, Award Winning Singer, Song writer, *The Color of Blue, Evidence of Life, Brave Bird*

"I found myself drawn into the work almost in spite of myself...You have a great deal of yourself invested in *Big Horse Woman*, and one way or another, you will find a place for it. With my admiration for this often-moving American Odyssey. It is your own *Ulysses*."
Selma Lanes, thingé, Renowned Children's Book critic, lecturer and editor, Author *The Art of Maurice Sendak,* and *Down the Rabbit Hole, Through the Looking Glass*

"I enjoyed reading Big Horse Woman so much. I can't wait to see the published version."
Pam Montgomery, Herbalist, Author, *Partner Earth, Plant Spirit Healing;* Green Nations Gathering, Plant Spirit Healing and spiritual ecology.

"Thank you! Your work is lovely...beautiful, and I've read and enjoyed it with appreciation and enthusiasm."
E. Barrie Kavasch, Herbalist, Ethno-Botanist, Author, *American Indian Earth Sense, Native Harvests: American Indian Wild Foods & Recipes, Equine Herbs & Healing: An Earth Lodge Guide To Horse Wellness*

"I became engaged with Water Willow very early in the narrative. What I found particularly enjoyable was the way you used your protagonist's growth, her passage through certain significant events in her life, to show your readers the way the tribe lived day to day in the 1830s and 40s. I felt that in reading this story I absorbed a great deal of information about the food and medicine the Ponca used, their methods of hunting, cooking and making war; also their social norms, their views of the seasons, flora, fauna, the cosmos, and their way of conducting inter-personal relations. An entertaining and hugely *instructive* story, one that reminds me most strongly of Mari Sandoz' *These Were the Sioux*. That slim volume taught me things about Native ways that a score of anthropological tomes had failed to deliver. I am no expert on Native histories... but what I read was convincing enough. Written with calm authority."
Alan Wilkinson, Author, *The Red House on the Niobrara* and *Cody, the Medicine Man, and Me,* Professor, American Studies, Durham, UK.

"Wonderful words of praise for your book, your love of big horses, your interest in indigenous native cultures, your desire to care for the only home we have, Earth..."
Pamela Rickenbach, Blue Star Equiculture, Draft Horse Rescue

"I love entering this world. I hate leaving it and finding myself on the subway."
Suzanne Louis Reddick, thiⁿgé, Artist, Jeweler, Midwife.

"I brought along Big Horse Woman to the beach with my girls (they are 17 and 12) and read it to them. They were *entranced*– sat listening like we all did (when you read to us.)"
Trish Marx, Children's Author, *Reaching for The Sun – Kids In Cuba, Echoes Of World War II, I Heal*

"All children should be taught this way."
Kateryna Prokopenko, Photographer, Ukraine

"Reading *Big Horse Woman* was like taking a long deep breath, but how it feels in the heart on the exhale. To follow her journey is like drinking from the well of understanding for the indigenous to this land, and it is mixed in with a brilliant view into the language and culture of the Ponca tribe during the mid to late 19th century. Barbara does an amazing job at intermingling poetry, storytelling, facts, and her own knowledge of this time period and tribal community, including her understanding of the land.
This book was an adventure from the beginning to end.
I am so excited to see what happens next!"
Emily Stegall Jasenski, Homeopath and Educator

"I am sitting in a coffee shop with *Big Horse Woman*. I've put the book down many times, so moved by your words that I couldn't continue or see through my tears. I appreciate your work, your research, and the lessons I continue to learn from you. I am just seeking wisdom and I find it in this story. I feel a true heart connection with Big Horse Woman; A knowing that connects us all as women. And feeling the urge and urgency of moving forward, through whatever comes. We must take a stand for what we believe in... Holding to center here, and my heart is full. Thank you, and our ancestors, from my heart to yours."
Shara Thome, Urban Renewal Massage, Artist

"I absolutely loved this book. It was engrossing, very interesting and left me wanting more - so much so that I was sitting up in bed and reading until the wee small hours of the morning, could not put it down and kept saying to myself "just a few more pages."
I really and truly loved your book and can't wait for Book Two, Three and Four!" **Jan Burton**, Writer, Editor, Australia

"You write with a fine sense of history and culture. You have a gift for language and your prose is clear, strong, honest, and memorable. You also write about your characters with respect and love, a point of view that inspires respect and love in the reader. *Big Horse Woman* gathers up all of your talents and puts them on beautiful display. An impressive work."
David Ebershoff, *author of The Danish Girl, The 19th Wife, The Rose City*, Executive Editor, Hogarth and Random House

The Author with her team of Percheron draft-horses, BARNEY and FRED.

Photo © Bonnie Burgeson

ABOUT THE AUTHOR

Ever since Barbara was very little, she wanted to make stories in words and pictures for the whole world. She earned her Bachelor of Fine Arts, from the School of Visual Arts, New York and spent her life learning about plants and horses and storytelling.

Big Horse Woman, first in a series of four epic novels, was a Finalist in the Leapfrog Press Literary Fiction Contest, and Winner of Chanticleer International Book Award, Prairie/First Nations, Laramie Prize for Western Fiction. *Big Horse Woman,* born in a dream, sparked Barbara's interest in Ponca Language, because she wanted to Name the Plants the way Big Horse Woman would. This led to her becoming a lifetime student of the Ponca Language.

Magghie, book two, was a Finalist in Chanticleer International Book Award, Laramie Prize for Western Fiction; excerpts published in literary journals, anthologies and *Nebraska Life* magazine. While writing Magghie, Barbara was also run over by a horse-drawn vehicle, and likewise, had to relearn how to walk. With the support of family and friends from four directions, she was able to move to Nebraska, continue her studies, and complete her novels. The simultaneous publication of *Big Horse Woman* and *Magghie* is the culmination of the dream that started it all, stories in words and pictures for the whole world.

An Herbalist, Big-Horse-keeper, and Language teacher, Barbara offers classes and consultation in traditional Plant Medicine, and Horse Care, and advocates for the revitalization of native language as a core element of cultural preservation and identity.

Barbara continues to scribble in her Dream Journal, which she started keeping at age thirteen, and to follow the characters she meets there.

www.bighorsewoman.com
Instagram @big_horse_woman
www.facebook.com/bighorsewoman/
bighorsewomanbooks@gmail.com

ALL RIGHTS RESERVED
STORY AND ART ©2022 BARBARA SALVATORE

WINNER - Prairie/First Nations
LARAMIE PRIZE FOR WESTERN FICTION
Chanticleer International Book Awards

LARAMIE
Western Fiction
1st Place
Best in Category
CIBA
Chanticleer International Book Awards

LEAPFROG PRESS
Publisher of Quality Fiction, Poetry and Non-Fiction

FINALIST LEAPFROG PRESS SPRING FICTION CONTEST

BIG HORSE BOOKS
PO BOX 414
VERDIGRE NEBRASKA
68783